Wall Street Blues

Other Books by the Author

Trump: The Saga of America's Masterbuilder
Kingdom: The Story of the Hunt Family of Texas
Dynamic Investing
Inside the Underground Economy
How to Profit from the Wall Street Mergers
The New Tax Law and You
Mind Over Money
The Optimist's Guide to Making Money in the 1980's
Everything the Beginner Needs to Know to Invest Shrewdly
Who's Afraid of 1984?
Here Comes Immortality
It Usually Begins with Ayn Rand
Radical Libertarianism

WALL STREET BLUES

A NOVEL

Jerome Tuccille

A Mario Sartori Book
Lyle Stuart Inc.   *Secaucus, New Jersey*

Published by Lyle Stuart Inc.
120 Enterprise Ave., Secaucus, N.J. 07094
In Canada: Musson Book Company
A division of General Publishing Co. Limited
Don Mills, Ontario

Queries regarding rights and permissions should be
addressed to Lyle Stuart, 120 Enterprise Avenue, Secaucus,
N.J. 07094

Manufactured in the United States of America

Library of Congress Cataloging-in-Publication Data

Tuccille, Jerome
    Wall Street blues : a novel / Jerome Tuccille.
      p.   cm.
    "A Mario Sartori book"
    ISBN 0-8184-0455-8 : $17.95
    I. Title.
PS3570.U233W35   1988
813'.54--dc 19   87-18122
                                                        CIP

To Oscar Collier, who provided the constructive encouragement
I needed during the year and a half I worked on this novel

Wall Street Blues

Prologue

The week between Christmas and New Year's Day is one of the busiest of the year in the investment business. It is the week when half the investors in the country decide to sell all the junk in their portfolios to take a tax loss for the year; the week when brokers get bombarded with urgent calls from panicky clients who waited until the last minute to take care of business they had all year to worry about. It is a week that most sane investment counselors take off to go skiing with their families and let their assistants take care of the year-end hysteria. It is a week I usually take off myself, but this year was different.

This year I was flat broke, tottering on the edge of bankruptcy, and I needed every scrap of business that came my way.

So I got to the office early each morning and stayed at my desk until well after the market closed in the afternoon. Most of the time I was preoccupied with my personal financial crisis, wondering what the hell I was going to do to resolve it. When Alex Jordan called me at three o'clock the day before New Year's Eve, he caught me in a thoroughly perplexed mental state.

"Paul! Alex here. Happy New Year, fella. How've you been?"

"Happy New Year, Alex. I'm fine I guess. Why complain?"

"Elaine and the kids?"

"They're okay too. And Barbara?"

Pleasantries out of the way, Alex Jordan got down to the real

9

purpose of his call. He was not one to spend a penny unless he had some business in mind.

"I'm getting together with some people after the holidays and was wondering if you'd care to join us."

"Oh? What's up?"

"A start-up situation, a new venture I'm thinking of getting involved in. We've got the financial backing to set it up and some talented people to run the show. There's an investment side to it and I thought you'd fit in nicely."

"Sounds interesting, Alex, but I'm jammed up with more business than I can handle now. When . . . when did you say you were getting together?"

"A couple weeks or so. We'll probably set up a lunch so everyone can get acquainted. You might want to join us just to see if there's anything there that strikes your fancy."

"Well . . . let me know when you've set a date. I can't make any promises, but if I can get away for an hour or so maybe I'll join you."

"Fair enough. This could be a very lucrative situation, fella, so you owe it to yourself to at least take a look and find out what it's all about."

"Will do, Alex. Thanks for calling. And again, happy New Year to you and Barbara."

After the conversation with Alex, I sat and stared at the wall chewing on the end of a paper clip for the better part of an hour. I had known Alex for three years but the more time I spent with him, the more I realized I didn't know him at all. He was always pleasant and charming, and always highly evasive. I caught glimpses of the man from time to time, a fleeting glance at one aspect or another of his persona, but never the whole man in focus at any moment. He was extremely rich; that much I knew about him. But how he got his money and exactly what he did for a living were still mysteries to me. There was no shortage of rumors circulating around him, stories about his business dealings involving some prominent members of the underworld, but no one had come up with any facts to prove them. Ostensibly he worked as the chief financial officer for a high-powered real estate developer, but that struck me as mere window dressing. He seemed to move in lofty circles on his own, and operated more like a mover and shaker himself than like someone else's numbers cruncher. Perhaps one day I would learn the full story about him. But I doubted it.

One thing I did know for sure: if I ever decided to become a crook to solve my own financial problems, Alex Jordan would be the first one I would call.

Chapter One

There were times when the weather was cold and the icy wind was howling in from the Sound that I wondered how I could get through another year of this self-inflicted torture. January and February were the worst months by far. Standing there on the platform in the arctic morning darkness with a hundred other zombies too numb to move was an exercise in masochism. The train was invariably late, and as we stood there with the sun barely up on the Sound, jiggling pathetically on the frozen platform in an effort to shake off the cold, it was easy to contemplate the unthinkable. Too easy. It was too cold to retrieve your newspaper from the briefcase, too dark and windy to read it if you did, nothing else to do but wait and jiggle, watch your breath fog the air before it was whipped to shreds by gales off the water, nothing else to do but think those titillating thoughts. What if? By the time the lights of the train were visible up the tracks, moving in slow motion as they approached the station, the frigid air had penetrated through my face right into the bone. My eyes were blurred with involuntary tears. I had a headache.

Boarding the train was hardly a relief. A hundred mummies turned into barracudas as they angled for the best seats, the ones on the end or against the windows, anything but the middle of a three-seater. They blocked the aisles as they stripped off their Arctic gear—bulky overcoats, hats, gloves, mufflers and tried

13

to stuff it all onto overcrowded racks already jammed with the paraphernalia of seated passengers who pretended to concentrate on their morning newspapers as the newcomers jostled in beside them. It was bad enough putting up with the indignity of it all without having to deal with some jerk who was scowling because you had the audacity to sit beside him. The next part was fun, elbowing for reading room as everybody folded their *New York Times* or *Wall Street Journal* in halves and quarters and tried to read some section of a page. I always tried to sit beside a woman if I could arrange it. There were more women commuting these days, and by and large they were more civilized than the men, not yet case-hardened into thugs by decades of bone-jarring commuting. The men were too eager to do battle over some perceived violation of their territorial rights.

Ordinarily I read my newspapers on the way into Grand Central, compulsively trying to squeeze in both the *Times* and *Journal* during the hour-long journey and feeling vaguely depressed if I didn't finish them. Lately, however, I was engaged in another kind of lunacy, believe it or not an extended engagement with my checkbook in an attempt to balance it—or, more precisely, to figure out why it was so tragically out of balance each month. It was so hopelessly out of balance, as a matter of fact, that I was beginning to experience some perverse sense of relief if the monthly shortfall was within a thousand dollars. Truly, I could not believe how I let things get so far out of hand. Here I was, a financial "expert" advising other people on how to manage and invest their money, allowing my own financial affairs to drift away beyond my control. Every time I took on a new mountain of debt to finance the Good Life—a second home, ski trips to Utah, European vacations, restaurants, cars, every piece of technological wizardry manufactured by man—I justified it with the rationale that it was all deductible. Borrowing money, thanks to Uncle Sam, used to be the best tax shelter of all. Now even that rationale was gone, thanks to the latest tax law. And the cash outlay each month, every month, had now reached the level of an uncontrollable Green Hemorrhage. No longer could I delude myself with the notion that I was a shrewd financial planner who had contrived to keep his tax bill down. I was a junkie, hooked on compulsive spending, a slave to the banks and credit institutions. My father, who had never earned more than fifteen thousand dollars any year of his life and managed to retire comfortably before his sixty-fifth birthday, looked at my six-figure income in wonderment, imagining that I was rich. But I wasn't rich at all. I was dead flat broke and living like a king. I had everything and owned nothing. When I added up all the money that I owed, and balanced it against my assets, I broke out in a cold sweat even though the temperature inside the train was not much warmer than it was on the platform.

Across the aisle I noticed an attractive blonde, thirty-six or thirty-eightish, concentrating fiercely on some legalistic report on her lap. I loved the look of the modern businesswoman, so crisp and neat and intelligent and somehow so sexually stimulating with that caged sensuality not quite hidden beneath the veneer of efficiency. Their smells were a welcome addition to the dehumanizing commuter train. The subtle odor of perfume and bath powder rounded off the sharp edges of the male effluvia—the early morning farts and bad breath and sourish exudations. The evening trips home were even worse with a day's worth of sweat and spicy men's room smells added to the stew of odors.

The women were the only welcome diversion from my checkbook problems these days. Money worries had expanded to a point where they were now beginning to take over my entire life. I was preoccupied with them on the way to work in the morning and the way home at night, and more and more at crucial times during the day when I should have been concentrating on business. There were the first and second mortgages on my house in Soundview plus the first and second on the ski house in Utah. Then there were the bank loans, the overdraft lines on three different checking accounts that were used up almost to the hilt, plus a dozen different credit cards that had all been run up close to their limits. It was costing me eight to nine thousand dollars a month just to live, just to clear up my basic bills, while my alleged six-figure income netted me a little over seven after a rogue's gallery of bloodsuckers, including IRS, had extracted their monthly nourishment. Anxiety gripped my chest like a vise at unexpected times throughout the day, and blood-chilling, ball-shriveling panic threatened to overwhelm me at approximately three-fifteen every morning when I awakened in a frigid sweat wishing I could go back to sleep and never wake up again.

It was precisely then when those unthinkable thoughts came creeping into my mind, when those unimaginable scenarios played themselves out like a horror movie in my head as I lay there in the early-morning darkness with my wife sleeping warmly by my side. Most frightening of all was the fact that the unthinkable no longer seemed so unthinkable. More and more, to my astonishment, the unimaginable was beginning to seem like a viable solution to my financial distress, and the realization that I might be capable of acting out my early-morning fantasies actually had a calming effect on me. What if? What if, indeed. I had what it took, whatever it took, to be a criminal. Absurdly, the acceptance of this notion was the only antidote for the panic that gripped me at those odd hours, the only tonic that soothed me enough so that I could fall back to sleep again. The moral side of it did not trouble me at all. Amoral as I was, I could do what I had to do to climb out of the hole I dug for myself during the past few years. That was enough to know, enough to chase away the demons of fear for at least a few more hours.

Grand Central was the usual madhouse, with battalions of charging commuters erupting from the bowels of the terminal into the main concourse above. They dashed past the shopping bag ladies and the homeless men reeking of excrement and piss into the surrounding streets, or into the catacombs of the subway system that would suck them in crowded cars at breakneck speed down to the financial district. I was one of the fortunates, if that's the proper word to describe the condition of those who worked within walking distance of the station. In fair weather and foul, I got my morning exercise by hiking downtown to 34th Street, then crosstown over to Penn Plaza on the other side of Fifth Avenue. Each morning I passed the demented derelict who had staked out the southeast corner of Madison Avenue and 41st Street as his personal fiefdom. His hair was matted with filth, and his face, ankles, wrists, and chest that was exposed to the numbing cold were imbued with heavy layers of grime. He wore the same outfit in summer and winter, impervious to the weather—a long heavy Army surplus overcoat open in front, no shirt, dirty urine-streaked trousers barely held in place with a limp leather belt, no socks, and unlaced shoes splitting apart at the seams. Empty cardboard cartons, his furniture apparently, were scattered on the sidewalk near the curb. One evening when I passed him on the way back to Grand Central, he was sitting on one of the cartons reading a newspaper and smoking a stubby cigar that he had picked out of the gutter. Pedestrians scurried around him on their way home from work, but he was oblivious to them all. In his own mind he was enjoying a cigar in the comfort of his living room, catching up on the news of the day before dinner. He was no different from the rest of us.

The best thing to be said about Manhattan in the winter is that the bitter cold overrides the rotting smells of summer. The wind chases the dirt and litter across the streets and sidewalks, and scatters the stink in a dozen different directions. In the warm weather the putrefaction hangs in the air like a miasmic cloud. The walk over to the west side is a journey through an urban minefield, a cityscape of crumpled cigarette packs, crushed beer cans, broken wine bottles, dogshit, and human piss stains against the sides of buildings. Garbage of every description is lined along the curbs, and the nerve-racking din of blasting automobile horns and raised voices keeps everyone in a state of perpetual tension. The anxiety intensifies as you approach the vicinity of Madison Square Garden and the Penn Plaza complex. The smells are a little gamier, the filth in the streets a bit more exotic, and the airborne clamor a bit more raucous. It is as though the bottom had fallen out of Times Square and the detritus spilled over ten blocks to the south.

Monica, my secretary of three months, was already at her desk when I got off the elevator on the sixteenth floor. At twenty-five, she was twenty years younger than I, a well-stacked, extremely attractive, and thoroughly fucked-up young woman from the Bensonhurst section of Brooklyn. Her face was not much to look at, somewhat plain and pockmarked with acne scars from her teenage years. But her body was special. She had a wonderful chest, full and high and erect, a narrow waist with wide hips, and absolutely gorgeous legs that she liked to show off with tight skirts split up the side. She was full and round all over without being the least bit overweight. One morning about a month after I hired her, she flabbergasted me when she walked into my office with a stack of mail. Usually, she would just drop it on my desk, smile, exchange a few pleasantries with me, then go back to her own desk. On this particular morning, however, she hung around nervously, lingering longer than she had to as though she had something on her mind and didn't know how to bring it up.

"Anything wrong, Monica?" I asked cautiously, sipping from a cup of lukewarm coffee I brought up with me from the deli on 33rd Street.

She looked down at my desk, fingering a paperclip absentmindedly, struggling for words. "I probably shouldn't tell you this," she finally said, staring straight into me.

"Tell me what?"

"I feel you're someone I can talk to, someone who's sensitive and understanding and won't make fun of me."

I got a little nervous, wondering what the hell she was leading up to. Monica was an intense person, a cauldron of seething conflicts and unresolved emotions, and I found her unpredictable. "You can tell me anything, Monica. I promise it won't go any further than this room."

"I . . . I've been dreaming about you lately."

"Dreaming about me? What kind of dreams?"

She looked right into me without a hint of reserve or embarrassment as she answered, "I'm sure you can guess."

The temperature in the room seemed to shoot up fifteen degrees. My face was flushed and my neck was on fire. This was totally unexpected. "You mean erotic dreams?" I asked stupidly. I was used to flirting, but this was different. We were enacting a scene out of a porn flick.

"Yes," she answered and looked down at the desk, blushing for the first time.

"What were we doing?" I was getting into it now. I was more than just a little curious and I was definitely aroused.

"Everything you can imagine." She stared straight into me again and I was the one who averted his eyes. "We were in a hotel room or an apartment, I couldn't tell. You brought me there, then you started to undress me and I didn't want you to stop. You pushed me back on the bed and . . . and put your face between my thighs and it . . . it was the most wonderful, the most beautiful thing that ever happened to me in my life."

How do you respond to this? Do you say, "I see, that's interesting, tell me more," as though we were discussing a story in the morning newspaper, or do you get up and close the door, turning your office into a confessional and yourself into a counselor? Actually, I did neither. Instead, I felt a voyeuristic thrill and a thousand calculations flashed through my mind in a second, all of them having to do with whether or not I should act out this fantasy with her in some out-of-the-way motel room.

"Was there any more?" My voice was barely audible because of the sexual tension that constricted my throat. I sounded disembodied, as though my voice were in the adjoining room by itself.

"Lots more." She was at ease now, trusting me with this cosmic fantasy of hers. "We did everything. I couldn't get enough of you. It seemed to go on for hours. When I woke up I was totally exhausted, sweating like crazy, but it was all so real, more real than it is in life if you know what I mean."

All the while I was undressing her in my mind, wondering what she looked like beneath the dark blue turtleneck blouse that hugged her chest and the tan skirt with the Oriental slit up the side. I knew it would be good, very erotic and highly emotional. I also knew it would be extremely complicated. There could be no casual roll in the hay with her, no passionate one-nighter with a kiss on the cheek and a fond goodbye after it was over. This one would not let go too easily once she sunk her teeth in.

"Was this the first time, Monica? The first dream you had like this or . . ."

"Oh no. It's been going on every night for over a week now. I wouldn't mention it otherwise. Every night it gets better and more real for me, like an obsession almost."

"Do these things happen a lot to you? I mean, have you obsessed over other men like this?"

"Never. That's what's so intense about it. I never do this to myself, never. That's why I think there must be something special about us, some unusual chemistry and attraction. I've never felt like this before in my life."

"I see." The instantaneous passion of the moment had passed for me. It was overwhelming and fleeting, and now it was gone. What was left was some kind of clinical detachment. This thing was impossible. It could not go any further. "I'm flattered, Monica, I really am. I don't understand why a sexy young woman like you would be so obsessed with an old fart like me. I'm twenty years older than you."

"You don't understand what you have, Paul. You're attractive and youthful, I don't think of you as old, and very warm and considerate. You make me feel like I can really count on you. And you're terribly sexy, you must know that."

"Still, there must be a million twenty-seven-year-old guys out there who would love to take you out to dinner and spend the night between your legs, take care of you, you know what I mean."

"What were you like when you were twenty-seven?"

The question startled me. It was perfectly logical but I didn't expect it. My answer was instinctive and truthful, Pavlovian almost. "I was a fucking asshole."

"Well, things haven't changed much."

"Unfortunately, we can't do anything about this," I said, having made up my mind without realizing it. "I would love to get involved with you, love to make love to you, but it can't be done. It's impossible."

"Why?"

"For one thing I'm a happily married man. I love my wife and I don't want to jeopardize that. For another thing, my life is too complicated right now and I can't handle any new complications. And if you need a third reason, there's no way we could hide it. It would be all over the office in about ten seconds flat."

"Would it make any difference if I didn't work here?"

Another good question. This kid was on the ball. She had thought it all out carefully beforehand. "Possibly. I don't think so. I can't be sure. I'm attracted to you. I'd love to fuck you and I'm sure it would be good. It just can't be done right now."

Monica and I became good friends after that unnerving encounter. It was out between us now and the tension was dissolved. We talked a lot about our "unrequited passion" and our "unconsummated affair" matter-of-factly. We joked every day about it, spicing up the conversation with a lot of four-letter words. We discussed a million other things as well, which was what she really needed more than anything else—a father substitute, a confessor, a shrink surrogate who listened to her convoluted stream-of-consciousness outpourings with genuine concern and understanding. And she had quite a tale to tell, too. Her autobiography was a classical Greek tragedy almost, an epic lament set in contemporary Brooklyn instead of some Attic plain. There was a heavy-drinking father who was rarely home and who never paid her much attention—didn't even know which school she attended—when he was there; a locomotive of a mother whose waking hours were spent in a frenetic state ranging between high anxiety and outright hysteria; a ne'er-do-well brother who either raped or came close to raping her, she couldn't remember exactly, so thoroughly had she blocked the incident from her subconscious mind, when he was sixteen and she was thirteen; a retarded younger sister whose condition Monica was brought up believing by her mother was somehow her fault. She had all the beauty and intelligence her sister lacked, and it apparently was her duty to atone for this injustice throughout eternity.

In truth, Monica's problems were a welcome diversion from my own, and I always listened to her patiently and attentively. There was something luxurious about playing father confessor to another person, particularly an attractive young woman, when you were buried beneath an avalanche of your own kind of grief. Listening to someone else's tale of woe was momentarily reassuring. It's not that we take pleasure in other people's misery, but it is good to know that someone else's sanity is being tested as severely as your own. Suicide is always premature, a friend once said to me. You never know what the hell is going to happen tomorrow that could turn your whole life around.

Lunch, when I went out for it, was usually eaten across the

street in Tommy Gilmartin's bar. Tommy and I had known each other for twenty-five years. We went to college and played football together, then dropped out of touch until I walked into the Dublin House five years ago and saw him standing behind the bar. He had joined the Navy after college, then worked at a succession of boring nine-to-fivers for a few years before he met the Dublin House heiress at a party in the Hamptons. Her father was the one who opened the original Dublin House in the Bronx during World War II, and built it into a chain of highly successful bar-restaurants that extended throughout the five boroughs of New York City. After Tommy got married he went to work for his father-in-law, managing one of his bars on Fordham Road in the Bronx before buying the one within a stone's throw of Madison Square Garden. Now Tommy was a rich man in his own right. His timing was perfect and he had picked his location well. He prospered during the economic resurgence of the 1980s that saw the west side of Manhattan evolve into a hubbub of sporting, political, and business activity centered around the Garden, the Penn Plaza complex, and New York City's new convention center. His bar was packed every day with businessmen and construction workers eating lunch and knocking back a few drinks, and he played host every evening to an endless stream of boxing, basketball, and hockey fans.

When I walked into the Dublin House this bitter cold January afternoon, Tommy was at the end of his bar pouring scotch for a group of fat, red-faced, white-haired men who looked like Irish politicians. They would have been equally at home in Boston. He saw me walk in, never missing a thing that went on inside his establishment, and wiped a spot clean for me as I elbowed my way through a raucous crowd of construction workers, black and white prostitutes getting oiled up before a tough night's work, and dark-suited stockbrokers from my own building across the street. It was high noon on a cold day in the middle of the winter, but it always felt like New Year's Eve at Tommy's bar.

"Where've you been? I haven't seen you in a week," he said.

"Trying to stay out of trouble, Tommy. Still recuperating from the holidays."

"I know what you mean. Try getting through Christmas with five kids some time."

"I've got enough trouble with two. How's the family? Everybody okay?"

"Fine, fine. What're you having?"

"Just a beer. Who're the Tip O'Neill types down the end? They look like Irish racketeers."

Tommy smiled and drew a beer for me. He was as big and burly as ever, but his hair was thinning now and he was running to fat. Still, you wouldn't want to tangle with him. He looked like the type of guy who would bite your ear off in a fight and buy you a drink afterward. There was never too much trouble in his bar despite the exotic and diversified clientele. Besides Tommy behind the bar, his staff looked like rebels on leave from the Irish Republican Army—which is exactly what many of them were. Tommy was fairly open about his IRA sympathies, and the Dublin House had in fact become a clearinghouse of sorts for the Irish revolution. There was always a table full of fair-haired men with thick brogues buzzing conspiratorially among themselves in the corner. It was no place for an aggressive Anglophile.

"Politicians, racketeers, they're all the same," Tommy said in response to my question. "All I know is, every time they leave I'm a little poorer than I was before they came in. Can I get you a sandwich?"

"I'll try some of that Irish roast beef you've got, the stuff that looks like it's been sitting out in the rain for six days."

"It'll make a man out of you, Paul, put some hair on your balls."

"That's not where I need it," I laughed and he joined in. Tommy and I had been checking out each other's receding hairlines ever since we met again.

I settled in at the bar, sipping my beer as he moved off attending to his customers' needs. Thanks to Tommy Gilmartin, my investment business had been flourishing handsomely for the past few years. One day, about three months after I ran into him again, he called me aside when the lunch hour bedlam had subsided.

"Paul, maybe you can help me," he had whispered confidentially. "This is between you and me. I know I can trust you."

"Of course, Tommy. What can I do for you?"

"This is a cash business," he continued, looking around left and right as though an IRS agent might come crawling out of the woodwork any minute. "I mean, I'm on the books here for twenty thousand a year. The fringe benefits are what make this business so interesting."

"I understand."

"My problem now is what to do with the cash. At any time I might have thirty, forty, maybe fifty thousand in my safe deposit box and it's getting harder and harder to get rid of it."

Everybody should have problems like that, I thought to myself. God bless America. And God bless the system if you knew how to use it correctly.

"I know what you mean, Tommy. You used to be able to bring in up to ten thousand at a time as often as you wanted to. Now it's getting tough. Anything more than once a year is subject to scrutiny and some places won't accept more than a few hundred at a time anymore. IRS is breathing down everyone's neck."

"The question is, can you help me?" Tommy looked directly into my eyes. He knew that what he was asking went beyond friendship. He was risking severing our relationship, and he was banking on my trust to keep it to myself. But Tommy knew me well. We had played football together, and you can size a man up pretty well when the crunch is on. I had a streak of larceny in me that ran every bit as deep as his. Managing other people's money has always been a borderline endeavor. It's a risk business, and one that's well compensated if you're willing to bend the rules a little.

"Yes," I said without hesitation. "But we'll have to be careful. No more than ten at any time and I'll let you know when to bring it in."

"Good," he smiled, relaxed now. It was apparent that he had a tough time broaching the subject with me. He had spent an idle hour or two debating with himself. "I don't expect you to take chances for nothing, you know," he added. "Whatever arrangement you want to make is all right with me."

"Don't worry, friend. I make my living doing this sort of thing. You don't ask me to discount my commissions, and I don't ask you where the money comes from. That's the usual arrangement."

So Tommy, my friend, my old college sidekick, was now my client. And a good client he was, too, trekking across the street to my office every few weeks or so in a beer-stained white shirt and shiny pants with a thick envelope tucked beneath his windbreaker. The first batch of cash he brought in was enough to make you drunk just smelling it. It reeked of stale beer and whiskey as though he had been mopping the bar with it. Soon he was referring his colleagues to me—restaurateurs and bar-owners from all over Manhattan, and eventually his cousins and in-laws from the Bronx. My fame was spreading far and wide, and the true nature of that fame was driven home clearly to me one morning when I answered my phone.

"I'm Jack Scanlon from Inwood," the caller, a man with a heavy brogue, nervously identified himself. "I'm a cousin of Tommy Gilmartin's, related by marriage."

"Yes?" Only a crazy greenhorn would introduce himself like that.

"Tom . . . Tom tells me you're the Chinaman."

"I'm the what?"

"The Chinaman. You know, the man who does the laundry," he said nervously, impatient with my obtuseness. I nearly fell off my chair.

"Well, that's the first time I ever heard it put that way, but, yes, I think I can help you."

"I'd like to come down and see you about three o'clock this afternoon, if that's convenient for you."

"Fine. See you then."

Thanks to Tommy and his network of cohorts, cousins, nephews, and in-laws, my standing as a professional "money manager" and "financial advisor" to the struggling masses yearning to live free of excessive taxation took on an added dimension. My business, comfortable to begin with, started to grow by leaps and bounds. Suddenly I was everybody's favorite Chinaman, the man who laundered money whiter than white. I knew more about New York's bustling underground economy than anyone else alive, and that knowledge carried with it a certain element of risk. After all, if one is inclined to abuse privileged information of that nature, one is likely to hobble around for the rest of his life on plastic kneecaps. But what the hell, I reasoned to my-

self, the risk comes with the territory in this business. Most of
the cash wound up in bearer bonds and unregistered paper of
one kind or another, a neat trick in itself since the government
was making it increasingly difficult to locate hard-to-trace investment vehicles. When some of Tommy's cousins turned out to be
New York City cops and firemen looking to hide pots of cash
from God knows what schemes they had going, my last vestige
of idealism flew out the window. Never again would I ever feel
the least bit protected by the boys in blue.

Chapter Two

It was always tempting to stop off for a drink in Charlie Brown's before catching the train out of Grand Central. The secretaries were in abundance on every third barstool, hoping to catch some upwardly mobile type fresh from a divorce or at least a well-heeled executive who wouldn't mind helping them out with their rent once in a while. I enjoyed observing the action even though I was not in the market for any extramarital activity. Flirtatious as I was I never cheated on my wife, whether out of a paranoid fear of catching something exotic or some lingering dollop of guilt from my Catholic school upbringing is hard to say. Probably a little of both. A drink or two in that atmosphere, surrounded by all the dark wood, forest green walls, frosted mirrors, and the constant chatter helped to take your mind off more pressing concerns like the threat of impending bankruptcy, for example.

This evening, however, I resisted the temptation and headed straight down the ramp to my train which was already boarding passengers for the journey back to Connecticut. I avoided the bar car on my way toward the first nonsmoker up front. I had witnessed some pretty incredible sights in the bar car, a lot of heavy drinking and flirting and general grabass that came pretty close to dryhumping when the train was especially crowded and boisterous. There was serious gambling, too, with some Wall

Street traders dropping as much as fifty or a hundred bucks in an hour-long poker game between Grand Central and Soundview. Occasionally I enjoyed the action, and indulged in the luxury of getting slightly inebriated amidst the clamor, the coiling cigarette and cigar smoke, and the damp exudations from the heavy breathers. There was always a lot of speculation about who was actually fucking whom among the commuters, who was going off to party late into the night after they called their respective mates to say they were caught up late at work, and about once a year a marriage or two did get wrecked when an illicit romance took a serious turn. The marina in Soundview was filled with boat dwellers, divorced husbands mostly whose ex-wives lived in four hundred thousand dollar homes with their kids while they staggered from the boatyard each morning in dark suits and briefcases to catch the 7:28 into Manhattan. It was one of the more bizarre spectacles of contemporary suburbia watching them parade single file from their boats in full business regalia. The main problem with the bar car, for me at least, is that two drinks on the way home invariably put me in the mood for more of the same later on, and I didn't feel like adding alcoholism to the list of problems I had to deal with. An alcoholic would be an easy thing for me to become if I wanted to give it half a try.

I hunkered down in a window seat in the first nonsmoking car and tried to take a fifteen- or twenty-minute nap during the ride home. Ordinarily, napping was something I did not have a problem doing, but lately it had become impossible. The money situation preoccupied me completely and I knew I was pretty close to taking drastic measures to resolve it. Each time I closed my eyes and tried to nod off, the panic seized me, literally seized me like a demon seizing a victim, and I started to quiver uncontrollably until I thought I would jump out of my skin. I dreaded running into someone I knew during these moments of quiet hysteria, afraid my voice would come out two octaves higher and they would observe me as I was in the process of doing a swan dive off the deep end.

Until now I had not discussed the situation with my wife Elaine. Elaine came from a family that was constantly walking a financial tightrope, and part of our current problem—or so I rationalized it at least—stemmed from my desire to give her all the things she had been deprived of in her youth. She was happy and feeling secure, having made it all the way to one of the poshest communities in the northeast from the violent, garbage-littered streets of the South Bronx. In doing so she had taken on a somewhat preppie suburban air and cleansed her speech of every trace of her heritage so that you would have thought she came from Anytown, U.S.A. It was a trait that annoyed me sometimes, especially since I had gone out of my way never to lose touch with my own working-class Bronx roots. But I understood her motivation. For this reason I hesitated to terrorize her with the facts of reality. I wanted to protect her from the sharp edges of life, let her luxuriate in the white-collar enclave of Soundview where the main concerns of the inhabitants were whether they should ski in Vail or Europe this year, and whether they should present their children with a Mercedes-Benz or a BMW on their sixteenth birthday. Most of this line of reasoning was bullshit of course. If I didn't want to wallow in all the creature comforts as much as she did, none of it would have come about in the first place. Elaine and I were birds of a feather beneath it all, which was the main reason why our marriage had survived sixteen years of emotional turmoil. Still, during my moments of self-pity an undercurrent of resentment began to percolate a little too close to the surface. At times like this I felt like a bubbling cauldron just about ready to explode.

When I pulled into the gravel driveway the little things caught my eye. The one thing wrong with gravel was that it tended to get rutted from the tire tracks; little mounds developed off to the sides and bare spots formed down the middle. This was another Saturday morning project that needed to be tended to; get out the fucking rake and smooth down the gravel. Why gravel instead of blacktop? Because in certain sections of Soundview blacktop driveways were considered low class. Elaine and I both grew up in Concrete City. Cement was called Guinea Gold, and anybody who was fortunate enough to have a postage stamp backyard cemented it over with a "patio" and strung a clothesline on it. The driveways were all blacktopped, and trees, if you could find them, were the next best things for dogs to piss on after fire hydrants. So, our driveway in Connecticut was strewn with six hundred dollars' worth of tiny round blue-gray pebbles.

The gutters were another item that had to be taken care of. I never did get around to cleaning them out in November after all the gorgeous red and orange and yellow leaves fell in them, so now whenever it rained the water cascaded over the side like a waterfall in an African rain forest. The waterfall made deep pools at the corner of the house near the cellar door, and the pools eventually seeped into the cellar adding to my flooding problems. This was yet another project, I made a mental note, that had to be tackled this Saturday or the next one at the latest. Have Barabbas Plumbing (the bastard might as well call himself) install a fucking water pump in the celler. Soundview was the only town I knew where the plumbers and electricians showed up in tweed jackets with leather patches on the elbows.

Naturally, a water pump had a dollar sign attached to it, an additional outlay of cash above and beyond my normal backbreaking living expenses. I was not in the best possible frame of mind when I entered my house and noticed that the temperature inside was approaching the level of a sauna.

"Hi, honey," Elaine sang out when she heard the door click.

"Hi yourself."

I hung my coat in the hallway closet and breathed in the eclectic smells. Elaine could make a house smell better than anyone else I knew. We were always the last ones to take down our Christmas ornaments, and two weeks after the holidays the air was still scented with pine from the tree and wreaths, and the aroma of food and spices on the stove. Since she always had three things going at once—a meatloaf or a roast in the oven, a pie cooling on the counter, and perhaps a sauce for tomorrow night's meal simmering on the burner—the combined essence of all this caloric exotica hung in the air like a warm, damp, delicious cloud. If I did not have an appetite before I walked in, I developed one instantaneously. The air was so thick you could taste it.

I walked into the kitchen and hugged her from behind, inhaling her hair and nuzzling her neck. Elaine was forty-three, two years younger than I, and her body was more perfectly sculpted now than it was when we were married. She worked out like a dervish, leaping and flailing away in aerobics class three times a week and punishing herself on the Nautilus machine to firm up the flesh. She was a hell of a woman, and the lecherous glances of other men constantly alerted me to that fact. She turned around and kissed me, smiling brightly with her large Chiclet teeth.

"How come it's so hot in here?" I asked despite my better judgment. I was a compulsive person and just could not help myself.

"Don't start complaining about the heat, please. We're all freezing."

I checked the thermostat and saw she had pushed it up around seventy-one. "Sixty-seven or sixty-eight is warm enough," I said.

"Paul!"

"Does Laurie have her socks on at least?"

"They're both bundled up with woolen sweaters and heavy socks, and they're still freezing." She was not about to give an inch. Even when you were right you never actually won an argument with her.

One time when my daughter Laurie came downstairs and asked me, "Can we turn up the heat, Daddy? It's freezing upstairs," I nearly went berserk. She was dressed in gym shorts and was running around barefoot. I controlled my temper with great effort and replied calmly, "Go upstairs, Laurie, and put on a heavy sweater, sweat socks and shoes. If you're still cold after fifteen minutes I'll turn up the heat."

She didn't like it, but accepted the logic of my proposal and did as I asked her. Since then we had an unwritten rule in the house. Everybody got dressed up warmly first; then if they were still cold the heat went up. It was a feeble victory, however, since everyone was always colder than I was no matter what the temperature. It was virtually a no-win situation for me, one's perceived level of comfort being a highly subjective evaluation, but at least I had asserted myself and established some sort of ground rule, flimsy as it was in practice.

I walked into the family room to check on the kids. They were watching MTV on cable, Mark, at fifteen the older by two years, all but hidden beneath a heavy blanket he pulled up around his ears like a Mexican wearing a poncho, and Laurie stretched out on the floor in an outfit that barely met my minimum requirements. She was the more audacious of the two, always testing my rules to see how far she could push them, see how much she could get away with before I snapped and lost my temper. She was also the athletic one, active in everything from field hockey to softball, while Mark, who read a lot for his age, had developed a streak of premature cynicism that, I felt, would serve him well in later years. Elaine and I argued about that quite a bit, she feeling that he was too young to be so sardonic and I replying that a healthy dose of either cynicism or paranoia should be everybody's first line of defense.

"Hi, kids."

"Hi."

"Hi, Dad." They said hello without lifting their eyes from the tube.

"Who's that weird guy you're watching?"

"Shhh!" Laurie hissed impatiently. "It's Billy Skunk's latest video."

Billy Skunk? Who the hell was he? I didn't know any of them anymore. I seemed to be stuck in some sort of a time warp that ended with Peter, Paul and Mary, Bob Dylan, and Joan Baez. Billy Skunk looked like a creature from Venus with hair that stuck out in all directions and makeup on his face. Boy George, a friend once told me, had the distinction of being voted simultaneously both the ugliest male and the ugliest female vocalist of the year a while back. There were so many of them to keep up with these days. Were there that many back in the fifties and sixties? It seemed to be a smaller universe of rock stars back then. The Beatles, the Who, the Doors. Maybe brain rot has eroded my memory somewhat. Whatever the case, these cretins with green and orange hair and eye shadow looked unhealthy to me. I didn't like my kids being exposed to them and influenced by them, but it was already far too late to do a damned thing about it.

"Satisfied?" Elaine asked cryptically as she came up beside me.

"About what?"

"Satisfied that we're not all sitting around half naked complaining about the cold?"

Elaine was like a dog with a bone; she just could not let it go. Provocation was a kind of foreplay with her. She came at you until you either gave in or told her she was full of shit. In the mood I was in tonight I was not about to give in to anyone.

"Laurie's wearing a summer sweater, and those sweat socks are so thin I can see her feet through them."

"Dad!" Laurie protested from the floor, still not diverting her eyes from Billy Skunk.

"What do you expect us to do?" Elaine persisted. "Dress up in ski sweaters and hiking boots inside the house like you do, then complain about how hot it is?"

I could see we were not going anywhere with this issue, would never resolve it to anyone's satisfaction if we thrashed it out for a hundred years. "It's not important," I said. "The house smells great. Which one of these many vapors are we indulging in tonight?"

"We're having meatloaf," she smiled, as happy to change the subject as I was. "The coq au vin is for tomorrow, and we'll finish the leftovers during the rest of the week."

I slipped my arm around her waist and walked her back to the kitchen. "You're incredible. You do it all, and you're still a lovely piece of ass."

"You're not bad yourself. A bit of a pain in the ass sometimes, but nobody's perfect."

As usual, she got the last dig in before we sat down to dinner.

Chapter Three

Elaine held back the bad news until afterward. Mark and Laurie were getting ready for bed, and Elaine and I were in the living room sipping the last of the wine from dinner. Laurie needed braces, she informed me. Dr. Mandel would do the job for twenty-eight hundred dollars, payable over eighteen months.

"And that's cheap," she said with emphasis, making her point before I protested. "Everybody else in town is getting three thousand dollars at least."

"It may be less outrageous, but it sure as hell ain't cheap."

"What are we supposed to do?" She was obviously ready to go the distance on this one. "She *needs* braces. My parents never let me have them when I was her age, and now I'm stuck with this overbite for the rest of my life. And Laurie's got *my* teeth."

"All right, all right, she needs braces!" I figured it was time for the shit to hit the fan. "God forbid she should go through life hating us because we deprived her of braces when she was thirteen. How about some psychotherapy, too, to help her cope with the horrible ordeal? We don't want her getting all fucked up because she has to walk around with her mouth looking like a birdcage for the next two years."

"I don't understand you." Elaine's cheeks were flushed with anger now—anger and a little too much wine. "You act like you're being persecuted every time we have to spend some money. We're not leading a conspiracy against you. I didn't *plan* for her to have my teeth so that we had to spend some money to straighten them out."

"It's not *just* the twenty-eight hundred for braces. It's the six hundred dollars worth of pebbles for the driveway. When I was a kid rocks were free. You got all you wanted for nothing. Now I have to pay some prick to pour stones all over my driveway. Then there's two hundred and fifty dollars for a water pump to pump the fucking water out of the cellar. I . . ."

"If you had cleaned the gutters when you were supposed . . ."

"Shut up a minute! I'm not finished. Before that it was three thousand six hundred and forty dollars and seventy-five cents for the new oil burner, the cast iron, super-efficient, flame-retention, anti-pollution firebox that's going to save us all kinds of money during the next twenty years. If it doesn't break down in three of course. Then . . ."

"Are you finished yet?"

"Hell no! I'm just getting warmed up. On top of that there's nine hundred dollars a month to carry a condo out in Utah we can't rent out because they've overdeveloped the goddamned town. There's two thousand dollars a year just to fly back and forth to visit the place, plus another thousand dollars worth of lift tickets every time we go out."

"You're the one who needed Utah. I would have been perfectly happy driving up to Vermont once or twice every winter."

"Then, of course, there's six thousand five hundred dollars we're still paying off for a trip to Europe you just had to have. You . . ."

"You wanted that as much as I did, you son of a bitch!"

"Bullshit! In addition to all that, we have another fifteen hundred dollars . . ."

"I'm not sitting here and listening to any more of this. I'm going upstairs to read. When you stop raving like a maniac I'll . . ."

"Don't go. Stay here. We have to have a talk, a calm, rational discussion about money. No yelling, no screaming, just facts. Okay?"

It had to come out sooner or later. It was way overdue. With the fire crackling in the fireplace in front of the sofa, and the flickering light glinting in the Christmas tree ornaments across the room, the setting could not have been more tranquil, more idyllic. But tranquility was not in the air tonight. Resentment, anxiety, repressed fury that had been building up for three or four years, hostility, anger, everything but tranquility permeated the air like a heavy cloud.

"The fact is we've got financial problems," I told her quietly, as calmly as I could manage. I laid it all out for her: the mountain of debt we had taken on to finance our style of living, the monthly shortfall that was continually eroding the little capital we had left, the need to keep borrowing even more money just to keep our heads above water, the whole picture. I hadn't wanted to hit her with it all at once. My intention was to give her just a peek, a hint that there was something unrealistic about her picture postcard view of our existence, but once the floodgates were opened it all came spilling out in an endless torrent until I exhausted myself. Behind it all, too, was a need (although I didn't recognize it at the time) to shift some of the burden onto her shoulders before I buckled under the weight. When I finished Elaine was truly bewildered and more than just a bit frightened. Nothing was more menacing for her than financial insecurity; it opened up a Pandora's box full of primal terror.

"But you make so much money," was her initial reaction, her eyes wide and glowing red, reflecting the dancing flames in the fireplace.

"After taxes it's not enough. It ain't what you make, it's what you keep." I was feeling weary from the ordeal.

"Why didn't you tell me before?"

"It's bad enough I've been losing sleep over it, Elaine. You didn't need a nervous breakdown, too. I didn't want to tell you. I'm sorry I had to tell you now."

She bit her lower lip, sipped her wine and stared intently into the flames, her mind working on overdrive. "We'll sell the place in Utah. We don't need it and, you're right, it is too expensive."

"To whom? People are trying to unload vacation homes all over the country. It's a buyer's market right now."

Again she bit her lower lip, lost in thought. She wasn't panicking, not at all. She was going to tough it out, I could see that already. I had forgotten just how tough she really was.

"Considering your line of work, Paul, there must be something you can do. I mean, I don't know anybody who knows how to manipulate money better than you do."

What was she suggesting? There was an unmistakable tone of ruthlessness in her voice. "There may be a few things I can do," I said cautiously, wondering where she was leading.

"We absolutely cannot lose this house, that's number one. And the kids have to be taken care of. I don't care what else happens and how it has to be done, but those are the top priorities."

Here was a woman who was determined to do anything to protect hearth and home and, most of all, her children. Underneath everything else, all the suburban polish she put on, she was still a South Bronx streetfighter. When threatened she was tougher than I, firing me up with the courage to think creatively, to come up with unorthodox solutions to our dilemma if everything else failed. Why not? I was the one who would be taking all the risks, the one whose neck was stuck out there beyond the perimeter. There was no doubt in my mind that she was prepared to sacrifice her husband to save her children, if it came to that. Startled as I was at first, I admired her instincts. I reached over and took her hand.

"Don't worry. Nothing's going to happen. I'll find a way, that you can be sure of."

Elaine leaned against me and kissed me passionately. I don't think she ever excited me more than she did then. We went upstairs without saying a word, and practically tore each other's clothes off the second we entered the bedroom. We were in a hurry to get at each other's naked body, to explore each other's terrain like two horny teenagers going at it for the first time. And then we fucked with great intensity and passion until a strong current jolted us into a violent climax.

Heavy dry snowflakes filtered down through the gray clouds onto the streets of New York City the next day. Momentarily at least, they covered the filth with a powdery white blanket, but I knew that exhaust fumes would turn the whiteness into black slush before the day was over. What a crime, a travesty of nature, I thought. It was an apt reminder that beauty is rare and fleeting. The reality of daily existence is quick to stamp its ugly marks on it.

I hailed a cab in front of the Garden and told the driver to take me crosstown to the Century Hotel on Park Avenue. There was a luncheon there I wanted to attend since the speaker was Kevin O'Malley, the Police Commissioner of New York City. Kevin and I had grown up together in the South Bronx, and I followed his career as he worked his way up through the labyrinthine legal structure of the city while I toiled—if that's the word—in the canyons of Wall Street. Kevin's father had been Police Commissioner before him, so it was a natural succession of sorts when he was appointed to that powerful post by Mayor Feldman. I hadn't seen Kevin since his pre-Commissioner days when I ran into him at a securities analysts meeting at the World Trade Center. Kevin was one of the heavies the city had lined up to try to convince the financial community that New York City bonds, despite the city's fiscal infirmities, were still a good risk for pension portfolios. To a great extent he had succeeded, using an adroit mixture of Thomistic logic and thinly veiled political bullying. He was a consummate actor, a brilliant scholar, and an Irish streetfighter all rolled into one.

When I stepped into the main ballroom it was already crowded, with most of the people clustered around the two portable bars in the far corners. I scanned the room looking for a familiar face, and spotted a few of New York's movers and shakers scattered among the crowd. Marty Finnegan, the owner of the Hudson Club, a lavish hotel and casino built out over the river in the West Sixties, was engaged in an intense conversation with the Parks Commissioner. Marty and I had gone to St. Anselm's High School in the Bronx together. After college he opened up one bar after another in Manhattan, developing important political contacts along the way, until he finally got the zoning changes needed to erect his hedonistic pleasure palace overlooking the river and the eastern shore of New Jersey. Exactly who the backers were who had fronted the tens of millions of dollars for construction was a subject of great speculation. Some things it was better not to know too much about. Marty nodded as I walked in, acknowledging everyone he knew as they moved past him without missing a beat in his conversation with Commissioner Rosen. The one guy I didn't want to talk to grabbed hold of my elbow as I sidled up to the bar. Harry Winkler, the popular financial writer and biographer, lived a few towns down the line from me in Cos Cob. I didn't dislike Harry, really, but I found him to be a terrible snoop who was always digging for information you didn't want to reveal. A mutual friend once told me that his marriage was almost wrecked by something he told Harry in confidence that later found its way into print. Still, Harry could be useful at times. He was a great source of information who was all too willing to share the most intimate details of other people's lives once you gave him a crumb or two he could use in one of his books.

"What're you doing away from your quote machine this time of day?" he asked as I ordered a beer.

"I came to hear Kevin tell us why the city's so fucked up, the same as everybody else."

"You don't need Kevin to tell you that," he said, slugging from a bottle of Heineken's. "The city's fucked up because half the people in this room have their hands in everyone else's pockets. You can't take a piss in New York without getting a permit first."

"How's your friend Donald Trump?" I asked, noticing that a few more gray hairs had found their way into his mustache and beard.

"Fuck him! Do you know how much it cost the taxpayers for him to build that domed stadium of his? Big entrepreneur, right, who's never risked a penny of his own money."

"I hear that sidekick of his, what's his name, the lawyer who represented him on that other deal, is dying of cancer."

"Cancer, my ass. The son of a bitch has got AIDS."

"Who told you that?" I asked, startled.

"It's true, believe me. It comes from an impeccable source as they say. Tell me. You're a pretty good friend of Kevin's, right? I hear he wants to run for mayor this year when Feldman retires. What have you heard about that?"

"Nothing. I haven't talked to Kevin in months."

"Really? I thought you two were pretty tight."

"It's true. I fell out of touch . . ."

"Anything you tell me is in the strictest confidence, I want you to know that."

"Excuse me, Harry. There's someone over there I haven't seen in a year. Talk to you later."

"Sure, Paul. We'll have lunch, right?"

I moved across the room looking for new faces. The crowd was pretty oiled up by now, and the din of conversation was a palpable presence in the air. I ran into Mike Fiorito, an analyst I knew at Merrill Lynch, and the two of us carried our drinks to one of the tables where we were quickly joined by others anxious to get started on their Lemon Sole or Chicken Florentine. For an extra four bucks you could have the Beef Wellington, an indulgence I was willing to leave to the cardiac arrest candidates.

Lunch was an uneventful affair. The booze and wine flowed freely and everyone scouted the table for possible new contacts who might be able to do them a favor in the future. Mike Fiorito was on my left, and my table companion on the right was Sally Harris of Prudential-Bache, one of the highest-paid women in the investment banking field. Sally was trim and petite with light brown bangs combed down neatly over her forehead. She looked like a minister's wife out with her friends for an afternoon tea. But she had a mind that worked like a computer, and her demure little body harbored the instincts and the morals of a cobra. I had seen more than one Wall Street veteran underestimate her at the negotiating table, only to realize when it was too late that she had just raped his bank account.

"What brings you uptown today?" I asked her. "I know it can't be the food."

"I like to rub shoulders with the big boys once in a while," she answered with a smile. Today she was wearing a pin-striped suit with a big red bow tied around her high white collar. I always had the feeling that beneath her librarianish demeanor she was probably a pretty fiery woman.

"You're sitting next to the wrong guy then," I kidded her. "I'm just a poor middle-aged stockbroker trying to scratch out a living."

"Yes, well we poor working stiffs need all the contacts we can make. Let's have lunch the next time you're coming downtown. I enjoy getting away from the office and swapping war stories once in a while."

"I'd love to."

Our attention was called to the dais by a portly gentleman rapping his spoon against a water glass and blowing into the microphone. On the dais beside Kevin O'Malley were the standard religious representatives usually found at these affairs—a dour-looking rabbi and a round cherubic priest. Protestants no longer had much input into New York City politics. The priest had a big fleshy face with no jaw or chin line. His cheeks just melted down like hot dough into his shoulders, and he had a stomach to match, a soft breadloaf that jiggled over his belt. The first thought that crossed my mind was that celibacy was just so goddamned fattening. His face was blood red and his eyes were a faded washed-out watery blue. There was an alcoholic beatitude to his entire demeanor, while the rabbi looked forlorn and long-suffering. Perhaps he had gas he was trying to hold in.

Kevin was introduced and the room rocked with loud applause. He was well liked and respected, a street kid from a tough neighborhood who had worked his way up with a combination of drive, intelligence, and political savvy. Tall and skinny, somewhat stooped, with graying hair powdering the thinning black curls, steel-rimmed glasses sliding down a sloping Bob Hope nose, he launched directly into his subject with flashes of sardonic humor. "Somebody asked me to come here and talk to you about white-collar crime," he said, "although why such a distinguished assemblage would be interested in that subject is beyond me." He was candid about his own political orientation, describing himself as a knee-jerk liberal who, upon assuming the office of Police Commissioner, had been mugged by the facts of life. The old political labels didn't fit anymore, he declared. There were too many neos around—"neo-liberals, neo-conservatives, neo-moderates, and neo-whatever is fashionable at the moment." He was a realist before anything else, he said, a pragmatist and problem-solver dealing on a daily basis with the unique conditions of modern urban life.

"Quite frankly, we can't even begin to worry about who's moving money from point A to point B without proper authorization," he said. "It's a question of time, manpower and money. Give us the men, the money, and the technology, and we'll take care of it. Right now, however, every cop on the beat, every plainclothesman and undercover detective is working overtime to control a condition that's unique to this moment in history. No longer is our job one of protecting the good guys from the crooks. In this society today, perhaps for the first time ever, we have a generation in our midst, and I'm talking about kids ten, eleven, twelve, and thirteen years of age, who are functioning sociopaths. They are totally amoral and devoid of any semblance of a value system. They can't even be called evil because they truly do not make moral judgments or distinctions. They see nothing wrong with walking into a delicatessen, for example, sticking a gun in the owner's face and demanding his money, then pulling the trigger just for kicks after they've gotten what they came for. They see nothing wrong with blowing away another life; they feel absolutely no remorse, no twinge of guilt or wrongdoing.

"In my opinion, this generation of sociopaths is completely irredeemable. These kids are beyond the pale of rehabilitation. A whole generation of youngsters is lost to us and, more than that, they have positioned themselves as the implacable enemies of society. They are truly the New Barbarians clamoring to tear down the gates of civilization as we know it today and terrorize the cities. How they got that way is not my area of concern. I have my own theories that would take a few hours to unwind, but my primary job is to control this cancer, to contain the erosion before we are all overwhelmed. And this is not just a New York City problem, make no mistake about that. We are looking at a modern-day phenomenon that is at least national, probably international in scope, and may possibly be linked psychologically to the terrorist mentality that permeates global politics. I don't know. I'm not sure. I haven't worked it out that far yet. But it is very real, very threatening, and it affects all of us.

"So, if I seem to have avoided the main topic of discussion today, please forgive me. I would love to have the luxury of coming up with solutions to embezzlement and crime in the corporate suite, but I'm afraid I just don't have the capability of doing so. If society thinks it's important enough to worry about, then society—you, me and other taxpayers—will have to make the money available to launch a full-scale attack on the problem. Right now, however, we are exhausting all our resources on the more immediate problem of trying to keep the next generation, the six- and seven-year-olds, from turning out like their older brothers and sisters."

The applause was thunderous and instantaneous, a standing no-holds-barred ovation. It was one of the most remarkable speeches I had ever heard delivered by a police commissioner, or by anyone else for that matter. It was also a brilliantly crafted political exercise. If Kevin was not gearing up for a mayoral campaign, then it had to be the Senate he had his eye on. I did my own instant analysis of Kevin's talk, trying to figure out exactly what he had accomplished. His performance, as offhand and extemporaneous as he tried to make it appear, was carefully orchestrated. He told everyone in the room exactly what they wanted to hear, and simultaneously avoided discussing the one subject that made them uneasy—the subtle machinations of white-collar crime. I doubted that he had a single enemy in the room at that moment.

"What do you think?" Sally leaned close and whispered with that impish grin on her face.

"I think if Kevin wants to run for mayor this fall he can raise a million dollars right here for his campaign chest."

I wanted to go up and say hello to Kevin before I left, but it was impossible to get near him. He was besieged from all sides by well-wishers and glad-handers, people swarming all over him vying for his attention. I don't think I ever admired his skills more than I did then, but there was something deeply troubling about his speech at the same time. Did he really believe what he said, or did he merely deliver a message calculated for maximum political effect? Either way it was alarming. If what he said about the hordes of allegedly barbaric youth terrorizing the cities was true, there was little hope for society; it was the bleakest and most pessimistic of all possible scenarios. And if Kevin was tailoring his views to suit his political ambitions, he was revealing an aspect of his nature I never saw before—a dark and ugly demagogic core that was all the more dangerous because of his wit and intellectualism.

The dark and ugly core of my own nature came a little closer to the surface later in the afternoon. The seed of larceny that had been gestating for weeks past now became a palpable, living presence. Without consciously entertaining any grandiose schemes about how or when it would be done, *if* it *could* be done, my subconscious had been working overtime on the dilemma. With apparent spontaneity the thought flashed into my mind, from the blue as it were, that I required a dummy account, one dummy account for openers at least. I had a client I didn't like, Joseph Pellegrino, a contractor from Queens, who had been using his dead brother Anthony's social security number for years. This tidbit of information he passed on to me one day with a confidential leer on his face, perhaps hoping to turn me into an accomplice of sorts. I told him that what he did was his business provided I didn't know about it, so I would pretend I didn't hear his last remark. He never brought it up again and I helped him carry on his illegal deception with my passive complicity. Every few weeks or so I accepted an envelope stuffed with cash from him which I dutifully invested in various types of bearer bonds. Joe recognized a true confederate when he saw one; despite my feeble protestation, we were cut from the same cloth; notwithstanding my dislike of him as a person, we were birds of a feather doing business together. Possibly I was even more corrupt than he since, presumably, I knew better and should have been held to a higher ethical standard.

So it came to pass that frosty afternoon following Kevin O'Malley's speech that I opened an account in the name of J. Anthony Pellegrino, using a social security number from a file of numbers I had been keeping for a rainy day; that day had finally arrived. The numbers belonged to former clients now deceased, others who had retired permanently overseas or disappeared to parts unknown, and some were phonies available on the black market complete with bogus names and addresses. The address for my dummy account was easy. For a few dollars a month you could have any one of dozens anywhere in Manhattan, and hundreds more throughout the country. These were little more than cubbyhole offices with mail drops for scores of "residents," and some of them even had a switchboard and would take messages for an additional monthly fee. Every few days or so you picked up your mail and phone messages. It was a regulated business, but there was also a subterranean market for such activity where the identity of the real tenant was closely guarded. Once the name, address, and social security number were established, it was an easy matter to walk into a bank with a hundred dollars in cash and open a checking account.

I had no concrete plan of action in mind when I did all this, but I felt better knowing the groundwork had been laid. I felt a vague thrill, a tremor of excitement rather like an errant husband slipping into a motel room in mid-afternoon with his best friend's wife. It was illicit and stimulating, and also a bit frightening when I contemplated where I might be heading. In the midst of this incipient impropriety, Monica came into my office and laid some paperwork on my desk.

"How're you doing out there, Monica?" I asked absentmindedly.

"I'm lonely and bored. I'd like to hide under your desk and suck your cock."

"Take off your dress, will you. I'm going to eat you into a coma."

"Really? Just tell me when."

"Get the hell out of here right now before something happens we'll both be sorry for later."

Chapter Four

We usually invited three or four couples over for a party on Superbowl Sunday, but this year we were on the receiving end of an invitation to the home of Jack Travis, the billionaire developer who owned everything from football and soccer teams to Las Vegas gambling casinos to the futuristic Travis Plaza, a complex of hotels, office towers, and condominiums at the foot of Manhattan. Jack lived in a rambling Victorian mansion on six acres of land overlooking Long Island Sound on Brimlow's Point. I had been introduced to him two years before by Alex Jordan, the Chief Financial Officer for the Kaufman brothers who, along with Donald Trump, were Travis's main competitors in the real estate world. Jack was still only in his early forties, a genuine Golden Boy with flaxen blond hair threaded throughout with an undercurrent of brown—vanilla fudge hair a friend of mine once called it. He was movie-star handsome, and his wife Jeanine was his female counterpart, a willowy brunette with a thick Georgia accent.

It was a cold blowy day on the Sound, and there was a pale moon in the afternoon sky hanging above the water's edge on the other side of Brimlow's Point. The first thing that caught your eye when you entered the Travis home was the ceiling mural that had been painted, Michelangelo style, by a local artist named Ann George. She had done the work practically for nothing, so happy was she to receive the commission to do the job. Her gamble had paid off handsomely. The Travises were delighted with her work and talked her up. Her reputation as their resident genius caught on immediately, and her job offers and fees skyrocketed with it. Jack Travis acquired a masterpiece practically for nothing, and in doing so he launched the career of a talented but previously unrecognized artist.

Elaine and I arrived about twenty minutes late, fashionably late enough so that the crowd was just starting to fill out when we walked in. I recognized many of the faces there from Rotary lunches, sports events, and fund-raising activities around town, and it was amusing to observe the heavy concentration of people from the usual bread-and-butter businesses. Suffice it to say that, if a bomb had fallen on Jack Travis's home this particular Superbowl Sunday, all activity in the town of Soundview would have come to an abrupt halt. The key politicians, builders and developers, real estate and insurance brokers, lawyers and assorted financial types all would have been blown away. A widely known real estate attorney with reputed mob connections—the one who supposedly was dying of AIDS or cancer, depending on the source—was holding court near the punch bowl looking as hale and hearty as ever. A few feet away from him was Mayor Paris talking to another clot of attentive listeners. He called himself Ned Paris these days, but I was perhaps the only one in the room besides his wife who knew him as Nunzio Sappienza, a former building inspector from the Gunhill Road section of the Bronx who had once been indicted, but never convicted, for accepting bribes from landlords in return for overlooking building violations. He knew that I knew him from that old life twenty years before, but neither one of us ever alluded to those days. Instead, he rewarded me with little morsels of gossip whenever we were alone, an unspoken bribe of sorts for me to keep my historical knowledge to myself.

"That fuckin' Travis," he said to me after a Rotary lunch just before Christmas. "He had the balls to call me up a few months back and ask me for permission to land his helicopter on his lawn. Imagine the gall."

"Just what the town needs, helicopters taking off at seven o'clock in the morning."

"All because that Chinese friend of his, Terry Ling, has a helipad on his own property. I told him 'No way, Jack. The neighbors are going crazy over Ling as it is. If I give you permission, too, they'll hang me upside down on top of the firehouse.' "

"Poor guy. He must feel like a second-class citizen without his own helipad."

"With all his money," Paris continued, "he's still scheming for new ways to make a buck. Would you believe he wanted to subdivide his property here into one-acre building lots instead of enjoying what he's got? The man just can't help himself. Thank God the Brimlow's Point Residents Association voted him down on that, too."

"How's his golf game? I hear he's a pretty good athlete."

"Athlete my ass. More P.R. bullshit. He golfed twenty over par the last time I played with him, then walked off and stiffed the caddy, he was so pissed off. Cost me twenty bucks out of my own pocket."

Terry Ling, Jack Travis's "Chinese friend," according to Paris, who was born in San Francisco and spoke not a word of Chinese, was also at the party. Terry had achieved notoriety back in the late sixties when his Ling High Growth Mutual Fund, with close to a billion dollars under management, went bankrupt. Millions of investors, many of whom had entrusted their life savings to Ling, were stranded high and dry without a nickel. It was the scandal of the decade; the wonder boy of the go-go years on Wall Street who had become a legend because of his supposed genius for stock selection turned out to have feet of clay. Bull markets make everyone look like a genius. But his real genius, it turned out, had been for self-promotion. When the dust settled and all the brilliant analysts with 20-20 hindsight took their blinders off and checked the record, they discovered that Ling had never been able to outperform the market in his entire life. The very analysts who had been praising him to the skies a few short months before, helping him establish his financial empire, suddenly became his most savage critics, dismantling his jerry-built reputation as though they were demolishing a building. It's one thing to con the public, but don't ever put one over on the professionals; they'll hound you until they've stripped your bones and left your carcass in the sun to rot.

While Ling's mutual fund may have gone bankrupt, it turned out that he himself was anything but. He seemed to have disappeared from the face of the earth for a while, then emerged five years later with a three-million-dollar house on four acres of land overlooking the water in Soundview. His next-door neighbor was Dinah Searls, the sultry black rock singer who was worth an estimated ten million dollars and was invariably late in paying her meat bill at Giacometti's, the local butcher. When social critics castigated Soundview for being a lily-white community, local boosters always pointed to Dinah as proof that the town was integrated. It would have been if there were enough blacks with three million dollars for a mansion on the water; buying a home on a building lot in the middle of town was another question entirely. Dinah was in attendance with her fourth husband, Nils something-or-other, a shipping magnate from Stockholm, while Terry Ling was chatting up Jeanine Travis and sipping a scotch and soda. Terry had absconded from Wall Street with his own fortune intact, snubbing his nose at the critics who left him for dead after the demise of his mutual fund, and he was now reaping the rewards of his new reputation as the brains behind the Travis empire, the man who spoke directly to God and passed on his pearls of wisdom to Travis himself. He was Jack Travis's best friend and chief financial consultant, living proof that you don't necessarily have to die first in order to be reincarnated.

Elaine spotted Alex Jordan and his wife Barbara over by the large TV screen, one of many scattered throughout the house, watching the game. We walked over to say hello and Alex leaned down to kiss Elaine before shaking my hand, a priority of his that never failed to irk me for some reason. I kissed Barbara and then said hello to him.

"Who's winning?" I asked.

"Three-nothing Giants. First quarter. How's Wall Street treating you these days?"

The first thing you noticed about Alex was the stench of tobacco that emanated from his pores like a malignant cloud. Barbara chain-smoked too, mostly I think in self-defense. They both had brownish-yellow teeth, and the first two fingers on Alex's right hand were stained brown from nicotine. Even his gray mustache was stained a sickly yellow from decades of filtering cigarette smoke. He was one of the few people I knew who still drank vats of brown whiskey, bourbon mostly. Everyone else had long ago switched to the light white stuff—vodka, white wine, and light beer ad nauseum. I admired his dedication to custom and habit, preferring the darker brews like Bass Ale and Dos Equis to the tasteless pale suds myself.

"Okay, I suppose," I answered. "Could be better, but why complain?"

Alex nodded and sipped his bourbon, his eyes fastened on the screen.

"How about yourself? I hear the Kaufman brothers want to build the tallest building in the world before Donald Trump gets around to putting up his monstrosity."

"Don't believe everything you read in the papers, fella. Everybody's doing a lot of talking right now, a lot of feinting and jabbing, but I don't see anybody rushing to actually build anything in this environment. The numbers just don't come out right."

Alex still retained more than a trace of the British accent he brought over with him twenty-five years before. It was ingrained in his very being like the tobacco stench, something he would never lose.

"I guess that means Donald Trump won't be moving ahead with his own plans either."

"Not bloody likely. It keeps their names in the headlines, though, just talking about it."

There was a moan from the group assembled around the television as the Forty-Niners passed into the end zone for the first touchdown of the game, then kicked the extra point for a seven-to-three lead. I left Elaine with the Jordans while I went over to fetch a couple of drinks, a beer for myself and a vodka-rocks for Elaine. Access to the portable bar set up in the main living room, Jeanine's "solarium" as she liked to call it, was all but blocked by Bill Walters, Soundview's six-foot-four-inch-tall and three-foot-wide Commissioner of Planning and Zoning. He was swaying already, shifting his weight from foot to foot, a not altogether meager accomplishment for a man with such a formidable center of gravity. I skipped around his right side as he bobbed to the left, and ordered my drinks. I loved eavesdropping at these affairs, and kept my antennae tuned to the rambling discourse he was delivering to a couple who listened politely but looked as though they would rather be talking to someone else.

"If . . . it was up to me," Walters hiccuped, "I'd lock 'em up an' throw away the key."

Breaking and entering was a major topic of conversation around town lately, that and drugs. Gangs of highly skilled and sophisticated robbers were driving up to Soundview from Brooklyn and Manhattan in late-model BMWs, Mercedes-Benzes and Jaguars, breaking into homes within a few minutes' drive of the highway exits, and taking off with cash, jewelry, VCRs, television sets, and anything else of value they could load quickly into their cars. They kept changing their pattern, concentrating on one neighborhood first then shifting their attention to a different one on the other side of town. Rape, assault and battery, drug abuse, and even murder were also on the rise in Soundview, alarming town residents who believed until now that they were insulated from the problems afflicting surrounding communities.

"Pay . . . we pay a fortune to live here an' now . . . now we gotta be worried about this . . . all this drugs an' everything. . . . Goddamn kids never had it so good," Walters added incongruously.

"I quite agree," said the gentleman he was speaking to, someone in a blazer, green slacks and docksiders despite the frigid weather, while his wife nodded and searched the room frantically for an escape route.

I carried my drinks away from the bar, marveling to myself about the complexities of the human mind. It was not so terribly long ago that Bill Walters himself had been charged with tax evasion by the IRS. There was some question about how a man, ostensibly earning fifty-two thousand dollars a year as a public servant, came to be living in a five hundred thousand dollar house, drove around town in a Cadillac that was never more than two years old, and vacationed in San Diego each year in his own home overlooking the Pacific. All this appeared in the local newspaper three days running, then just as quickly disappeared. The issue was apparently resolved quietly to Bill's satisfaction since nothing seemed to have changed in the interim; his level of living had not declined, nor had his salary as a town bureaucrat gone up appreciably. According to the original newspaper accounts, IRS was charging him with failure to pay taxes on hundreds of thousands of dollars of unreported income during a five-year period. Then nothing, silence. Two years passed and Walters still had his job, his cars and homes, his reputation as a solid citizen and a pillar of the community. He talked drunkenly but passionately of life-long incarceration for hoodlums who ripped off two or three thousand dollars worth of merchandise at a time, while those around him who knew his past nodded solemnly in agreement. I thought about Kevin O'Malley's speech the previous week, focusing on his piquant reference to those who move money "from point A to point B without proper authorization." What a facile and seemingly innocuous description of perhaps the most subtle and hard-to-detect criminal activity of our age. Hundreds of thousands, even millions of dollars changed hands in a split second with no obvious thuggery involved, no assault and battery, no cuts and bruises, no lacerations or concussions, just battered bank accounts, bruised egos, bewildered victims, and an incredulous and somewhat admiring public marveling at the genius and complexity of it all. Now you see it, now you don't. Poof. Pots of legal tender vanishing without a trace.

"Did I miss anything?" I asked when I returned to the group.

"Seven-six San Francisco," said Alex. "The Giants pushed all the way down to the two-yard line and had to settle for three. Bloody criminals. Don't tell me they don't have their eyes on the point spread."

Alex was another mystery to me, as he had been for the three years I'd known him. Elaine and Barbara met at a high school cake sale and started off as tennis buddies. Eventually we were invited to their house for dinner, and they to ours. As couples we evolved into fairly fast friends as these things go, getting together for drinks or an evening at the theater once a month or so. Yet, as long as I had known him—as long as I would ever know him, I felt—I had only been able to catch glimpses of the man. There was a reserve about Alex; *deceptiveness* was too harsh a word without something more tangible to go on. He told people precisely as much as he wanted them to know, and not a syllable more. Many high-powered, well-connected people are somewhat vague about exactly what it is they do for a living, but at this stage of our friendship I should have been able to penetrate a little further behind his shell. "Oh, I'm just a numbers cruncher," was the most I had ever been able to get out of him. "I do the sums to make sure they all come out right in the end." Elaine and I had more than one discussion about Alex, a discussion that invariably threatened to deteriorate into an argument when she got, I thought, needlessly provocative.

"Alex must make tons of money," she commented about a year after we met them.

"I'm sure he does, but there's more there than meets the eye."

"What do you mean?"

"Have you ever been able to figure out what he does for a living?"

"Something in real estate finance I think. Isn't he a CPA or something?"

"Or something. Working for the Kaufman brothers has got to be a somewhat shady occupation, I'd say."

"In other words, you think he's a crook," she snapped, staring directly at me with a challenge in her eyes and voice.

"I didn't say that and I hope you never repeat it to anyone. I'm merely suggesting that he operates on a very high-powered level and he's quite mysterious about the things he does and the people he comes in contact with."

"Of course I'm not going to repeat it. I wish you wouldn't talk to me as though I'm an idiot. But you seem to think that everybody who has more money than we do has to be a crook or something close to it."

"Look at the way they live, Elaine. They've got three boys in college simultaneously. That's, say, forty thousand a year after taxes. Besides the house they live in, they own three other houses in Soundview that they rent out, not one of them worth less than four hundred and fifty thousand. They vacation all over the world as often as they want to, plus . . . hell, you don't do all that on any kind of a salary, not on three hundred thousand, not on four hundred thousand dollars a year."

"Has he ever said anything to you that would indicate he's not on the up-and-up?"

I thought a minute about that. There was nothing specific, nothing concrete. But . . .

"No, not really. I suppose I could find out though. He's been after me for some time to have lunch with him, meet with some of his people to get acquainted, toss some ideas around, that sort of thing."

"And?"

"I've never taken him up on it because, well, I'm not sure why. I'm always busy with my own clients in the middle of the day."

"Maybe you should," she said emphatically, her green eyes flashing with a bright intensity.

"Well, we'll see. Maybe I will one of these days."

Three years into our friendship, nothing much had changed in the interim. We still met them for dinner and drinks, still spent an evening at the theater with them, still ran into them at affairs such as this Superbowl party, still talked about every conceivable subject except anything too personal. I liked Alex and Barbara, but found my friendship with them so superficial, it felt frustrating and incomplete. I could not really "get into it" with them, as I liked to do with others I knew, and I felt deep inside that his interest in me was mainly opportunistic; somewhere, somehow, he would find a way to use me. Elaine accused me of being paranoid but, then again, I have never denied that paranoia is my first line of defense.

The game ended San Francisco 24, Giants 20, a curiosity of more than passing importance since the point spread was three-and-a-half in favor of the Forty-Niners. "I knew it, I bloody well knew it," Alex fumed, his face turning a blotchy purple. It was the most emotional outburst I had ever heard from him.

"I don't understand football very well," Elaine said to Barbara.

"Neither do I, but Alex seems to feel it's all very predictable, very scientific."

"I need another drink. Come on, fella. You look like you're running on empty too."

Alex stormed toward the bar and I followed behind him, admiring the self-absorption and single-mindedness of the man. He was motivated almost exclusively by money, and every action he took, every movement he made was tailored with his primary goal in mind. I loved money, too, and desperately needed more of it to finance the lifestyle I had drifted into, but in many ways I felt that I was a perpetual student in life, an irredeemable observer driven to learn from the actions of others. I lacked ruthlessness, I knew that, and sometimes I regarded this as a personal weakness that kept me a half-beat out of step with the tempo of the times. It worried Elaine, too. She never said as much but it was evident in the tone of her voice, especially since our conversation about money a few nights earlier. People like Alex took action without worrying about anything except the benefits for themselves. I tended to look at six different sides of a situation, weighing the pros and cons, the legal and moral aspects of what I was thinking of doing until the opportunity passed. I needed to believe strongly enough in the existentialist code if I ever hoped to rise up out of my personal quagmire.

We ordered drinks at the bar and I observed, again observed, Alex smiling, shaking hands and exchanging pleasantries with those near him like a man running for public office. He knew everyone and he had a gift for being able to size up and dismiss in a second those who would be of no use to him. His chitchat was never idle or without purpose.

"What have you been up to lately?" I asked him. "Anything exciting?"

He sipped from his bourbon and soda and lit up another unfiltered Pall Mall. "I met some chaps a few weeks back. An absolutely brilliant group who are starting up their own company. If I had five million dollars I'd put every penny into their operation. You ought to meet them yourself. Could be a very lucrative situation."

"Maybe I'll take you up on your long-standing lunch invitation. What day looks good to you?"

Alex hesitated a moment, drawing on his cigarette then sipping his bourbon while exhaling smoke through his nostrils. "Will you be around the next week or so?"

"I'm not going anywhere until the second week in February when we head out to Utah for some skiing. Anytime before or after that is just fine."

Alex stared straight into my eyes, as directly as he ever had. "I'll call you," he said, "I'll set it up and give you a call."

Then he excused himself and moved off across the room toward a group of men clustered around the buffet table. He did not invite me to come along so I stayed at the bar observing, always observing, studying the little cliques of people scattered throughout the room engaged in isolated conversations. It was an enormous party with perhaps two hundred people there, but there was no general ebb and flow, no continuity of social intercourse. The crowd was broken up into clots of three, four, or five, with one or two people splitting away from one group at any time and joining another somewhere across the room. Jack Travis himself spent a moment or so with each individual clique, shaking hands and exchanging a few words. Whenever he approached a particular group, all conversation ceased and attention focused exclusively on him. I watched him work the room like a professional statesman, a diplomat spending a little more time here and a little less time there, but never an inordinate amount of time with anyone. Jeanine circumscribed the party from the opposite direction, doing her own bit of magic everywhere she stopped. It was an extraordinary performance, perhaps the best study in political gamesmanship I had ever witnessed.

"What did you think of the party?" Elaine asked me as we drove down the long winding driveway. The sky was inky black behind us as it blended with the horizon.

"Fascinating. There must have been a billion and a half dollars in that house today."

"Incredible. Did you meet anybody interesting?"

"Interesting? Well we'll see. I'm having lunch with Alex in a week or so. He has some people he says he wants me to meet."

"Oh?"

"It'll be interesting to find out what that's all about."

Elaine nodded and looked out the window as we exited past the guardhouse into more plebeian surroundings. She didn't say anything, but I could tell she obviously approved. Having lunch with Alex Jordan, she believed, was a smart thing for me to do.

Chapter Five

I knew my anxiety over money was getting critical when I started to think more and more about my cousin Vito. Vito was a semi-hood forever lurking around the periphery of organized crime. He owned a home improvement business in Mount Vernon a few years back—kitchens, bathrooms, Vinylume siding, patios, that sort of thing—and when he couldn't find a buyer for it at his price, he did what any red-blooded American hoodlum would do: he burned it to the ground for the insurance money. The investigators came around sniffing for a hint of arson in the wind, palms were greased and a deal was cut, and Cousin Vito walked away with a smile on his face and some added ballast for his bank account. They called him "Coconuts" after that (Coco for short) because he proved he had a pair of big ones. He made it look so easy. The Vito Solution: if you can't sell it, burn it. He did and he got away with it. It happened every day, hundreds of times a day all over the country.

Would the Vito Solution work in Utah? I wondered. In my perplexed state, I focused on the condo in the mountains as the primary cause of my cash-flow problem. Mortgaged up to the rafters, I no longer had a nickel's worth of equity in the place. It was evidently unsalable and unrentable in the present economic environment. It was costing me a small fortune to carry it. Poof! Why not turn it into a pile of ashes and collect from the insurance company? Of course, the downside risk with the Vito Solution was a lengthy tenure as the guest of Uncle Sam in some federal penitentiary. Or else, the way my luck had been running lately, I might succeed only in burning down one wall instead of reducing my pile of glass and redwood to a black hole in the snow. Besides, I was emotionally attached to the elegant and expensive toy way out there in Mormon country. It would be like burning my best friend at the stake. I could not do it under any circumstances.

Arson was not my only solution. There was also bankruptcy and default. Let the bank foreclose on it and sell it at auction. Let the banks own all the unsalable, unrentable condos in the country. But this was equally unacceptable. It was the solution for a man without imagination, a man totally devoid of creative skills. I was capable of entertaining unorthodox ideas. What would Alex Jordan do if he were in my shoes? What was the Alex Solution to the problem? Clearly, Alex would say, it is far superior to make so much money that you can afford to have it all—houses, vacations, whatever you want—without feeling a pinch. Why not make all the money you need rather than do something crude and stupid? Why not move money from point A to point B if you are in a position to do so? It's the major enterprise of our time and you're not participating, Alex would reason. Banks were laundering hundreds of millions of dollars in drug money every day in Florida, Texas, and as far north as Boston. Brokerage firms kited checks and earned tens of millions of dollars in illegal interest. Advisors to the President of the United States bartered powerful jobs in Washington in return for some help with their own financial problems. Top executives made millions by trading on inside information. District Attorneys with a reputation for their toughness on street crime took kickbacks from mob figures. Big Bob Thompson, the top law enforcement officer in the country who delighted in tromping through marijuana fields with a flamethrower, pandered to the real estate developers in his native state. Credit companies and department stores charged customers nineteen percent while they themselves were borrowing money at nine percent. On and on it went. And what was the official response to all this? The banks and brokerage firms and other institutions received a slap on the wrist occasionally, while prostitutes and muggers went to jail for ten years.

Yes, the Alex Solution was clearly superior to the others. Points A and B were such a short distance apart, a split-second journey. It was like beaming Mr. Spock up to the *Starship Enterprise*. All I needed was a beaming device, a mode of transportation. Actually, such a device had already been established with the creation of my dummy account. Point A walked into my office three days after the Superbowl party in the person of my less-than-favorite client, Joseph Pellegrino, the contractor from Queens. Point B, of course, was fixed quite firmly in my own mind, or more accurately in my own bank account. That much, at least, had never been in doubt.

Joe introduced me to his "friend" with a wink. She was a small, attractive Oriental woman named Connie who had shiny white teeth that looked as though they were capped. She sat quietly beside him and fished a cigarette from her purse. I lit it for her and pushed the ashtray within her reach. Joe Pellegrino was the kind of man who enjoyed flaunting his sexual conquests. He was not bad looking but his face, to me at least, was scarred by that all-knowing leer he wore in place of a smile. He was slickly dressed with a bulbous pinky ring on his left hand. A strong odor of spicy after-shave lotion wafted from his persona. He struck me as someone who read *Gentleman's Quarterly* or *Uomo* for tips on the latest fashions, but no matter how he adorned himself he would always look like a 1950s gang leader. Without ceremony, he tossed a bulging envelope on my desk as though it were filled with single dollar bills instead of fifties and hundreds.

"I got a great poker hand here, four nines," he said, glancing at his friend to make sure she appreciated the joke.

"Right up to the limit," I smiled.

"Is there any way we can up the ante? Not that I don't like comin' in to see you, Paul, but it would be a lot easier for me if I could bring in twen'y or thirty at a time."

"I think maybe I can help you, Joe. I think I've got a way."

"Really?"

I nodded.

"How?"

"Leave it to me. Finding the loopholes is my job. That's what you're paying me for, right?"

"That's what I like about this guy," he said, flashing a smile at his girlfriend who was studying me with great curiosity through a veil of cigarette smoke. "You got a problem, come to Paul. He's the guy who knows how to fix it."

I noticed that he had refrained from calling me his Chinaman in front of Connie, although the effort must have been strenuous for him.

"Be right back," I said, picking up the envelope and leaving them alone for a few minutes while I went out to the cashier's cage. Without hesitating or giving the matter a second of thought, I deposited the cash into the dummy account I had opened in the name of J. Anthony Pellegrino. The wheels were already in motion and the act seemed all but inevitable. I had no specific plan in mind when I originally opened the account, but my subconscious must have been working overtime without my realizing it. Every detail was suddenly crystal clear to me. It was as though I had a voice inside me giving me instructions, plotting out my behavior with intricate precision. I knew what had to be done instinctively as it were, without having worked out anything like a Grand Scheme in my conscious mind. Perhaps my conscience could not have handled anything that was too obviously calculated. I had to chart my course on automatic pilot.

"Here's your receipt." I handed him a receipt for $9,999 made out in his own name. "I'll buy the usual and have it shipped out to you."

"So you think you can handle more than ten?" His eyes were wide, alive with thought. "I can send a lot more your way if you can help me out."

"No problem. Just bring it in," I smiled, keeping it as casual as possible. Nothing to it.

After he and Connie left. I bought $10,000 face value of bearer treasury bonds at a discount with a lower coupon rate than usual. The transaction came to $8,946.74 and the confirmation for the trade would be mailed to the fictitious J. Anthony Pellegrino at his equally fictitious address. It was a simple matter to type out a phony confirmation on a blank slip, listing the cost of the transaction as $9,989.40, which I mailed to Joe at his real address. The bonds, too, would be shipped to Joe in a week or so with an altered delivery slip, but the $1,052.26 in surplus cash would remain in the false account. Later on, whenever I felt the time was right, I would have the money wired to the checking account I had opened for J. Anthony Pellegrino, and then write a check to myself to complete the journey from point A safely home to point B. It was so simple I almost laughed giddily. Foolproof. The worst that could happen was that Joe might groan a bit about the yield he was getting, lower than what he was used to. But most of these cash-heavy entrepreneurs were unsophisticated when it came to the financial markets. A bunch of Wall Street mumbojumbo about yield curves and similar jargon would make their eyes glaze over quickly. They were happy to get rid of their greenbacks without having too many questions asked. I was so exhilarated I could almost feel my heart leaping out of my chest, or so I imagined. I was intoxicated, high on the thrill of it all. I couldn't stay in the office a minute longer. Grabbing my coat from the rack, I left work early and practically ran across the street to the Dublin House for a late-afternoon drink with my old buddy, Tommy Gilmartin.

The lunch-hour freak show had thinned out considerably, with only a few diehard drinkers scattered around the bar. Between noon and two the Dublin House sometimes approached the level of a psychotic pig-out, with sequined prostitutes, clownish pimps, grimy construction workers, dark-suited businessman, and off-duty cops clustered together in their assorted outfits. A visitor from more conventional parts might have thought he had inadvertently dropped in on a masquerade ball. I walked down to the far end of the bar and waited for Tommy to break off his conversation with a man nursing a scotch and water and smoking perhaps his thirtieth Camel of the day. The jukebox in the corner behind me emitted some high-pitched wailing that was a poor substitute for music. Through the marvels of modern technology, three Englishmen made themselves sound like five black women in labor.

"Beer, Paul?" Tommy asked after he had broken loose from the customer who didn't want to go home.

"No, I think I need something stronger right now. How about

some of your finest unadulterated Jack Daniels on the rocks with a twist."

Tommy made the drink, rubbing the lemon peel along the rim of the glass with a flourish. "The pressures of Wall Street got you down?" he asked with a grin.

"Not really. I feel pretty good today as a matter of fact. How're things going with you?"

Tommy looked over both shoulders to make sure no one was listening, then leaned closer and said, "I had to fire three bartenders yesterday for stealing."

"Really? How did you catch them?"

"See that guy down the other end, the one wearing the brown jacket and hat?"

"Yeah."

"He's my spotter. Comes in and checks the action to make sure all the money winds up in the till. A lot of the bars in the neighborhood use him."

"And?"

"He caught three of my best bartenders running a scam on me. Between the three of them they were hitting me for over a thousand a week."

"Ouch! That hurts."

"What hurts even more, Paul, is I trusted these guys. Patrick, the ringleader, was with me for two years. I brought him over from Ireland and gave him a job as a favor to my cousin. He was like family. I couldn't believe it."

"What did he say when you confronted him?"

"He didn't bat an eyelash, didn't even try to deny it. Looked me straight in the face and said, 'It's all been for a good cause. I wouldn't have done it otherwise.' "

"Raising money for the IRA?"

"IRA my ass. He's saving up to buy a bar down the street and go into competition. He never stole a nickel for anybody but himself in his life."

"Amazing."

"Can you believe it, Paul? You bring people into the country, set them up with a job and treat them like your own, and they pull something like that."

" 'God protect me from my friends; my enemies I'll take care of myself.' That was the smartest thing my father ever said. That and his advice to marry for money. 'It's just as easy to fall in love with a rich woman as a poor one,' he said when I was in college. I thought he was terribly unromantic and insensitive. The true wisdom of the man is only beginning to register with me now."

"You can't trust anybody, Paul. I learned my lesson the hard way, believe me. God knows how long they've been getting away with it. Over two years they might've hit me for a hundred grand. Jesus!"

"Well, Tommy, don't make yourself sick thinking about it. It's over now. You've got them out of here."

"Yeah, it's over. Until I catch the next one with his fist in the register. It's a crummy business, Paul. I should've done something nice and clean, put on a suit and tie and got on the train every day like a solid citizen."

"Bullshit, Tommy. You're talking to your banker, remember? You think you could tuck away a nest egg like you've been doing working for a salary?"

"I don't know. I wonder sometimes if it's worth it, all the headaches and long hours. You want a refill?" He nodded toward my empty glass.

"Why not? I'm in the mood today."

When Tommy returned with my freshened drink, I leaned closer and said to him in a lower voice, "Listen, Tommy. Pass the word among your friends. I found a way to take in more than ten grand at a time. They can bring in as much as they want to now. That goes for you, too."

"Oh yeah?" He stared at me quizzically, a hint of suspicion in his eyes. He was not in the most trusting of moods today. "How can you do that?"

"It involves some funny bookkeeping, a little sleight-of-hand like a financial shell game. But it's completely safe. I've got it all worked out."

He thought a moment before replying. "If you say so, Paul. I just don't want to take any more chances than I have to. I feel . . . I feel a little funny about doing this in the first place."

"Feeling guilty, you mean?" I was getting a little annoyed with him. "You're a big boy, Tommy. You know what your options are. You either declare it all and pay IRS what you owe them, or you tuck it away like you've been doing. Hell, I'm the one taking all the risk. It's my license on the line."

Tommy smiled and backed off. The street fighter in him got the better of his Irish Catholic conscience. "Fuck IRS!" he said vehemently. "Every time I turn around some prick's got his hand in my pocket. You know how much real estate taxes I pay on this building? I just sent in my sales receipts the other day. The taxes on booze keep going up but my customers expect me to hold the line on prices, otherwise they'll take their trade down the street. Then there's payroll taxes on these creeps . . ."

I listened to his litany of grievances against the city, the state, the feds, his suppliers, and every other middleman he dealt with, and I knew that he would be all right. Just getting him talking on the subject was more than enough to override any qualms he had about hiding money from Uncle Sam. Everybody felt guilty, but everybody was also highly pissed off—fortunately for me, otherwise I would have to go out and actually work for a living instead of flipping money around like flapjacks on a skillet. I was starting to get in my cups now, starting to feel the bourbon. Two drinks was all it took these days. Whenever I got a little high my mind wandered down different paths simultaneously. I recalled a client of mine, a lawyer who called me up one day to complain about the commissions I was charging him.

"You Wall Street guys are the biggest crooks in the country," he said.

"No we're not," I replied without hesitation, answering his barb with pure instinct. "We're fourth. You lawyers are first, doctors are second, accountants are third, and we're number four."

There was dead silence on the phone for a full ten seconds, and then he exploded in a bellowing roar of laughter. "You're hot shit," he finally said. "I've gotta remember that one. You're only number four after lawyers, doctors, and accountants." Ho, ho, ho. He hung up the phone laughing as hard as he ever had in all the time I knew him, and I could imagine him calling up six of his lawyer, doctor, and accountant friends to tell them the joke. Happily for me he had a sense of humor, otherwise I might have lost a good client with my smartass remark. Then I thought about the astrologer who dropped into my office one afternoon to discuss the bond market. She started off by asking me what sign I was. When I told her I was Gemini with Libra rising, she sat back in her chair and relaxed. "I'm Aries," she informed me, "and I absolutely cannot do business with an earth sign." Gemini was just perfect, thank God, for this pixilated little woman had just inherited four hundred thousand dollars from her father's estate that she wanted to invest in bonds. "But not until September," she announced. "At that time Uranus will be in conjunction with Mercury, and the bond market will start a rally that's going to last until the following August when Mars transits Neptune." That was just fine with me. It all added up to a six-thousand-dollar commission, three percent split fifty-fifty with my firm, regardless of what the stars and planets were doing at the time. I told her to send her friends around too, if they like dealing with someone who understood the intricacies of astrological investing, but sadly enough there weren't too many of them with rich parents about to expire.

Perhaps the most memorable visitor of all was the diamond merchant from Antwerp who was referred to me by a client of mine in the garment business.

"I vant to buy bunds," he declared in his rather quaint accent, a blend of Belgian, Yiddish, and New York City.

"I can get you eleven percent with thirty-year corporates."

"Zat's all? Elefen perzent is nozzink, it's shit."

"Well, that's all the bond market's paying now. If you don't mind taking a bit of risk, I can get you eighteen percent on South African gold stocks. But you'd be gambling on an explosive political situation down there."

"Eighteen perzent! Now you're makink me hot! Eighteen perzent! I call you and let you know."

Two days later he called back with his decision. "Go ahead and get me ze eighteen perzent. My friends in Souze Africa tell me the government can hold out for three more years. So I buy now and sell in two."

He wound up with his eighteen percent and some sleepless nights I would not have wished on my enemies. But he loved the risk almost as much as he enjoyed collecting the dividend checks. He lived with risk every day, juggling diamonds back and forth between Europe, the United States, the Middle East, and South Africa. Eventually he went broke when the value of diamonds and other hard assets collapsed during the Reagan years, and the last I heard he was trying to get back on his feet again at age seventy-two by importing fabric, tiles, and God knows what else from the Orient. I always had a warm spot for him, as well as for my lawyer, my astrologer, my cash-heavy entrepreneurs, and others like them. Without them I could not have afforded condos in Utah and other trappings of the Good Life—the Good Life that was now burying me beneath an avalanche of debt that had grown beyond my control. My appetite for material consumption was prodigious; it bordered on gluttony. Now that I had acquired just about everything I ever thought I wanted, I suddenly realized I didn't own a damn thing. The banks were my senior partners in my homes, cars, my expensive meals and vacations, and the only way to get rid of unwanted partners is to buy them out. To do that I had already begun to step over the narrow divide that separated outright thievery from garden-variety skulduggery.

Chapter Six

Alex Jordan called me at my office the next day to ask me if I would be free for lunch the following Monday. Next Monday was perfect as it turned out. It gave me time to open several more dummy accounts in various names, complete with fictitious addresses, social security numbers, and checking accounts. I was becoming a connoisseur of checkbooks, selecting various pastel shades for my "clients," some embellished with sailboats, flowers growing in a meadow, and other motifs that banks make available for an additional charge. I would never dream of using personalized checks for my own account, but for some reason I derived a perverse pleasure out of picking the precisely correct style and design for these pseudonymous investors. It seemed to be in keeping with the endeavor.

While I was doing all this, I also had an entire weekend prior to the lunch to contemplate just how far I was willing to go. How larcenous was I willing to be? It was important to have one's limits firmly in mind before sitting down with Alex and his cohorts to discuss business. One thing I clearly would not do was steal from friends like Tommy Gilmartin and other people I liked and respected. The Joseph Pellegrinos of the world and others of that ilk were all fair game, however. Anyone other than friends or relatives (well, most relatives anyway) sent my way with satchels full of undeclared cash was ripe for the picking. Such were the rudiments of the thieves' code I started to develop for myself. Without ethical structure and a proper value system, the ramparts of civilized society would crumble to the ground.

Alex selected a fine seafood restaurant in the Grand Central area called Captain's Cove for our Monday lunch meeting. The place was renowned for its huge lobsters and enormous portions of whatever fish was running at the time. The lobsters greeted you from a tank near the entranceway as you walked in. The restaurant was dimly lit and festooned with acres of bogus fish netting and coils of heavy rope that struck me as ludicrous anywhere too far removed from the island of Nantucket. It was out of place in midtown Manhattan, the noise and grime capital of the world, but everyone else apparently loved it. Reservations were taken weeks in advance, and you had to know the maître d' to get a decent table along the walls or in a corner. Prices were outrageously high, a consideration that did not seem to bother the regulars in the least. Alex was evidently a regular here, judging by his choice vantage point behind a large circular table directly across from the bar. He was in the process of ordering drinks for himself and three men who sat with him around the table.

I ordered a Bass Ale for myself, and was introduced to the other guests. Ron Bishop was a tall, painfully thin black man with round horn-rimmed glasses. He looked like an ex-basketball player from Harvard or Princeton, a man in his mid- or late-thirties built entirely of bone, sinew and muscle. There wasn't a hint of fat on him. Mike Rosenbaum, on the other hand, was his polar opposite—short, white, grotesquely fat. He had to weigh three hundred pounds or more. His body jiggled like cottage cheese, and his muscles had all turned to blubber when he was six years old. The third member of the trio was George Burnham, a strikingly handsome redhead about my own height, an inch on either side of six feet tall. He could easily have been a gigolo or a playboy had he chosen that line of work. Even at age forty or thereabouts he was refreshingly youthful and virile, a man who looked as though he worked out at the gym three times a week. All in all they seemed to make a fairly compatible group, joking easily among themselves and with Alex.

It took me about ten minutes into the conversation to sort out their various roles in whatever enterprise they were involved in. Ron Bishop was the star of the show. The others kept alluding to his "brilliance" without being too specific about exactly what he had accomplished. Mike Rosenbaum was obviously the legal beagle or accountant, probably both. He spewed out numbers in a never-ending stream like a computer gone berserk. George Burnham was sales, public relations, and marketing rolled in one. He was charming and quick with a smile—no genius, for sure, but clever with words in the way of a glib professional salesman who was always turned on. And Alex? Alex was the deal-maker, the mastermind who sought out the right people and brought them all together to powwow and see what they could come up with. My own role in this affair, exactly where I fit into it all, was not immediately clear to me.

The waiter came and took our orders. Alex, the perennial Englishman despite his twenty-five years away from home, wanted a well-done steak. Ron ordered a two-pound lobster, the smallest they had. Mike looked as though he wanted one of everything on the menu, but he contented himself with the surf 'n turf, a baked potato, and most of the bread in the basket. I had never seen anyone eat bread the way he did. He didn't spread butter on it; he actually laid on a separate pat of butter for each bite he took, consuming eighteen pats in all on six slices of bread before his salad arrived. George ordered broiled sole with just a wedge of lemon, no butter or sauce, and I settled for blackened Pompano Cajun style with seafood gumbo for a starter. I like food hot and spicy whether it is good for me or not.

Midway through our entrées the true purpose of the gathering was made clearer to me. "Ron has come up with a truly marvelous concept," Alex said, directing his remarks to me as he knifed into his charred meat. "If I had five million dollars in cash I'd put every cent of it behind him."

"Really? I'd like to hear about it," I said, smiling, easing into the general tone and purpose of the meeting.

"I've put a lot of deals together, Paul. I've played midwife to dozens of start-up operations that grew into fairly substantial public corporations a few years later. But I've never . . ." and here he paused for emphasis, knife and fork held aloft as he gazed into my eyes, ". . . never come across anything quite as exciting and dynamic as this. It's absolutely brilliant, a guaranteed winner."

The others nodded in agreement and fixed me with their stares. There was a hunger in their eyes, an urgency that was catching.

"What exactly is it, Alex?"

"It's going to be . . . oh hell, Ron can give you the details far better than I can," he answered, returning his attention to the petrified meat on his plate. I had the distinct impression that a fair amount of rehearsal had taken place before my arrival.

"Quite simply, Paul, we're putting together a company whose primary function is doing deals, highly lucrative deals with guaranteed profits built in." Ron Bishop leaned forward, resting his weight on both elbows. Mike Rosenbaum stared lustfully at the half-eaten lobster on Bishop's plate. He summoned a great deal of self-restraint to keep himself from attacking the sweet white tail meat before it got too cold. George Burnham chewed his fish slowly behind a perpetual smile. He was selling even while he chewed.

"Dealmaking is the primary enterprise of our time," Bishop continued. "Everybody wants to do deals. Mergers and acquisitions, leveraged buyouts, risk arbitrage, you name it. Entrepreneurship's the name of the game today. Kids used to grow up dreaming about being President of the United States. Now they want to start their own company, be their own boss. It's the national religion."

"That's true enough," I agreed cautiously, washing down the pompano with a swallow of ale. "I see it every day in my own business. The idea of keeping your nose clean and working your way up the corporate ladder so you can retire when you're sixty-five is passé."

"Exactly! And that's where we come in. The professionals. The dealmakers. Acquiring our own companies and hiring managers to run them. Conducting seminars in New York, L.A., Chicago, Dallas, D.C., all the big cities, and teaching others how to do it. Charging them acquisition search fees and seeking out suitable candidates for them to do their own LBOs. Building a network of interlocking companies, each one with its own unique function related to the whole—the dealmaking enterprise, the college for entrepreneurs, the investment banking division, the acquisition search department, all of it fitting together like parts in a well-oiled machine—and then taking it public a few years down the road. We'll all own stock in the umbrella corporation—the Zurich Group is our working corporate title unless someone comes up with something better. Once we go public . . . well, I don't have to tell you what that means. We'll all be able to spend the rest of our lives on the golf course, the ski slopes, or sailing around the world, whatever turns you on."

Bishop smiled broadly, indicating he was finished for the moment, and the others smiled at one another and nodded as though they had just heard the most cataclysmic declamation since the Sermon on the Mount. For my own part, it usually takes me about forty-eight hours to get the point. Elaine once told me I had a slow moon; I always uncovered the hidden meaning behind a situation after everyone else found it first. The best way to handle a failing like that is to say nothing, smile shrewdly, and put off making any decisions until your brain was unclogged. That's exactly what I did, fixing an inscrutable grin on my face and nodding sagely. I didn't offer any comment.

"He likes it," Alex informed the others. "I've known Paul long enough to tell when he's impressed by something."

"I'd be lying if I said I wasn't interested." I committed myself just enough to keep my hand in the game. I still had not figured out what my role was supposed to be. Why did they invite me to the party?

"We're still in the development stage," Ron pushed on, encouraged by my seemingly positive reaction. "Right now we're in the process of drawing up a business plan, nailing down all the details, specifying our individual functions in the operation. When everybody's happy we'll sit down with the lawyers and move into the contract stage. I take it from your response so far that you're interested in exploring this a little further with us?"

"I'm intrigued by what you've said so far. I'd like to get a little more detail and learn about my own specific functions as you put it."

Ron turned to Alex, deflecting my inquiry back to his court. Alex took his time answering, lifting his napkin from his lap and mopping his mouth, then sipping his bourbon and lighting a cigarette.

"Ron mentioned an investment banking aspect to the enterprise. We're going to be doing everything from raising venture capital for start-up companies to making our own stock offerings to lending money to our clients to help them finance their own LBOs to . . . you name it. And that's where I see you fitting in, Paul. I told everyone here at this table before you arrived that you're one of the best people I know for this slot. I think they'll all back me up on that."

The others nodded together.

"You've got access to clients with an ongoing need for investment vehicles for their cash, you've got all the necessary licenses we need to establish our own broker-dealer and investment banking company. You know the financial markets, you've got Wall Street connections, a client base with a substantial amount of money already under management. Hell! I can't think of anyone with better credentials to head up this side of the operation."

He might have added that he had also detected in me a streak of larceny that would have made Barabbas blush. So there it was. The point was as clear as day in something less than my normal forty-eight hours. Elaine would be proud. Our individual contributions were clearly defined. Alex was the maestro, the conductor who was orchestrating the entire performance. Ron Bishop was the idea man with a head for generating a quick buck in return for a minimum of labor. Mike Rosenbaum was the legal and accounting department, the numbers cruncher or fudger depending on your perspective. George Burnham was the salesman who would make it all sound like a once-in-a-lifetime opportunity for the public. And yours truly? I was the financial wiz, the investment expert, in other words the fucking Chinaman, the guy who would do the laundry. What the hell did I expect? It was a talent I had been sharpening, although on a lesser scale, for almost two decades.

"I like what I've heard so far, gentlemen," I said. "I'm heading out to Utah next week for a few days of skiing. Let me give it some serious thought while I'm gone, and I'll call you as soon as I get back."

In reality, I did not need a few days in Utah or anywhere else
to arrive at a decision. I think I had made up my mind to join
them in whatever scheme they concocted before I met them for
lunch. I spent the remainder of the week fine-tuning my laundering skills, siphoning off a percentage of the cash I took in
from clients into my various dummy accounts, and mailing out
phony confirmation slips for the trades. I had perfected the
whole procedure to the level of high art. It was amazingly simple
and virtually undetectable. Even if I should somehow get
tripped up along the way, the people I was dealing with were
hardly in a position to blow the whistle on me. They were grate-
ful for the opportunity to hide larger amounts of cash than I originally took in for them, and it was understood that they had to
pay hefty fees to compensate me for my risk. Some of the larger
banks, as a matter of fact, were quite candid about skimming a
flat ten percent right off the top from all large cash deposits. My
main lament was that I did not start earlier. All that time and
opportunity lost to trepidation and caution while major financial
institutions were raking in millions for providing the same services I was. Maybe Elaine was right; perhaps I did have a slow
moon. Outdated moralist. Fearful of what? People didn't go to
jail for stealing from thieves. Well, it was never too late to start
making up for lost time. By the end of the week I had over
thirteen thousand dollars scattered among five different dummy
accounts. And I was only just getting started. My mind raced
ahead. In a year I should have between a hundred and a hundred and fifty grand. In five years I would be able to walk away
from all of it a semi-rich man, with an income of seventy or
eighty thousand a year before I even woke up in the morning.
Not too shabby. Not too shabby at all.

"I'm going to miss you," Monica disrupted my reverie as she
entered my office late Friday afternoon. "When are you
leaving?"

"Tomorrow morning. We're flying Western Airlines to Salt
Lake City, then we pick up a car and drive to the mountain."

"Can't you hide me in your luggage? I won't make any
trouble. Just take me out and fuck me when your wife is off skiing or something."

"Sounds like fun. Maybe I'll take you up on it one of these days."

"Promises, promises. I'm jealous. I'd love to spend a week with you snowed in at some mountain retreat. We'd never get out of bed except to eat. Not even then. We could have food sent in three times a day."

"I'm getting old, Monica. I'm not sure I can get it up more than once a day anymore."

"I'll find a way to rejuvenate you. I'll suck your cock so hard it won't have time to get soft."

Monica had closed the door behind her when she walked in, something she never did. It was not a casual act. She was pushing. How far could she go with it? I got up from my desk and walked over to her. She thrust herself forward and I leaned down to kiss her. She was warm through her sweater, trembling. She dropped her left hand to my groin and rubbed me. When I kissed her she shook violently in my arms.

"Jesus, Monica. Somebody could walk in here any minute."

"What are we waiting for, Paul?"

"I . . . I don't know. Maybe I'm crazy. It's my slow moon."

Her hand was still on my erection, rubbing it up and down as hard as she could.

"When I get back, Monica. When I get back."

"Promise?"

"Promise."

"I can't wait."

"Get out of here now before I fuck you on the floor, before I can't control myself and start tearing your clothes off."

"Think of me when you're out in Utah, Paul."

"I will."

"Really?"

"I won't be able to help myself."

In a second she was gone, back to her desk outside my office with my door wide open again. My head was spinning. Was I really going to push it all the way with her? Until now I enjoyed the game, was flattered by her attraction to me. But she was too fucked up emotionally for this to be a hit-and-run affair, a no-strings-attached sexual explosion with no repercussions. Was I willing to throw caution to the winds in this area, too? Was I growing reckless in my middle age? Or was I merely taking advantage of financial and sexual opportunities that others would have grabbed at without thinking twice about it? Behind it all was a nagging feeling that I had been a sucker all along, a fool for worrying about such arcane matters as morality, integrity, and fidelity in a world that put power and prosperity at any price before all other considerations. There were no easy answers, too many variables to sort out. Whatever ethical code I had was crumbling rapidly. I was being propelled ahead by a floodtide of uncertainty. A momentum was building up. My life was moving beyond my control. And I didn't care. I liked the feeling of being swept away by forces bigger than myself. It relieved me of the pressure of making decisions, of taking responsibility for my own actions. I felt as though some Grand Puppeteer had me dancing on strings.

The flight to Utah was a welcome respite from the asylum of everyday life. That's exactly how I felt as I boarded the plane with Elaine and the kids, a man on leave from the snake pit. It's amazing how tranquilizing an airplane ride to paradise can be. Pressures and worries drop away like leaves from a tree. Everything seems possible again. Crushing concerns shrivel to nothingness, and the road ahead is filled with visions of total pleasure and relaxation. For the next week I wouldn't have to worry about anything except what trails to ski each day and what restaurants to eat in at night. For an instant I recalled Thoreau's constant refrain, the code he governed his life by: "Simplify! Simplify! Simplify!" How good it would be to simplify life. All it takes is a minimum of half a million dollars invested at twelve or thirteen percent, and you could live almost anywhere you wanted without too much to think about. Turn your brain into a vegetable and wallow in the sun.

Snow was falling lightly when we landed in Salt Lake City, and my spirits continued to soar with my first glimpse of the majestic Wasatch Mountains that served as a backdrop for the Mormon capital. We retrieved our luggage and skiing equipment without a hitch, picked up our car from the rental agency, then began the forty-five minute climb up Interstate 80 toward Deer Valley. Not even Laurie's question, "How soon will we be there, Daddy?" which she repeated every five minutes, darkened my mood. Mark, as usual, managed to piss me off a trifle when I glanced into the rear-view mirror and observed him reading a book. We were passing through some of the most spectacular terrain on earth, a veritable paradise if your tastes ran to winter sports, and he had his nose buried in a science-fiction space thriller.

"How can you read now, Mark, when it's so goddamn beautiful right outside the window?"

He ignored me.

"Mark!"

"Leave him alone," Elaine said.

"It's boring," he finally answered.

"How can mountains be boring?"

"They're the same mountains I saw last year."

"And the year before that," Laurie joined in.

"I just don't understand kids," I said to no one in particular. Elaine smiled and rested her hand on my thigh.

"Relax, honey. We're on vacation." She stared at me until the tension was dissipated.

Right, we're on vacation. Block it all out for a solid week. Block out Alex Jordan and Joseph Pellegrino and Tommy Gilmartin and Monica and her big tits and wonderful ass and all the fears that come with moving money from point A to point B without proper authorization. Block out Laurie's nagging question as we drove up the mountainside. Relax and let Mark be Mark and read a book if he wanted to instead of staring out the window mesmerized by the glories of Mother Nature. Concentrate on the moment, on the fact that you're still young and healthy, and you're out here on a mountain road in Utah with your family who loves you. The snow was falling in big dry powdery flakes as it always does in Mormon Country, and the wide sweep of rugged mountains around us was blanketed in the purest white, so white it hurt your eyes even as it thrilled you when you looked at it.

"It doesn't get any better than this, kids," I called out.

"How much longer now, Daddy?" Laurie asked for the sixth time.

"We're almost there, sweetie. Another ten minutes or so."

"I'm hungry," Mark said, putting down his book for the first time and rubbing his eyes. "Hey look. It's snowing."

Elaine laughed as I turned around and made believe I was going to whack him. "He's putting you on," she said.

"Look at all that gorgeous snow," Mark continued his game.

"Isn't it spectacular?" Laurie mimicked me.

"I've never seen such gorgeous snow in my entire life," said Mark.

"They don't get snow like this on Mars," I said.

"They get better snow on Mars," he said. "It's red, the most gorgeous red snow you ever saw."

"I'll bet it's spectacular," said Laurie.

"I'm hungry, Pop," said Mark.

"I'm hungry too," said Laurie.

"We're hungry," they laughed together. "How much longer till we get there?"

Elaine looked at me shaking with quiet laughter. The mood was good, the tension was gone. We were on vacation. The weather was perfect for skiing and we were off to a rollicking good start.

We arrived at our trailside condo by mid-afternoon. The maintenance crew had shoveled a path through the six-foot-high snow leading to the front door, and the snow was banked in higher drifts around the sides of the house. We unloaded the car and turned up the heat when we got in. The kids checked out the television set to make sure it still worked, then looked around for something to eat.

"It's early enough for a couple of runs," I said to Elaine.

"The kids are starved. I'll take them to town for a hamburger or something."

"I want to hit the mountain before it gets too dark."

"I'd rather wait till tomorrow. The kids would rather eat than ski right away."

"I'll be finished around five or so," I said. "I just want to test my legs a bit."

"What should we do for dinner? Do you want me to bring back some steaks for the grill?"

"We'll go to Texas Red's for ribs. I love their ribs and that red ale they have on tap."

Elaine took off in the car with Mark and Laurie, and I unpacked my skis and poles from the heavy blue nylon bag. They were Atomic 180s that I had been using for five seasons, still in great shape thanks to the ice-free Utah slopes. The conditions in Vermont would have pitted the edges by now. I exited through the back door, stepped into the bindings, and pushed off onto the broad easy slope that led down to the double chair lift a few hundred yards below. It was snowing more heavily now than when we arrived and the temperature was in the twenties, about as ideal as it could be. I took it easy on my first run down, sticking to the groomed intermediate trails with packed powder. I was not a deep-powder skier, having learned to ski in the northeast on sickening stretches of glare ice that resembled sheets of glass with sharp ruts cut into them. Packed powder as free of moguls as possible was what I loved best. You could fall on your neck without getting hurt, as though you had landed on a down-filled mattress. My second run was even better. My legs and knees remembered what they were supposed to be doing without me concentrating too intensely on style. It all came back quickly, the lessons and experience reasserting themselves after lying dormant for a year. I picked a more difficult trail for my third run, a wide black diamond hill with a panoramic view of half of Utah. The sun was fading lower toward the western range, glowing pale yellow through the swirling snow. The air was laced with the smell of winter and a distant whiff of woodsmoke. Halfway down I hooked off onto a connecting trail that met up with the broad tapering path that curved past my house. When I snapped off my skis and propped them in the outdoor shed built into the side of the building, it was five twenty-five and the snow was still falling in dry weightless flakes.

"How was it, honey?" Elaine asked. The three of them were bundled around the fireplace watching television.

"About as wonderful as I've ever seen it. Why don't we get up early tomorrow and start before the lift lines build up?"

"That's what I'd like to do. I like it better in the morning and then resting about one or so."

"Not too early," Mark interjected without removing his eyes from the television screen.

"You and Laurie can do what you want to do. You have your skis and lift tickets and you're on your own. Mom and I are getting up early, though."

"We don't want to ski with you anyway," Laurie said. "You ski all the easy trails like old people."

"They might as well come down in wheelchairs they're so old," Mark agreed.

Later that night, after a hearty dinner in Texas Red's in the old mining town of Park City, Elaine and I enjoyed a brandy in front of the fireplace. The fire was cooling down with just a few glowing red coals still crackling beyond the screen. The kids had gone to bed and it was quiet time, decompression time for just the two of us.

"I love this best of all," I said. "Just you and me and a chance to relax for a change."

"I love the kids, they're wonderful, but they *are* a lot of work."

"A bit rough on the nerves sometimes."

After a silent moment or two, she brought up the subject that had been on both our minds for nearly a week. "Did you decide yet what you're going to do about Alex and his partners?"

I let it sit for a minute and then replied, "I'm going in with them. I guess I decided that before we left Connecticut."

"Are you sure that's what you want to do?"

That annoyed me quite a bit, but I made an effort not to show it and spoil the mood. She had been nudging me for months to cozy up to Alex and let some of his magic rub off, and now she was acting as though I had sidestepped into this deal totally on my own.

"It's best for all of us," I said more sharply than I intended. "It's a chance to make more money, lots more money, maybe even get rich. I don't see any other way of doing that."

"You don't see anything . . . anything a bit off-center with the set-up?"

"You mean crooked? For Christ's sake, Elaine. High-powered

deals with lots of money involved are always pushing up against
the edges of the law. So far I don't see anything blatantly fraudu-
lent or illegal about it, if that's what you mean. If I do, I'll walk
away from it."

"Just as long as you feel comfortable with it, honey. That's the
main thing."

She slipped her hand into mine and snuggled closer against
my side. We had said all there was to say about it, and it was
time to slide back into the enjoyment of the moment. I put my
brandy down and leaned over to kiss her, undoing the buttons
on her slacks. We made love there in front of the dying fire, slow
gentle considerate love at first that worked its way into a passionate roll on the shaggy bearskin throw rug. Elaine and I had
come a long way together, and now we were on the threshold of
the biggest gamble of our lives. It was as though everything had
been building up to this minute, the big plunge, a traumatic roll
of the dice that would either set us up financially for life or else
ruin everything we had worked for up till now. I had never fancied myself a reckless gambler or risk-taker, but that apparently
was what I had become. I doubted that Elaine understood the
true dimensions of it all. If she did, her sense of equanimity was
nothing less than astounding.

The rest of the week in Utah was a skier's dream, the days
filled with innumerable runs down dry virginal snow that
swirled down nonstop from the sky, and the evenings with beer
and wine and too much food in the saloons along Park City's
main drag. Packing up to leave was all the more difficult because
of the perfect time we had, all the more difficult knowing that I
was leaving this snow-covered wonderland for the icy winds and
the sharp, unforgiving edges of the real world.

Chapter Seven

She was there when I returned as I knew she would be, searching my face for signs of whether or not I had changed my mind.
A flush of guilt ran through me when I sat behind my desk for
the first time in more than a week and contemplated the road
ahead. There was the usual foot-high pile of papers that always
accumulated during a vacation, as well as a towering stack of
phone messages. I sorted through these first, putting aside the
less important callers for the moment and arranging the others
in their order of urgency. Alex Jordan, Tommy Gilmartin, Joe
Pellegrino, Mike Moran, Patrick Walsh, Jimmy Dixon, Roger
Touhy, half the ginmill owners in the city with bursting sacks of
cash that needed to be funneled down into the undergound
economy. Now you see it, now you don't. There were three
messages from Harry Winkler, the nosy writer who was probably looking for an angle for a story, which I deposited immediately in the circular file. I saved Alex Jordan for last and spent
the rest of the morning setting up appointments for my cash-
heavy clients to come in and see me. By noon I had waded
through them all and I was left with only one important call to
return, the one to Alex. He had just left for lunch, as I hoped he
would have, and I left a message with his secretary for him to get
back to me. He would not be returning until one-thirty or two,
so I was able to buy some time. Time for what? I wasn't sure.

There was no question I was looking for a miracle in the next two hours, some word that a lost relative had died and left me a million dollars. Fuck you money. Enough money to thumb your nose at the world, let your dick hang out if you wanted to, and go your own merry way. The American dream.

Monica had been sidling around the periphery of my consciousness all morning, waiting for the right moment when I cleared through most of the backlog before she descended on me.

"So?" she asked, planting herself in front of my desk about twenty after twelve and smiling down at me.

"So?"

"So how was it?"

"Spectacular. The best skiing ever. The best skiing and eating and drinking in the history of mankind."

"Did you think about me while you were gone?"

"Every day," I lied. The truth was, I had managed to put her and everything else related to this place totally out of my mind for the whole trip. Now that her plump tits were three feet from my face, however, it was a different story entirely. In the space of three-and-a-half hours it felt as though I had never left the office. Utah was rapidly becoming a distant dream.

"Did you really?"

"Yes."

"Do you remember what you said before you went away?"

"Every word of it."

"And?"

"Have you had lunch yet?"

"No. Why?"

"Why don't you and I go down to Toots Shor's for a steak sandwich or something?"

"Things are looking better already. I'll get my coat."

When Toots Shor lost his original establishment in the west fifties, some investors bought his name, opened a new place on West Thirty-third Street, and propped him up inside the doorway to greet people as they walked in. He looked ancient, a frail old relic of his former self, and several wags joked that he had been dead on his stool for two weeks before anyone noticed. Now the place was Tootsless, Toots Shor's in name only, a big featureless barn with no distinction and no celebrity following to speak of. But it was convenient to my office and we managed to get a table in a remote corner where we could quaff some beer and discuss whatever had to be discussed.

We sat side by side instead of across from each other and she immediately kicked her shoe off and ran her stockinged foot up my shin underneath my trouser leg. I introduced her to the wonders of Bass ale, not that she needed an aphrodisiac of any sort; a cup of beef bouillon would have meant as much to her. By the time we ordered a second drink and sliced London broil sandwiches for lunch, her left hand was on the inside of my thigh moving ever closer to the magic zone.

"Take it out," I said, briefly hating myself for what I was doing even as I thrilled to the illicit eroticism. She did not say a word, but proceeded to unzip my fly beneath the tablecloth and take it out, massaging it firmly with both hands.

"I'll do anything you want me to," she said huskily, her voice hoarse with sex. "I'll suck you off right here at the table if you want it."

I moved my hand up beneath her skirt, feeling her with my fingers through her panties. She was warm and sopping wet and she shuddered as I stroked her.

"I can't stand this," she whispered. Her eyes were closed tightly and she bit her lip.

"Tomorrow, I'll drive my car into the city and we'll go to a motel in Brooklyn after work."

"I'm ready right now. We can get a room in that hotel across the street."

"Sure, and advertise it to the whole office. Tomorrow's better. We'll drive out to a motel near the airport."

"Afraid to be seen with me in Manhattan?"

"You bet I am. I'm not so much afraid of Elaine leaving me as I am of her trying to get even. My wife's a very vindictive woman."

When Alex's call came in a little after two o'clock I was half drunk from the ale and from the heady excitement of fingerfucking beneath a tablecloth in a crowded restaurant. It was easier getting through what passed for a normal day lately with a buzz on, and increasingly difficult to do it sober. An alcoholic haze seemed to soften the edges of things.

"Are you all rested up, fella?"

"I was up until about four hours ago. By ten o'clock it felt as though I had never been away."

"I was afraid you'd be so entranced by the wonders of the Rocky Mountains that you might forget about us and become a ski bum."

Maybe in five or ten years, I thought. Maybe when the kids are through with college and another million bucks or so has been pissed down the great rathole of life. Then it will be time to simplify, simplify, simplify. But right now it can't be done. Right now I'm a slave to my kids, to the banks, to my lifestyle, to the whiphand of the Great Practical Joker in the sky.

"Not much chance of that, Alex. Got too many bills to pay. I did think things over while I was gone, though, about our lunch meeting before I left."

"What did you come up with?"

"If the offer's still good I'm ready to move ahead with you. I'd be kicking myself if I didn't."

"Splendid! I'm delighted, Paul, and the others will be too. We're getting together Thursday night at the Palm. There'll be some new faces there, a couple of money men with yards and yards of long green. We'll nail down all the details and get things off to a rolling start."

"Sounds good, Alex. I'll be there."

"Speaking as a friend and not a business partner, fella, we've got a golden opportunity to make a bloody killing." Alex's voice dropped a pitch or two, taking on a confidential tone. "If all goes the way I think it will, in three or four years we'll be sitting over drinks in Palm Springs without a worry in the world."

"I don't see anything too upsetting about that scenario," I laughed. Neither did he apparently. Neither would any other reasonably sane person I could think of.

I left home early the next morning to avoid the rush-hour traffic into Manhattan, and I was nearly sideswiped by some maniac in the lane to my left. He was tearing down I-95 seventy-five miles an hour reading a road map that was propped up on the steering wheel. I screamed at him and honked my horn repeatedly, finally breaking his concentration on the map. It was hardly a propitious start to the day. Perhaps it was an omen, a portent of things to follow. I was anxious enough about all these new developments in my life without having to worry about forces beyond my control.

The day was filled with appointments with impatient clients eager to have their hard-earned cash converted into more respectable investments. I fancied myself as the keeper of one of the gates leading down to the underground economy. There were just so many chutes or sinkholes out there, and one of them was mine. If I needed moral justification for what I was doing, which I did not most of the time, I took pleasure in the notion that I was doing my bit to starve a government that was bloated with corruption, bureaucratic arrogance, and an insatiable appetite for the earnings of its citizens. And in doing so, of course, I was balancing my own sizable budget deficit.

It turned out to be a highly productive day. I managed to siphon off another five thousand dollars into my dummy accounts, bringing the total so far to nearly twenty thousand. I was so busy toting up my pirated booty that I had no time to comment on Monica's ensemble for our evening tryst until late-afternoon. Her sweater was the first item that caught the eye, an aquamarine knit that was so tight it practically revealed the little wrinkles on her nipples. She set it off perfectly with a clinging bright-yellow stretch skirt with a slit up the left side, revealing her lean sinewy legs halfway up the thigh. She wore her hair in an upsweep that was held in place by a dark green comb. Even her perfume was different for the occasion, a dry scent with a hint of lilac in it. The impact was devastating when she entered my office toward the end of the day. If there was even a slim chance that I would change my mind, she succeeded in obliterating it completely.

"You look and smell delicious," I said. "Positively edible."

"It's about time you noticed," she replied confidently. She had obviously been turning heads all day long. How she managed to get to work without being violated in the subway was a mystery.

"I've been so busy I didn't mention it."

"Busy making money?"

"One day a week like this for the rest of my life would suit me just fine."

"I thought I'd better check on you to make sure . . . to make sure you . . ."

"To make sure you didn't get all dressed up for nothing?"

She smiled nervously.

"Why don't we get something to eat first and let the rush-hour traffic thin out?" I said. "Then we'll head for the hinterlands."

The look on her face was almost demure. She was beginning to assume the role of the pursued instead of the pursuer. What a transformation, and right before my eyes. From seductive trollop to blushing virgin in one easy motion.

We had dinner in a small Italian restaurant in the west thirties near Ninth Avenue. It was a plain old neighborhood trattoria with low prices and excellent food. The calamari in medium-hot sauce over linguini was tender, and Monica's veal was lean and tasty. Every time I looked at veal I thought about the first time I visited Texas, back in the early seventies. I went to a steak and ribs place with a business associate and asked the waiter if he had any veal instead of all those thick red steaks. He looked at me with infinite disdain, this city boy from the east with his three-piece suit, and informed me in his twangiest drawl, "We don't carry no slick meat here." I developed a taste for chicken, ribs, and bloody slabs of beef in a hurry after that, particularly when I was west of the Hudson River and east of California.

Monica sat beside me on the bench along the wall but the short red-and-white checkered tablecloth precluded any foreplay under the table. It was just as well. I was so horny just observing her in her skintight green-and-yellow ensemble that I didn't need any preliminaries to put me in the mood.

"Do you mind if I ask you something?" she asked, staring into the golden highlights on her wineglass. "I'm curious."

"About what?"

"Why did you finally give in? I came on to you so strong and you kept putting me off. I really didn't think there was a chance. And . . . and then you suddenly changed your mind. How come?"

"I guess I was finally overcome by your quick mind, your sparkling personality, and your lovely round ass."

"No, seriously. I've got to know. Why did you give in?"

Oh hell. I had almost forgotten how intense she could be. Beneath that lusty exterior was this confused young woman with a need to know. How? Why? What? Determined to understand the meaning of things. Not content to merely fuck her brains out and be done with it. Then again, I knew from the start it would be somewhat entangling if it ever got this far. Why should I expect anything else?

"Are you disappointed now that I turned out to be an easy lay?"

"Easy like hell," she laughed and loosened up a bit. Just a bit. "I really had to work on you. Why did you change your mind?"

It was so complicated I hadn't bothered to sort out the conflicting emotions myself. Once I decided to become a full-fledged thief, I suppose I saw no reason to continue to keep my libido in check. In for a nickel, in for a dime. Why hold back? Rake it all in, money, sex, and whatever else comes along. That sort of thing. That's the frame of mind I was in. I could not tell Monica, however, that she was part of my master plan for general dissipation.

"You're incredibly attractive, Monica. I can't wait to get you alone and take your clothes off. I'm sick and tired of the self-denial. I've been driving myself crazy for weeks. Does that make any sense to you?"

"I like that," she smiled and snuggled closer to me, winding her arm around my neck and kissing me on the cheek. "Lust conquers all."

"Something like that."

"How about your wife? What did you tell her you're doing tonight?"

Please don't bring Elaine into it! I'm having enough trouble with guilt as it is.

"Elaine's used to my comings and goings. She's never had any reason not to trust me."

"Until now."

"Monica, if you don't shut the fuck up I'm going to send you home alone."

"I'm sorry, I guess I talk too much. I can't help it." She tightened her hold around my neck and stroked my leg above the knee with her free hand. "I'm just jealous, that's all."

"Let's get going. It's late enough that I think we can take our chances with the traffic."

We inched our way in silence onto the West Side Highway, easing into a gap in the traffic between a black Jaguar with New Jersey plates and a fruit-and-vegetable truck that looked as though it had been through combat. Traffic was still fairly heavy but it was flowing downtown steadily at thirty to thirty-five miles an hour. The bottleneck at the entrance to the Brooklyn Battery Tunnel was not clogged too badly; cars and trucks funneled into it slowly from six different approach lanes with no serious jam-up. I shut the windows tightly to keep the exhaust fumes outside, but some of the noxious vapors filtered in through the vents under the dashboard. The air inside my Buick was a nauseating blend of lilac-scented perfume and diesel oil. Neither Monica nor I had spoken a word since leaving the restaurant. I glanced over at her sideways as we inched along at ten miles an hour through the underwater passageway that would lead us into the Redhook section of Brooklyn. She looked tense and fidgety, as though she wanted to say something but didn't know how to bring it up.

"You're so quiet all of a sudden," I broke the silence. "Anything on your mind?"

"I've made you angry with me. I can tell by your attitude."

"Angry? I'm not angry, Monica. I just want to keep this as uncomplicated as possible, that's all."

"You probably think I'm a slut, the way I've been acting."

Slut? I hadn't heard that line since I was sixteen years old growing up in the South Bronx. The borough mentality hadn't changed a bit in thirty years.

"If anyone's a slut here, it's me," I said.

She looked startled. "You? Why do you say that?"

"I'm the one breaking the rules. You're free and single. You can do anything you want."

"That's the first time I ever heard a man call himself a slut," she laughed.

I reached over and took her hand and I could feel the tenseness leave her body. She leaned over close to me and wrapped her hands around my right thigh and rested her head on my shoulder.

"I guess I take things too seriously," she said.

Once we emerged onto the Brooklyn-Queens Expressway the lanes opened up and I swung into the passing lanes and revved the car up to sixty-five miles an hour. I was always exhilarated by the drive along the Brooklyn waterfront. The ships were big and gray in their berths along the Gowanus Bay, and the lights from the shoreline danced brightly in the choppy water beyond them. The smell of salt water spiced with gasoline drifted inside the car, dispersing the noxious tunnel fumes. I took the long way out around the Shore Parkway, hugging the shoreline that curved around the stately homes of Bay Ridge where many of the city's racketeers and politicians lived. The bay grew wider and more expansive here as it merged into the Atlantic Ocean and the smell of gasoline faded away leaving only the clean delicious aroma of salt water. We passed beneath the Verrazano-Narrows Bridge, the long ribbon of lights and spires etched against the pitch-black winter sky, and continued along the Belt Parkway that followed the water's edge past Coney Island and Brighton Beach and further along past Sheepshead Bay. Here the smell of fresh fish from the charter boats in the marina blended with the salt air. We drove along the Belt past the U.S. Naval Air Station, Monica with her head on my shoulder and a firm grip on my thigh as I thrilled to the ocean smells, then further east along Jamaica Bay on our way toward the glowing lights and droning aircraft noises of JFK Airport. The area adjacent to the airport had been developed according to the scorched earth policy; it appeared to have been leveled first with flamethrowers and then built up with ugly motels with blinking neon lights scattered among blocky concrete industrial structures. I had a definite place in mind, a cheater's motel a stone's throw from the airport where you could rent rooms by the hour or by the night, depending on your needs. The walls and ceiling were paneled with mirrors and for a few dollars extra you could view X-rated films on the closed-circuit cable system. The erotic quality of the films was questionable, featuring as they did an assortment of sleaze-balls who looked as though they had been plucked from the bowels of Times Square.

The parking lot was crowded with cars of every description. I found a space between a white Cadillac Seville convertible, be-longing perhaps to some fur merchant stopping off for a quickie before going home to the Five Towns section of Long Island, and a long black Lincoln that could have been my cousin Vito's. The motel featured a shuttle service for traveling businessmen with a couple of hours to kill between connecting flights. Those without a bed partner of their own did not have to search too far to find one; the cocktail lounge was staffed with a collection to suit everyone's taste. There were white and black hookers on ev-ery third stool and a sprinkling of mocha-colored lovelies whose primary language was Spanish or Vietnamese. Perhaps their command of English was limited, but every one of them knew how to count all the way up to one hundred. The lighting was dim enough to tone down some of the wrinkles and bruise marks on their arms and legs.

The piano player in the corner had about six months left to live. His maroon jacket was two sizes too large, his toupee re-sembled a racoon that had climbed up on his head and died, his skin looked like green polyester, and the liquid in his drink glass on the piano lid could have been one hundred percent formalde-hyde. Of course he always had a cigarette burning in the ashtray beside it, one of fifty he consumed throughout the day and night. In short, the Hideaway Inn was exactly what its name im-plied, a place for cheaters to engage in an hour or two of illicit sex with no more chance of running into someone they knew than there would be on the planet Jupiter.

Monica was mesmerized as we entered the lobby and walked up to the lady in the cashier's cage. Cash was king out here. There weren't too many business travelers who were anxious for credit card receipts from motels called the Hideaway Inn deliv-ered to their homes while they were on the road. I have a friend whose wife divorced him several years ago after she opened his American Express bill and found a charge to the Shangri-La Mo-tel in Atlantic City on the same night he was supposed to be in

Boston on business. Carelessness, he learned the hard way, can be injurious to one's marriage—and extremely expensive.

The lady in the cashier's cage quoted me the rates for three hours or by the night, as well as the rates for a plain room, one with mirrored walls and ceiling, and the deluxe special with mirrors plus closed-circuit cable television featuring a wide selection of "adult" films. The woman was unsmiling and as forlorn as her environment. Her neck skin was inching down like a slow-motion mudslide. In a few years it would encircle her shoulders in folds, a triple-strand necklace of decaying flesh. I took the deluxe special for three hours at a total cost of sixty-nine dollars, a fitting sum indeed considering the nature of the activity we had in mind. I paid cash and took the key and as I ushered Monica down the hallway to our room we passed three hulking giants who were obviously there to maintain law-and-order on the premises. One of them was sitting in a torn lounge chair across from the cashier, and he was reading one of the weekly scandal sheets modeled after the *National Enquirer*. The main headline on the front page spoke of a man dressed as Santa Claus who punched an old woman in the face and stole her gold crucifix, and another described a disturbed young man who put his puppy in the oven and roasted it alive. I was beginning to think that I should have taken my chances in the Plaza Hotel in the middle of Manhattan. This joint was too depressing for words.

Monica was in a trance when I locked the door behind us. She had not said a word since we left the parking lot, and I could almost feel her absorbing all the sights, sounds, and smells as we passed in dream-like silence from the civilized world into this tenderloin district near the airport.

"Home sweet home," I said as jocularly as I could manage. She stared at me with a bewildered look, as though someone had just punched her between the eyes.

"What's on your mind?" I asked.

"This place . . ." she stammered. "Where did you find . . . I mean how do you know about . . ."

"Out of the newspapers, believe it or not. The *News* and *Post* are filled with ads for places like this. Right back there in the middle of the sports section. Sportfucking belongs with sports I guess."

She shook her head from side to side with a half-smile on her lips. "I don't believe you. I knew you fooled around. I knew it was all an act. How many times have you been here before?"

"Just once, with Elaine."

"With your wife? You brought your wife here?"

"It's true. A couple of years ago we dropped our kids off at the airport and sent them down to Florida to stay with my brother and his wife. It was our first time without them since they were born. For a lark we stopped here before driving back to Connecticut. Made believe we were sneaking off for a lay on the side. We had a ball."

She laughed at that and searched my face to see if I was lying. I could see she did not believe me completely, but the notion that I might bring my wife to a place like this made it easier for her.

"I just can't figure you out," she said, still shaking her head.

I crossed the room and turned on the TV and instantly a movie-in-progress popped into view on the screen. A plumber knocked on the front door of a house somewhere in suburbia; it could have been my own split-level ranch in Soundview with the circular driveway and the kid's bicycles on the lawn. The lady of the house, a surprisingly attractive brunette dressed in the briefest tennis shorts I've ever seen, let him in. Two frames later he was fiddling around with a pipe beneath the bathroom sink when her long willowy legs appeared beside him. The camera followed his eyes as he took her in slowly, all the way from her ankles up to her crotch, to her chest, and finally to her face; she was staring down at him with an unmistakable look in her eyes. An instant later she threaded her fingers through his black curly hair and pulled his face into her groin while he slipped her shorts slowly down her legs. I could not get the image of Elaine out of my mind, Elaine alone in the house in Soundview with the kids off to school and some plumber or electrician arriving to do a job. Some job. The thought of Elaine in the role of the seductress on the screen excited me terribly. I was surprised by the intensity of my own passion, surprised and relieved; somehow I felt better about being here with Monica. What a way to handle guilt. Goddamned Elaine, fucking half the tradesmen in town while I reined in my lust, killing myself with self-denial.

I turned around to see if Monica was as moved by the performance as I was and my eyes feasted on topless Monica coming toward me, Monica with her aquamarine sweater off and her bra undone, Monica with her very large breasts hanging naked on her chest. Her nipples swollen and hard, hard as the erection that bulged inside my trousers straining to get out. Monica pressed against me, wrapped an arm around my neck and kissed me while she rubbed my hard-on with her free hand. I lowered my face and took her left nipple between my lips, pressing it and licking it as hard as I could. I never tasted one so big and hard before, and there were goosebumps all over the surrounding flesh. She spoke my name softly, "Paul, Paul," nothing more, just "Paul" several times. I told her I wanted her badly. Until now I believed I could take or leave her, give in to her advances or ignore them as I chose. Now I knew I needed to make love to her slowly and deliciously, needed to taste her whole body, needed to drink her in and savor every crevice and aperture, needed to lick and probe and learn about her flesh until it was as familiar as my own.

We were on the bed a moment later with the light from the television flickering on the unwatched screen across the room. I stripped her skirt and panties down her legs while she reached beneath my belt, inside my briefs, and held me in her hand. I kissed her all over and licked her soft white belly slowly, then licked the sensitive skin on the insides of her thighs. Her hair down there was light brown and curly, ginger-colored more than brown, and the smell of her vulva and the opening inside was strong and spicy. It simply drove me wild. She smelled like sex itself, smelled like the essence of lust, and when I probed inside her with my tongue and took her clitoris with my lips her body quaked out of control as though she had been jolted with electricity. She made crying sounds deep inside her throat and called my name out loud repeatedly. When I finally entered her slowly at first and then with quickening strokes, my penis wanted to explode. My groin was on fire. Then I came inside her with a glorious hot rush, my whole life flowing out of me. She came with me, came with me again and again in a long succession of convulsive and climactic spasms. Then she lay still.

We stared up at the ceiling and observed our prostrate bodies spreadeagled side-by-side on the bed. I felt depleted, exhausted, totally spent. I didn't think I could get it up again for a week and a half. But after ten or fifteen minutes Monica began stroking my inert penis with her left hand, then she knelt beside me, bent over and took it in her mouth. The sensation was startling. I thought I was asleep down there but she sucked me with such a hunger and intensity that I began to respond unexpectedly. Monica climbed on top and straddled me and guided me inside her. She pumped up and down until perspiration shone on her face, shoulders, and breasts. She worked herself into a renewed frenzy, doing all the work with her eyes closed as I lay back enjoying this new surge of passion. I was hard again but in no danger of coming for a while. I had it under control, imagining I was serving aces every time I came close to ejaculation. My next eruption would surely be the last. After several minutes we got onto our hands and knees and I entered her from behind. We observed ourselves in the mirrored wall to the left, and the reverse image of both of us drenched with sweat as we fornicated as though we would never quit excited me even more.

It was inspiring. I wanted to fuck her forever and never leave the room. I noticed the little belly roll of fat jiggling around my waist and made a mental note to ease off on the beer and get some more exercise. Monica's body was nearly perfect. She was full all over but very firm, with no trace of extra flesh. We tried two different positions after that and then we sixty-nined it, Monica sucking my cock while I held both her cheeks in my hands and licked her from behind. I even jabbed my tongue into her rectum, something I tried on Elaine several times but she always pushed away from me. Finally we came again missionary style, me on top with both her legs thrown over my shoulders for deeper penetration. This second time I thought my balls had fallen off. It was the best workout I had had in eight or ten years.

We rested for a while, Monica with her head on my chest as I stroked her hair and shoulder. She told me she loved me and I think she meant it, but it was not something I wanted to deal with. "Was it as good for you as it was for me?" she asked. I told her it was like dying and going to heaven; it was better than I anticipated.

"I knew it would be like this," she said. "I knew it would be wonderful and I wasn't disappointed."

"After tonight I couldn't stay away from you if I wanted to," I said.

We showered together, then dressed quietly in the bedroom. We managed to use up the full three hours almost to the minute. I was not a financial wizard for nothing; sixty-nine dollars buys a thousand dollars worth of pleasure if you know how to invest it. Monica was astounding. I was in no danger of falling in love with her, or out of love with Elaine for that matter. But I was definitely in love with the sexual romp we had just enjoyed together, in love with the taste and smell of her. If she could bottle her aroma and sell it through Frederick's of Hollywood or a similar emporium she would be a millionaire. Monica's Own. Essence of Lust. Effluence of Sex. The emanation from her damp crotch was an aphrodisiac. The sight of her enlarged vulva from behind and her round cheeks poised above my face was the meaning of life. Seek no further for I have uncovered the Great Mystery of the Universe. It is contained within a half ounce of cloth that encircles Monica's rump. Smell it, lick it, bury your tongue within it—and die. It was easy to see that I had just gotten addicted to Monica's sweating body.

We held hands as we crossed the parking lot to my car. I turned on the ignition, then leaned over and kissed her slowly. She responded eagerly, no doubt ready for another round or two if I was. There was no end to her appetite. I believe I could have gone back inside with her and fucked myself into a coma.

"There's never been anything like this before," she said.

By God, I do believe she's right. She owned me from the waist down. I might as well cut off my cock and slip it inside her purse.

"Let's get you home to Bensonhurst before we get started again," I said.

When I dropped her at her front door in the old Jewish-Italian neighborhood that had not changed a bit in forty years, we had already made a date for an encore the following week.

Chapter Eight

The inside of the Palm smelled like a five-day-old cigar butt when I arrived for the meeting with Alex and the other partners. The Palm charged outrageous prices for the largest steaks and lobsters in North America served up in an atmosphere that resembled a high school gymnasium. The waiters were from the old school—surly, obnoxious, even hostile. None of them had cracked a smile since they left Italy eighty-seven years ago. It was all part of the act and the clientele apparently loved it; the restaurant was filled to bursting every day for lunch and dinner. When you ordered a steak, that's exactly what you got. If you wanted a potato and some creamed spinach to go with it, that cost extra—a lot extra. The waiters did you a favor by serving bread and water for nothing. It was not a place I normally went to when I was picking up the check myself; tonight, however, somebody else's expense account would be dealt a powerful blow. Oh well, it was only funny money as we Wall Street types were fond of telling one another.

I shook hands and exchanged smiles with Alex, Ron, Mike, and George. We were partners now, business chums. Ron and George asked me about the skiing in Utah while Mike finished off the last of the rolls and waved his arm for extra butter. The skiing was spectacular, I told them. George lamented that he had not been able to schedule in a ski vacation this winter, and

Ron remarked that he would like to take up the sport some day when he had more time. The first time I took my children ski-ing, Mark kept staring with hypnotic intensity at a black woman coming down the slopes. "What are you staring at?" I asked him. "She's bwack! She's bwack!" he said, unable to pronounce his "l's" yet. "So what?" "She's beautiful, Daddy," he exclaimed in pure innocence. "Bwack people wook nice against the snow." I thought of his comment now while discussing the subject with Ron Bishop and wished I knew him well enough to relate the incident to him. But I let the moment pass, fearing that it might be misconstrued. It seemed inappropriate at best. Alex sat back and observed us all, sipping from a large dark bourbon on the rocks with a cigarette burning between his fingers.

"The investors should be coming by in a few minutes," he said after the pleasantries were out of the way. "Just to bring you up to speed, Paul, we formed our corporate umbrella, the Zurich Group, while you were away. I'm CEO, Ron's Chief Operating Officer, Mike's Chief Legal Counsel and Secretary, George is Marketing and Public Relations, and you're Chief Financial Officer and Treasurer. In effect, we're all equal partners each controlling ten percent of the outstanding stock. The other fifty percent belongs to the investors and their representatives, Miles Ross and Julian Castro, who're joining us tonight."

"How many investors are there all together?" I asked.

"That's open-ended right now. We'll create stock as we have to to keep the balance fifty-fifty. As far as we're concerned, we'll be dealing exclusively with Miles and Julian."

Miles and Julian. Exclusively. Representing an amorphous pool of faceless investors. God knows where the money was coming from. So far everything was shaping up exactly as I thought it would.

"Sounds fine to me," I said. "How soon do we open shop?"

"Within a month. By the end of March at the latest."

Miles and Julian arrived fifteen minutes later. Miles Ross was one of the strangest-looking men I have ever seen. He was barely five feet tall and impeccably tailored in a double-breasted pin-striped suit cut severely to his diminutive body. There was not a wrinkle or a ripple to be found. His straight black hair was plastered back with nary a strand out of place; it appeared to be sculpted out of ebony. He wore clear rimless glasses that gave him the look of a pint-sized Robert McNamara back in the days when he was part of the Kennedy administration. Julian Castro was big and shaggy, somewhat gruff and disheveled. Put a beard on him, replace his gray business suit with a set of army fatigues, and he would resemble his namesake down in Cuba. Miles and Julian comprised a fascinating duo.

Alex introduced me to the newcomers somewhat pointedly, I thought, as the "financial expert," a close friend of his with "yards and yards of Wall Street experience." Miles greeted me with the limpest handshake I had encountered in years; his hand felt like a cold dead mackerel. Julian was more effusive, flashing a smile that was meant to convey warmth and camaraderie, but succeeded primarily in turning my blood to ice water. Miles ordered an extra-dry Tanqueray Gibson "with lots of onions" and Julian ordered a Chivas on the rocks with a twist. We lifted our glasses together in a salute, toasting the great success of our joint venture. Julian, I thought, was especially solicitous toward me, eager for some reason to ingratiate himself right from the start. His attentiveness only made me nervous.

Over dinner Alex outlined the broad plan for everyone's benefit. The Zurich Group was the holding company for an interlocking network of subsidiary organizations that would offer separate but related services. Zurich Learning Systems would conduct seminars—for a fee of roughly five hundred dollars per person—in various cities around the country dealing with the benefits of buying an existing business rather than starting a new one from scratch. Students would be taught how to do leveraged buy-outs and acquire a business for as much as ten million dollars with no cash down. At the end of the two-day seminars, which would be held on weekends from nine to five, our salesmen would mingle with the students, identifying likely prospects for our Acquisition Search Program. Those signing up for the fifty-nine-thousand-dollar program, payable in easy installments as the deal progressed, would have access to Zurich's inventory of businesses for sale. Zurich would do the financials, crunch the numbers, negotiate terms with the seller, represent the buyer at the closing, and generally do all the detail work until the deal was consummated.

Next, Zurich Financial Services entered the picture, serving as a bank and financial institution for the buyer, offering loans at competitive rates, perhaps a point or a point and a half over prime. Besides making loans, Zurich Financial would also be chartered as an accounts receivable factor and an inventory broker. To generate the necessary cash to do the deal, ZFS would actually buy accounts receivable from the seller for seventy-five to eighty cents on the dollar, and discount his excess inventory by as much as fifty or sixty percent. The third major leg of the operation was Zurich Securities, a licensed broker-dealer and investment banking firm, member of all the major stock exchanges as well as the National Association of Securities Dealers. Zurich Securities would be responsible for taking many of these newly acquired firms public, and it would also market shares in other Zurich products such as mutual funds, annuities, and real estate limited partnerships. This was my bailiwick, the broker-dealer and investment banking end of the business. It would be up to me to help structure the deals, develop a network of registered reps, and sell these products to the public. I would be working closely with George Burnham, whose primary job was to wine and dine and otherwise serve as a high-level pimp for portfolio managers and institutional investors throughout the country, something he was clearly adept at. Ron Bishop, who had created the Grand Design or Master Plan in the first place, would supervise the entire operation and see that everything ran smoothly. Mike Rosenbaum would take care of all the SEC filings and make sure the deals were blue-skyed to comply with the securities laws of each state. Miles and Julian would funnel the money from the "investors" into the financial services division—the banking and factoring institutions. Money from parts unknown seeping its way into the system and throughout the economy until it was all but untraceable to its source. And Alex was the maestro taking care that everyone got along and performed their individual jobs with a minimum of friction. When he finished his presentation he sat back, pushed his unfinished steak away, and lit a cigarette.

"It sounds smooth as silk," I said, breaking the brief silence. "I'm just curious about exactly how the LBO end of this is going to work. Let's say we hold a seminar and sign up out of five hundred attendees, oh, perhaps fifty people into the fifty-nine-thousand-dollar program. What happens then?"

Alex looked over at Ron, the expert and resident genius. This was Ron's domain. He put down his knife and fork, linked his fingers under his chin, leaned forward on his elbows, and spoke with great deliberation. He was apparently pleased with the opportunity to demonstrate his brilliance in front of Miles and Julian.

"That's a good question, Paul, and one I'm sure that's on everyone else's mind. Right now we've identified a minimum of fifty thousand entrepreneurs out there who started their businesses twenty-five or thirty years ago, and are looking to cash in and retire with their wives to Florida or San Diego. You're looking at a guy who built his business from the ground up, a self-made man who's proud of what he's accomplished and who has a definite price in mind for what he thinks his business is worth. Usually it's a nice round figure like a million, or three million, or five million dollars, depending on the size of his operation. So he advertises his business for sale in the *Wall Street Journal*, *Money* magazine, *INC.*, and a dozen association trade journals. Six months go by and the entrepreneur is bitterly disappointed. He thinks his business is worth a million, let's say, to use an easy number to work with, but the best offer he's gotten so far is five hundred grand from somebody who's less emotionally involved in the business than he is. Are you with me so far?"

I nodded yes, as did the others. It was an intriguing scenario and he unfolded it well. It sounded like something that probably happened every day, a hundred times a day, all over the country.

"At this point the guy is desperate. He wants a million bucks so he can sit in the sun with his wife and play golf five days a week, and he thinks he's earned it. A million bucks throwing off a hundred grand a year for the rest of his life before he gets up in the morning. He's worked long and hard for it, and now nobody wants to give it to him. This is precisely the point where Zurich steps in. You want to sell your business? Well we represent people who want to buy it from you. You want a million dollars for it? No problem. In the art of negotiation, price is the easiest thing in the world to agree on. We'll give you your million dollars. But these are our terms. We agree on price but it's the terms that drive the deal. That's where the real negotiations begin. He already knows he can't get a million from anyone else. We've offered to pay him the money, but this is how we're going to do it. It has to be on our terms or no deal. The entrepreneur has no choice. He has to listen. Either that or sell out for half as much to somebody else, and skulk off with his tail between his legs. We give him a chance to hold his head up high and tell his buddies on the golf course that he got a million for his business, just like he wanted, only he won't be too specific about exactly what the terms were."

"I have a feeling you're setting us up for the punchline," I said, smiling. Miles and Julian were staring at Ron with heightened respect. The others had heard it all before, but this was the first time Miles and Julian, and myself for that matter, had been treated to more than a sketchy outline.

"The punchline, if you want to call it that, is this. We'll pay him two hundred thousand dollars down and the other eight hundred grand in notes over time. We take a look at his books and see that he has fifty thousand sitting in a checking account somewhere. That part is easy. That's fifty thousand already toward the two hundred thousand downpayment."

"You mean you're going to pay him with his own money?"

"It's not his money anymore. He's selling his business, right, with all the assets and liabilities his business contains. Part of the assets is the cash on hand as well as his inventory of goods and his accounts receivable—monies owed him by his customers thirty to ninety days down the road. So we take that fifty thousand cash out of the business and give it back to him as part of the downpayment. Next we look at his accounts receivable and see that he's got three hundred thousand due him within the next couple of months or so. We factor these receivables for eighty cents on the dollar and raise another two hundred and forty grand right out of his own balance sheet. Already we've got more than enough to make the downpayment, two hundred and ninety thousand so far, and we're just getting started."

"Why doesn't he factor the monies due himself, write himself a check for the two-ninety plus whatever else he can liquidate, and be done with it? Why does he need us?"

"Two reasons. First, liquidation never raises full value for anybody's business. He might raise three-fifty, four hundred thousand if he's lucky by liquidating, but not a million. It's only the future profits from the business that make it worth a million over time to a buyer. Second, he's got to think of taxes. All that ordinary income in one year, and a big chunk of it goes to Uncle Sam. He doesn't have anywhere near his million, only a few hundred grand minus the income tax. Poor man is semi-broke after all those years of hard labor. He's got no more business left and he still doesn't have the wherewithal to live his dream life on the golf course. We make it possible for him to take his cash out in installments and hang on to most of it."

"So we've raised two hundred and ninety thousand right from the balance sheet so far. What next?"

"Next he's got notes receivable, short-term credit he's extended to his customers that's going to be paid off within the next year. In this case we'll say our businessman has fifty thousand dollars worth of notes that can be sold to a mortgage broker, our own financial division for example, for eighty cents on the dollar. So we raise another forty thousand which makes three hundred and thirty thousand dollars toward the purchase of the business."

"Ingenious. Three hundred and thirty grand and our buyer hasn't come up with a nickel of his own money yet."

"And we're not finished," Ron continued. "We still have our inventory left to work with, and this is where it gets a little tricky. Most entrepreneurs fall in love with the product they've been making most of their lives. They've been churning out these widgets for years and they think they're the best widgets ever made. They've got a whole warehouse full of them and they want to get full value for every last item in stock. Only, the buyer of the business may not love those widgets as much as the seller does. It's all unsold product to him, and some of it may even be obsolete. Too much unsold inventory becomes a liability if you can't get rid of it fast enough when the economy gets soft.

"This is where most negotiations break down. The seller says I want two hundred thousand dollars for my widgets, and the buyer says you're out of your mind, you've got too many widgets in stock, half of them are obsolete, and I'm only going to give you one hundred thou for them. Next thing you know these guys don't even want to talk to each other anymore. But Zurich is the professional deal-maker. Zurich doesn't get emotional about widgets. We look at them and try to determine how much we can get for them. There are two things you can do with inventory. You can sell off part of it to a broker, the excess part you won't be needing for the next six months, or you can borrow against it. Normally you can borrow up to seventy-five percent against unencumbered inventory, so in this case Zurich Financial will lend the buyer a hundred and fifty thousand toward the purchase price with the inventory as collateral."

"So now we're up to four hundred and eighty thousand, but it's still not a million and we're running out of balance sheet."

"Not quite. We've still got his fixed assets left to work with. The seller owns equipment and machinery, perhaps even the building he operates in. Generally speaking, it's better not to get mixed up in a real estate deal. That's a whole separate transaction. So we'll stick to equipment, machinery, and other tangible assets like furniture and whatnot. An independent appraiser comes in and evaluates it all at two hundred grand on an orderly liquidation basis. You can usually borrow up to fifty percent against fixed assets, so in this case the buyer comes up with another hundred thousand which brings us up to five-eighty."

"Five-eighty and we said we'd give him a million. So how do we close the deal?"

Ron smiled, enjoying his role as educator as he moved into the home stretch. "The rest is easy. We said we'd give him two hundred thousand down which we do, so that leaves the buyer with three-eighty which he promptly turns into eight hundred thousand through the miracle of a zero-coupon bond and a single-premium deferred annuity. At today's rates, the seller could withdraw about ten percent of the principal each year, that's thirty-eight thousand on top of the twenty-four grand a year he'll be earning on the downpayment money, and the three hundred and eighty thousand dollar investment will grow to eight hundred thousand, the balance of the money owed him, in about fifteen years. Presto, he winds up with a million dollars for his business and an income of approximately sixty-two thousand a year to support him in retirement while he's waiting to collect the balance. Not too shabby considering his alternatives. For a sweetener we might even let him keep some of his perks like a company car and some paid trips to the Bahamas for, say, three years, and put him on a ten-thousand-dollar annual retainer to sit on the board of directors for a couple of years. After all, the buyer's going to need someone to help him run the business in the beginning, and nobody knows more about it than the guy he's buying it from."

"What's all this debt the buyer's taken on to finance the deal going to do to the balance sheet?" asked Miles Ross. Until now Miles and Julian had remained silent as they listened carefully to Ron's presentation.

"It'll take stockholder equity down to zero, maybe even to slightly negative."

"And that's not a problem?"

"Not at all. Don't forget, future earnings are not impacted. As long as the cash flow remains positive after the balance sheet is recast the income statement is still in the black."

"Even with the higher debt load?" Miles persisted.

"You've got to keep something else in mind. Most private entrepreneurs have a whole different accounting system than public corporations do. Public companies are beholden to the shareholders, so they pump up earnings wherever they can while entrepreneurs like to hide earnings from IRS to keep their tax bill low. One way to hide earnings is to inflate the cost of doing business. They pad the payroll by listing their wives, maybe a son or two, and Aunt Suzie as phantom employees. You look at the income statement and you see five hundred thousand dollars a year in salaries at the top of his expense column. But the buyer's not going to be paying Aunt Suzie or the man's family a red nickel in income. It's all smoke and mirrors. So after you do a little refiguring you determine that the real salary expense to the business is maybe three-fifty, let's say three-seventy-five a year. Already we've saved a hundred and a quarter a year in expenses."

"How about other items like advertising?" Behind his rimless

glasses Miles' eyes were black agates, hard and unblinking. If he
was trying to intimidate Ron, it wasn't working. The thin man,
perhaps a foot and a half taller than Miles Ross, remained
unruffled.

"Advertising will probably go up the first year at least," he answered. "After all, this guy's been thinking about selling his
business for a year or two. The last thing in the world he was
concerned with was increasing his ad budget. If he's cut it back
to fifty grand a year, say, the new owner will want to increase it
fifty percent or so during his first year in operation. So we saved
a hundred and a quarter a year in salaries and gave back
twenty-five in higher advertising expenses. But we're still ahead
by a clear hundred thou."

Miles nodded without smiling, apparently satisfied with Ron
Bishop's answer.

"The next entry we see under expenses is a hundred grand a
year for automobiles and entertainment. Well, the new owner is
not interested in driving around in a Cadillac or Mercedes-Benz
to impress his friends at the club. He's not interested in re-
warding the former owner's management people who've been
with him for twenty years with expensive cars and trips to
Hawaii. A plain old Ford or Chevy and an annual meeting in
Florida will suit him just fine. So we cut back another thirty or
forty thousand a year in this department. You buy the logic of
that so far?"

Miles nodded yes without removing his eyes from Bishop's.
Julian fiddled with his swizzle stick and looked around for the
waiter; this was all academic to him. Alex and the other partners
looked at Ron approvingly. He occupied the hot seat for the moment and was handling himself without a false note so far.

"Other expenses like insurance, rent, supplies, telephone,
utilities, and so on are going to remain pretty much the same. So
all in all, when we recast his income statement, we'll normally
find in a business this size that the former owner's been hiding
about a hundred thirty or forty thousand a year in profits. That's
about the norm, varying a little according to the type of business. By scaling back here and there and firing some of those
phantoms off the payroll, there's more than enough left over to

carry the extra debt load and pay most of it off within two or three years."

Ron Bishop leaned back in his chair, confident that he had given a good account of himself. Miles stared at him for a moment longer, then looked at Julian Castro and smiled for the first time since his arrival. In doing so he revealed a set of tiny pointed teeth that looked as though they belonged in the mouth of a hen.

"I like it," he said flatly and simply, causing Julian's face to erupt in a hearty grin of his own. Evidently that was all the Latin needed, a nod of assent from Miles Ross. Julian snapped his fingers, calling for another round of drinks. Our deal or business venture, whatever you wanted to call it, was sealed as we raised our glasses in a toast. The rest of the evening was taken up with less weighty business matters and a fair amount of jocularity. The tension was dissipated. We were all in it together, for better or worse. I had the uneasy feeling as I touched my glass to the others' that something irreversible had taken place this evening. We were in it for the long haul. There was no backing out from here on in. All the hedging was over. It was too late to buy any more time. During the past week I had committed myself in both my personal and business life to a wholly new course of action. In a sense I was breaking with the past, even though there were no outward signs of it. At least I hoped there weren't. I was enjoying the greatest high I had ever known and I could only hope I would not live to regret it.

Chapter Nine

"There's nothing wrong with him that a little more attention from his father wouldn't cure."

"Please, let's not get started on that again. I'm getting tired of listening to it."

It was Saturday night in Soundview and Elaine and I had just finished an outrageously expensive meal in one of the town's most pretentious French restaurants. The evening started off badly when I suggested throwing on a pair of jeans and sucking up some raw oysters at Jimmy's Harborside on the waterfront in Norwalk, while Elaine insisted on something more formal. I gave in as usual, partly out of guilt and partly because I thought it would take some of the sharpness out of her disposition. It was a miscalculation on both counts.

"I don't know any father who spends more time with his kids than I do," I defended myself.

"It's not the amount of time, it's the quality of it that's important."

"What the hell have you been reading lately? Some of your two-bit psychology books? What incredible bullshit!"

"Keep your voice down, will you," she hissed. Around us, candlelight flickered in the dimness and well-dressed diners carried on their own subdued conversations, pretending not to hear. Two months had gone by since the beginning of my affair

with Monica and, while I was the model of discretion taking
great care to keep it from being discovered, there was no question that my marriage was suffering. Why? I couldn't quite put
my finger on it. There was not the slightest indication that Elaine suspected anything. Our own sexual relationship remained
unchanged. Nothing different had entered the picture except
that once a week Monica and I slipped off to any one of four or
five motels on Long Island for an evening of erotic acrobatics.

If anything, my activities with Monica rendered me even
more sexually active on the homefront. Sex with Monica was an
aphrodisiac, a constant turn-on that made me crave more and
more of it with Elaine—and, to be honest, with other women I
came in contact with regularly. So far Monica was my only
extramarital indulgence, but I was increasingly aware of flirtatious signals that I previously ignored. Yet none of it affected my
attitude toward Elaine and the kids. Despite all this Elaine had
been getting more contentious, nagging me about an expanding
variety of subjects including my relationship with my son. I discussed the problem with Tommy Gilmartin, whom I had appointed to the role of my only confidant. He had a gift for cutting
through the clouds of confusion with his blunt common sense.

"If you want my advice, Paul," he said matter-of-factly one afternoon when I stopped in for a pick-me-up, "get rid of the girl
and everything'll be the same again."

"Monica? But why? Elaine doesn't have the faintest clue I'm
seeing her. It has to be something else."

"They know, Paul. They always know."

"Shit, Tommy. I'm paranoid enough without you giving me
something else to worry about."

Tommy moved his face closer to mine and stared straight into
my eyes. "Your trouble with Elaine started right around the
time you took up with the other one, right?"

"Well, yes, but I've been very careful not to . . . "

"They always know, Paul. You think you're acting the same
with her but you're not. The way you look at her is different, the
way you talk to her. Hell, you may even be doing something a
little different in bed that you weren't doing before. Think about
it. Some little trick you picked up from Monica that you wanted
to try out on Elaine. Wives notice things like that. They don't

talk about it right away but they start picking on little things instead of zeroing in on the one thing that could blow the whole marriage apart."

Tommy was right, of course. It had to be that. Nothing else made any sense. You can tell yourself for months that nothing is different, but deep down inside you know that you're overcompensating for the guilt; you've been trying too hard to make everything look normal when you don't know what normal is any longer. Following that conversation with Tommy I remembered the way Monica always threw her long legs over my shoulders for deeper penetration, and the time I asked Elaine to do the same. Only it didn't work with her. The fit was wrong, the angle of dangle was too far askew. Idiot! I introduced a new sexual variation with Elaine after years of consistency. How many other subtle changes had taken place that I was not aware of? She had to be wondering what was going on even if she did not know specifically that I was seeing someone else. So here we were in an expensive restaurant on a Saturday night arguing about a subject, our son Mark, that was not even the primary issue. Yet neither one of us dared to confront the real problem directly.

"You never play ball with him or take him fishing like other fathers do. All you do is have deep philosophical discussions with him like he was forty years old, and then you complain because he's always got his head buried in a book instead of outside playing with other kids."

"Skiing isn't a sport? We always go skiing together. Besides, I did try to teach him to play baseball. The first time the ball hit him on the head he threw his glove down and told me he didn't like the game. I also took him camping and fishing and he said it was boring. So what am I supposed to do? *Force* him to play baseball for Christ's sake?"

We played our charades with increasing frequency wherever we happened to be, over drinks after dinner, in bars and restaurants, during idyllic walks through the back country of Soundview. The only compensation was the fact that now the money was rolling in. Suddenly we had plenty of long green to pay for any indulgences we wanted, and Elaine invented new ones I hadn't dreamed of before. We were swamped with legal tender which meant at least that we didn't have to argue about money any more.

The Zurich Group opened shop in early April, just a couple of weeks behind schedule. We rented an entire floor of offices in the new Trump complex on the westside of Manhattan overlooking the Hudson River. The rent was enormously high, the highest price per square foot ever paid for commercial real estate anywhere. I thought it a terrible extravagance for a fledgling company just opening for business, a company with no real customers yet, but Miles Ross insisted on "the best address, only the best," and money was apparently no problem. A view of the Hudson from Fort Lee, New Jersey, would have made more sense to me, but who was I to complain? I was only the financial expert continuing to service my clients in much the same fashion as before, only now under the auspices of Zurich Financial Services. My clients were suitably impressed by my new surroundings and elevated me a notch or two in their esteem. Zurich was extremely casual, to put it gently, about its reporting policies for cash deposits; in fact we went out of our way to encourage them, the larger the better, which made my job a lot easier as well as riskier. By the middle of April over thirty thousand dollars had been shifted permanently from point A to point B and my financial anxieties were rapidly becoming a thing of the past. New anxieties, however, quickly moved in to take their place.

Monica, as one might have anticipated, made the move uptown with me as my administrative assistant. Unfortunately, my early trepidations about her emotional instability proved to be prescient. I worried in the beginning that a relationship with her was destined to be complicated. No hit-and-run affair, no casual roll in the hay seemed possible. Well, at least I was not unprepared for the direction our affair was taking. She became hysterical when I suggested that maybe we should cool things down a bit; perhaps it would be better for her full social development if she tried to meet someone closer to her own age who was in a position to marry her and present her with a couple of kids. She treated me to graphic descriptions of how she would take her life if I ever tried to leave her. One day she favored an overdose of sleeping pills, the next day a leap from the Verrazano Bridge that would flatten her body against the waves, a week later she threatened to turn herself into red pulp beneath the grinding wheels of a subway train. I listened to it all in fascinated horror. Surely she should have grown tired of me by now, tired of my aging body with the relentless belly roll and the chest hairs turning grayer by the week. I played up our age difference and the fact that I would be a wrinkled sixty when she was in her prime at forty, still with child-bearing years ahead of her. All to no avail. She desired me to the exclusion of all others, she said. So what if I was married? Some day I would leave my wife and family and live with her, she believed. Meanwhile she would wait.

Truthfully, I was just as addicted to our madness as she was. I did not love her, could not reasonably love someone who was crazier than I. But I was addicted to the look and feel and smell of her. She demanded sex at the oddest times in the strangest places, and her eccentric cravings were a weird turn-on for me. It was as though by my consenting to eat her and fuck her wherever and whenever she wanted it—at high noon on the floor in my office, on my desk, even once in a telephone booth in Penn Station—I was proving that I really loved her after all. Well, maybe I was. I could not figure out exactly what it proved except that, possibly, we were both out of our minds. I was the one taking most of the risk, the one with the most to lose. I was the one whose marriage was suffering as I plunged headlong into the dark waters of criminality and adultery, and I made no move to reverse direction and undo the damage. If that's not lunacy, what is?

Our first seminar was held in early June at the Grand Hyatt on 42nd Street and Lexington Avenue. We advertised it every day for two weeks straight in the *Wall Street Journal*, *New York Times*, the *Post*, the *News*, as well as in all the suburban papers throughout New Jersey, Long Island, Westchester County, and Fairfield County in Connecticut. LEARN HOW TO BUY YOUR OWN BUSINESS WITH NO MONEY DOWN, the headline trumpeted. FULFILL YOUR LIFETIME DREAM. BE YOUR OWN BOSS. DISCOVER THE SECRETS OF THE

LEVERAGED BUY-OUT THAT HAVE MADE FORTUNES FOR SOME OF THE RICHEST PEOPLE OF OUR TIME. DO YOUR OWN DEALS. WHY START A BUSINESS FROM SCRATCH WHEN YOU CAN BUY AN ALREADY PROFITABLE ONE FOR NOTHING DOWN?

You can quibble about the literacy of the ad copy but there was no arguing about its effectiveness. By the Friday before the seminar we had already received checks confirming reservations for over nine hundred attendees. By signing up beforehand they saved a hundred dollars off the regular seminar fee of five hundred and ninety-five dollars a person. On Saturday morning the corridor outside the lecture hall was jammed with more people looking to sign up at the door at full cost, and we turned many away when our maximum capacity of twelve hundred was reached by eight-forty. We were prepared to call the weekend a success with as few as four hundred people in attendance.

It was a curious assortment of students that we attracted. They ranged from down-at-the-heels types with unruly hair and unshaved faces who looked as though they plunked down their life savings to be here to well-dressed middle managers ready to branch out on their own. They were young, they were fiftyish and sixtyish, they were male and female, they were scrawny and obese, they were disheveled and they were groomed and prosperous-looking. In brief, they ran the gamut of humanity, dissimilar on the surface but with one overriding goal in common: the desire to be entrepreneurs, to do deals, to get in on the action they read about every day in the financial section of the newspapers. And we were there to show them how to do it.

The literature we handed out was glossy and impressive. It contained photographs of Zurich's founders in full business regalia, complete with credentials and resumes of achievements, some of which bordered on fiction. The message was unmistakable. The students were about to be treated to a rare privilege: they were going to learn the formula for successful deal-making directly from the pros. Our lead pro, Ron Bishop, led off the ceremonies with an overview of Zurich's *raison d'etre.* Ron was impeccably tailored in a three-piece suit that looked as though it were made of cast iron despite the fact that the temperature outside was pushing ninety. When he finished,

Ron introduced Alex, Mike, George, and myself who were sitting in strategic locations at the rear of the hall; no one could leave the premises without passing by one of us on the way out. Finally Ron introduced our "hired performer" for the weekend, a professional spellbinder, snake oil salesman, and platform dynamo named Cal Roberts who specialized in "You Can Do It If You Believe You Can Do It" psych-sessions for various corporations around the country.

Five minutes into Cal's performance I knew I was in the presence of a true wizard. Cal Roberts stood barely five feet six inches high, but he commanded the lectern like a colossus bestriding the earth. Dark of mane and countenance, with a lush black beard trimmed carefully along the edges of his cheeks, he bounced and gesticulated, manipulating his voice like a musical instrument, sometimes shouting and then lowering it to a whisper so you had to inch forward on your seat to hear him, carefully weaving a spell over his audience and enveloping all of us as one in a hypnotic web. He was frightening, he was awesome, and most of all he was monumentally effective. He turned deal-making into a religion and every soul in the audience into a true believer. If he had nefarious political ambitions he would have been dangerous. He dominated the audience with his will, with his persona, with the sheer power of his presence. It struck me sometime around mid-morning that he could have been reciting the names in the Hoboken telephone directory and still managed to enrapture the crowd. The fact that he was telling them everything they came to hear made him all the more mesmerizing. YOU CAN DO IT! YOU HAVE THE POWER WITHIN YOURSELVES TO ACHIEVE ANYTHING YOU SET YOUR MIND TO. ONCE YOU LEARN THE FORMULA THE ZURICH PROFESSIONALS HAVE CREATED AFTER YEARS OF HARD WORK AND EXPERIENCE, NOTHING—ABSOLUTELY NOTHING—WILL BE BE-YOND THE RANGE OF YOUR ABILITIES. By the time noon rolled around and it was time to break for lunch, I doubted there was anyone in the audience who did not believe he could go out and buy General Motors on Monday morning without laying out a nickel, if only he set his mind to it.

Saturday night and Sunday morning were taken up with the more practical matters of how a deal would actually be structured. PRICE IS THE EASIEST THING IN THE WORLD TO AGREE ON. THE TERMS DRIVE THE DEAL. THE ONE WHO DICTATES THE TERMS CONTROLS THE DEAL. Most of the individuals in the audience took notes at a feverish pace, filling up reams of paper with their scrawlings. As I gazed around the hall at the attentive faces, at this assortment of individuals who had laid out close to five or six hundred dollars for the privilege of being here this weekend, I recognized that every last one of them was getting good value for the money. Whether or not any of them ever went into business for themselves was almost irrelevant. They had come to a revival meeting and they were being properly uplifted and invigorated. The substance of the message could have been boiled down to an hour-long conversation over doughnuts and coffee, but it would not have been nearly as satisfying. It was not the main point. The medium was the message. The packaging. The hype. Deal-making as an art. And besides. How much could you charge for a breakfast discussion without the performance?

Cal Roberts began his wrap-up and sales pitch at three-thirty Sunday afternoon. The Zurich Acquisition Search Program. YOU CAN GO OUT THERE AND DO IT ON YOUR OWN IF YOU WANT TO. Here the cold glaring light of reality dawned over the audience for the first time. The party was coming to an end. Now it was time to go out and DO DEALS. For only fifty-nine thousand dollars Zurich would hold your hand after the weekend was over. Zurich would go out into the cruel world with you and help you put it all together. Think about it. Talk it over with the Zurich professionals at the rear of the hall before you leave. That's what we're here for. To serve you. To help you realize your goals and dreams. To hold your hand step-by-step along the way toward financial independence.

Of the twelve hundred attendees we had thirty-two firm commitments before we disbanded for the evening, and appointments to meet with dozens of others during the following week. If this first weekend was any indication, the Zurich Group was off to a rollicking start. Our first seminar was a smashing success.

We took in over six hundred thousand dollars in fees, minus a hundred thousand or so for expenses, and we stood to attract somewhere in the neighborhood of five million dollars over the coming weeks into the Acquisition Search Program. Already we were making plans to take our show on the road. Chicago, Atlanta, Los Angeles, Kansas City, New Orleans, Dallas. Being the pros with the right formula for success was going to be a lucrative business.

Chapter Ten

The spacious ultramodern offices of the Zurich Group with their expansive views of the river were a whirlwind of activity. The large windows facing out in four directions let in streams of yellow light. The intricate phone system could do anything, it seemed, short of brewing up a pot of coffee. Computer terminals hummed and blinked on every desk. A gorgeous redhead of indeterminate age presided over the reception center with a glittering smile, alerting us promptly when important visitors arrived. The executive offices lined the western wing of the tower with commanding views of the endless river and the New Jersey skyline. All of it was made possible by the magic of money which swept through our corridors like air through a wind tunnel.

To say that our highly efficient operation was nothing more than an elegant financial laundromat might have had an element of truth to it. But it would have been an inadequate description for such a sparkling enterprise. Suffice it to say that the "investors" were evidently pleased by the style, the high tone and sophistication of the organization. Miles Ross was a frequent visitor to the premises and the look on his doll-sized face was as close to a smile as he was capable of expressing.

Locating businesses for sale for our clients to consider was hardly a problem. Ron Bishop had been right; there were thousands upon thousands of them on the market all over the country. There was a great abundance of supply which meant we could be selective in our search, culling out the garbage and building up a file of substantial candidates representing every type of industry imaginable. Within weeks we entered into our computers an inventory of businesses that would keep us busy for years, and the files grew larger every day. We had them cross-referenced a dozen different ways—by industry, geographical location, asking price, length of time on the market, sales volume, profit margin, economic potential—and we graded them according to how well they measured up in each category.

Since Zurich Financial would be providing the banking and factoring services for many of our clients, lending money against inventory, fixed assets, and cash receivables, it did not take a great leap of the imagination to contemplate the possible consequences. In effect the Zurich Group, or more accurately its silent and anonymous cadre of investors, would wind up with a controlling financial interest in hundreds and thousands of small businesses throughout the country. It was generally known that organized crime had a symbiotic relationship with restaurants, funeral parlors, carting companies, gambling casinos, and other businesses of that type. But Zurich, serving as a cash laundering machine for the mob, funneling tens and possibly hundreds of millions of dollars at some point into its investment banking division, made it possible for its so-called investors to extend their reach throughout an ever-broadening spectrum of American enterprise.

The enormity of the situation, and the ingenuity of it, struck me full force one afternoon as I stared out over the river with a stack of fifty and hundred-dollar bills on my desk, the latest installment from Joseph Pellegrino. How had I gotten myself so deeply entwined in such a dangerous undertaking? It all started months before with my desire to rid myself of the financial anxiety that threatened to undermine my health and my emotional stability. I had come down this road fully aware of the direction I was taking. I made a decision to become a thief, a white-collar criminal in order to resolve my dilemma. But the true dimensions of what I was doing only hit me now, when it was too late to turn back even if I wanted to.

No longer was I stealing a thousand here and a thousand there from others like myself, a bunch of penny ante connivers trying to put one over on Uncle Sam. Now I was collaborating with some very dangerous people in their efforts to control a bigger and bigger portion of the nation's economic pie. When I dwelled on the potential ramifications a new wave of anxiety rushed through me that dwarfed the ones I suffered when I couldn't pay my bills on time. That was a child's game compared to this. A case could be made that it was actually subversive, and certainly punishable by much more than a mere fine and a suspension of my license. The ante had gone up from thousands to tens of millions. I had graduated from the minors to the big leagues. And the staggering proportions of it all chilled me to the marrow.

"What do you mean you're in over your head? I don't understand."

"This business, it's difficult to explain, but it's much bigger, much more insidious than I ever imagined."

"Paul, you're a big boy. You're not some naïve bumpkin from the sticks. Didn't you evaluate all this beforehand? Didn't you go into it with your eyes open? How can you have come this far not knowing, then get up one morning with a . . . with a great awakening like somebody threw a bucket of cold water in your face?"

"Christ, Elaine. I knew I wasn't going in with a bunch of Boy Scouts. I knew we were setting up some elaborate con, not blatantly illegal really, but a sophisticated shell game with a lot of financial manipulation going on. But I wasn't prepared for this. I don't care how naïve it sounds. I didn't expect it to be a front for the mob, a . . . a laundering operation for tons of money coming in from drugs, from racketeering, from God knows where else."

"Are you sure, Paul? Are you sure your imagination's not off in left field someplace? Is it possible you're blowing it out of proportion a little?"

The waves slapped up against the sides of the boat and gulls wheeled overhead in a glaring blue sky. The sun glanced off the water and off the railing on the deck and hurt my eyes when I looked at it directly. Elaine had wanted a large power boat for trips to Block Island and Nantucket, and I fought for a sailboat just big enough to breeze around the Sound in. So we compromised on this twenty-two-foot tub with both a mainsail and an inboard engine, a hybrid that was supposed to have the characteristics of both sailboat and powercraft but in fact served neither purpose well. It had all the sailing maneuverability of a giant cake of soap and the inboard engine sounded like an Albanian tank with a broken muffler. The kids hated it and were ashamed to be seen anywhere near the marina with us. Elaine and I both hated it, too, but were unwilling to admit it.

"I thought about that, Elaine. I've asked myself a hundred times if I'm not making things up, if I'm really seeing things clearly or if maybe paranoia is getting the best of me."

"You do tend to exaggerate things a bit."

"But not now. I'm convinced. I know I'm right. It's ingenious and insidious and it's almost impossible to prove. It's very elaborate and complicated."

"I can't believe Alex would be involved in anything as serious as that," Elaine said suddenly, surprising and annoying me.

"You've always stood up for Alex," I snapped. "I don't understand why you're so defensive of him. I've told you all along the man's a crook and you never wanted to believe me."

Elaine shrugged and looked out across the water, sipping from a white wine cooler and not replying. She was wearing a pale green bikini to remarkably good effect for a woman her age, for a woman twenty years younger for that matter. She was three pounds lighter now than she was when we got married and her thighs and stomach were as firm as a sailboard, a result of her hour-long workouts at the club three days a week. I knew I was insane for cheating on her and jeopardizing our marriage and yet I didn't want to stop.

"Well I don't know what to tell you, Paul. You've gone ahead this far and gotten involved in something that you say is dangerous and maybe even subversive. I don't know how to deal with this, who to go to or what to say. I think you should just keep quiet about it and not say a word to anyone. Is it too late to quit, to just walk away from it?"

"That's what bothers me more than anything."

"What do you mean?"

"I . . . I'm not sure I want to."

Now it was her turn to get angry. "I don't understand you!" she yelled. "I don't know who you are anymore. You're a bright intelligent man and you can't make up your mind about anything. You don't know if you want to be a crook or not. You can't decide how big a crook you ought to be. You don't know if you should keep on doing what you're doing or get out and do something else. And you can't make up your mind if you still want to be married to me or not."

The entire outburst came as a surprise, but that last line nearly knocked me over the side of the boat. She had evidently decided to confront me head-on, to home in on the real issue that had been festering between us instead of skirting around it the way we had been doing for weeks past.

"What are you talking about?" I played dumb.

"You know very well what I'm talking about. What kind of an idiot do you think I am anyway?"

"I still don't know what you're getting at."

"Who are you fucking, Paul? That stupid young trollop who answers your phone every time I call?"

I stared at her with my jaw slack for what seemed like an hour and a half. "You're out of your mind," was the best I could manage.

"Am I really? That woman . . . what's her name? Monica? . . . her voice turns to ice water every time I get her on the phone. Come off it, Paul, will you for God's sake! I know you've been sneaking off behind my back for weeks now. It must be her."

"I swear, Elaine."

"Don't lie to me. You're not the only one who can play that game you know."

What was she getting at? The slut! Don't tell me she's been screwing around on the side too.

"What're you driving at?"

"Do you know how many opportunities I have to get laid in this town? Half the men you know call me up when you're not around."

"You . . . you haven't . . . done anything, have you?"

"Why should I tell you anything? You're not honest with me so why should I be with you?"

I knew all along that she was the type to get even so I was not surprised. I knew my women well.

"Well, you're wrong," I said. "I've never cheated on you. I can't help it if Monica's a little bit in love with me. Maybe that's why she resents you. But I've never been to bed with her."

"You're a liar as well as a thief and I can prove it."

Proof? What kind of proof? My whole life was coming unglued.

"What . . . what are you talking about? How can you prove something that's not true?"

"Proof, Paul! Three thousand dollars worth of solid undeniable proof sitting in a safe deposit box where you can't get your hands on it. I knew weeks and weeks ago that you must have found yourself a girlfriend. You're as transparent as . . . as that fiberglass windshield over there. I couldn't believe it, Paul. I couldn't believe you could do this to me after . . . after all this time . . . after what we had together with us and the kids. You bastard! I had to know for sure so I hired someone, a professional detective to follow you around, and I couldn't believe what he came back with."

The entire world became a still life. Sea, sky, gulls, boats, noises from the beach and marina, all of it was frozen in time. There was only Elaine and I sitting a foot and a half apart, Elaine suddenly tense and upright on her deck cushion glaring at me with green fire in her eyes. Those eyes were glassy hard, a bit moist in dead center. The look in them was a roiling mix of hatred and injury, of disbelief and determination, of confusion and despair, and most of all of unforgiving hardness that prevailed above all the other emotions.

"Elaine . . . I . . . it's not true, none of it."

"Liar! Do you want dates and places? I can give them to you. How about the Island Motor Inn in Great Neck three weeks ago on a Wednesday night? I've got pictures of the two of you, you and that slut holding hands in that tacky cocktail lounge before you went upstairs to fuck your brains out. Do you want more?

I've got it. A telephone booth in the middle of Penn Station, you rotten pig. You couldn't even wait until you got to the privacy of a motel room. I hate you, Paul, for what you've done to me and our family. Do you hear me? I hate you for what you've done to me and to us."

And then she collapsed into herself as my world collapsed around me. The hard determined look in her eyes turned into a floodtide of grief, the firm set of her face and jaw shattered into splinters of despair and her entire body was wracked with a convulsive agony. She cried the wrenching and unstoppable cry of someone who has lost it all, of someone whose whole reason for being alive has just exploded before her eyes. And I cried too, a silent river of scalding tears that carried all the lies and dishonesty and the guilt and self-loathing down my cheeks and marked me with their indelible stain. I reached out to touch her and console us both but she recoiled from my touch, shivering with revulsion. I couldn't believe I had done this to her, to us, to our private universe. I could not believe it had come this far and so much damage had been done. I thought that I could stop it all in time when I had to, whenever it threatened to get too close to home. I thought I had it under control and all the while the reverse was true; events controlled me. You cannot lose your integrity without paying a price and my bill was overdue.

"I love you, Elaine, you've got to believe that. Despite everything I love you and want to keep you."

"Why, Paul, why? That's what I don't understand. We had so much and you . . . you just threw it all away. Are you getting tired of me? Is that what it means?"

"No, honey, believe me. I don't understand it myself. I was getting desperate. The money problem was driving me crazy. So I decided to change things around. For us. Only it spilled over into this other area, too."

"How dare you lay it on me? You've been sneaking out and fucking some tramp and now you're saying you did it for us?" The tears were over and her mood swung back again to outrage and revenge.

"I didn't say it was your fault. But the money problem affected all of us. You were instrumental in getting me involved with Alex and his bunch. You've been pushing my buttons for years to do something with him. You can't deny it."

"What's that got to do with you and your girlfriend?"

"But . . . it's all part of the same thing. It's all tied in together. Don't you see that?"

"That's the most disgusting thing I've ever heard. You're not even man enough to admit you were wrong and at least apologize . . . although I don't know how much good that would do at this point."

"Elaine! My decision to . . . to become a thief as you put it . . . was as much yours as it was mine. Admit it. It put me in the frame of mind where I was more vulnerable to the other thing."

"You're disgusting! I don't even want to talk to you anymore. Take me back to shore. I want to go home to *my* house. Under the circumstances, I think it would be best for everybody if you moved out for a while until . . . until we have a chance to calm down and sort things out a bit. I don't know what the hell we're going to tell the kids. That's the worst part of all. You bastard! And for whatever it's worth, I think your taste in mistresses stinks."

"You don't mean it."

"You bet your life I mean it. I've never been so sure of anything in my life."

"You're throwing me out?"

"I want you out, Paul, before you contaminate the kids with your . . . your . . . just get out and leave me alone for a while."

"You want to break up this marriage? I can't believe it, Elaine. We've got something special. We love each other and we've got a good solid family life with the kids. I fucked up but it's not irreversible. Don't destroy everything we've got. We can work it out."

"How can you sit there and accuse me of destroying everything? That's what bothers me more than anything, your pathetic attempt to lay some of the blame off on me. We have to resolve this thing and we can't do it together. We need some time by ourselves."

"I don't want this, honey. I love you, please believe that."

"I . . . I love you too. That's what hurts so much every time I read that report and look at the pictures. Every time I feel myself weakening I pull out the folder and . . . and then I want to kill you."

Once again her face disintegrated beneath a torrent of tears. She stared down at the deckboards, shielding her eyes from my view with her hand as she shook her head slowly from side to side. A curse rang out from ten feet away as I swerved hard right to avoid hitting a small catamaran on my port side. Irrationally, I shouted back a string of obscenities, taking out my misery and frustration on some potbellied weekend sailor and his wife. My entire world fell away from me. All the strength drained out of me and I became hollow inside. Everything I cherished was being stripped away. If someone shot me then and there I would have welcomed it since my whole purpose for living had been shattered and destroyed.

The two of us cried like babies, separate in our grief, while I made a feeble attempt to keep our lumpish craft under some semblance of control. We cried ourselves empty knowing we had lost it, knowing that whatever direction our marriage took in the future something vital had gone out of it. Finally we were spent, too drained and exhausted to argue any longer. It was time to discuss our plans quietly with as little rancor as possible.

"I can't talk you out of this?" I asked.

"Not now, Paul. We have to get away from each other for a while. There's too much pain and resentment. Just for a while until I sort it all out. I need time to think and be alone."

"Okay then, if that's the way it has to be. I'll take a small place, probably in the city near my office. We'll tell the kids I'm traveling a lot and I'll come up to see them as often as I can. Is that all right?"

She nodded yes. "Just let me know a day or so before you come up. I . . . I don't think I want to be around when you visit them."

So it had really come to this and Elaine was better prepared for it than I. I was the one being uprooted while she lived home with the kids and I assumed the pathetic role of the part-time father, the guy who comes to take them for a walk in the park on a lonely Sunday afternoon. God, it was ironic. How often had I observed the visiting fathers at the zoo buying popcorn for their kids, spoiling them on their one or two days a week with them, never dreaming that I would be joining their ranks not too far in the future? I had become that cliché myself, not believing it was possible. My kids! My family! Blown to bits in the winking of an eye. Or so it seemed as I floated dead upon the water, listening to the sounds of life and breathing in the salty smells, bathing in the warmth of a summer sun that had grown as bleak as winter.

Chapter Eleven

Kevin O'Malley announced his candidacy for Mayor of New York City on the same day that I cheated on Monica for the first time. I felt that I at least owed it to Elaine to be unfaithful to Monica as well as to her. I was lying on a rumpled bed in an East 63rd Street highrise beside a thirty-three-year-old divorcee named Janet when the eleven o'clock news came on. Janet was a bit on the heavy side but otherwise attractive in a raunchy way. When I first met her in P.J. Clarke's earlier in the evening she looked as though she had just climbed out of bed. Best of all she was available and she was new, and if there was anything she enjoyed better than sex I had not discovered it yet. She talked openly about the variety of men she had been to bed with in the year and a half since her marriage dissolved as I watched my old buddy from the South Bronx telling the country why he wanted to be mayor.

Renewal and commitment. That was evidently going to be the theme of his campaign. Renewal of the spirit that made New York the envy of every city on earth, and commitment to the principles of clean and honest government. He did not mention Mayor Feldman directly, but the man who appointed him to the post of Police Commissioner was retiring in the midst of one of the worst scandals in the city's history. The early promise of the Feldman administration was overshadowed in the end by a pervading pall of corruption. One by one the mayor's appointees were forced to resign as tales of kickback schemes and illegal profiteering made the headlines every day. The mayor himself was not involved, but he owed too many people who had no scruples about profiting from public power.

Only O'Malley among the mayor's senior appointees received a clean bill of health. Mr. Clean. The nuns had done a good job on his Catholic grade-school conscience and now he stood to benefit politically because of it while his colleagues were toppled in disgrace. Disturbingly enough for someone in my position, Kevin was doing a hundred-and-eighty-degree turn away from the speech I heard him deliver in mid-winter. White-collar crime had emerged as the leading domestic issue of the time. Kickbacks. Bribes. Insider trading. Laundering of cash. The Feldman administration was awash with all of it, and Kevin was pledging "an all-out war against the corporate criminals in their three-piece suits" who were "poisoning the moral climate of the age." I stirred uneasily on the bed as I digested his message.

Apparently Janet liked food second-best to sex. She treated me to a recitation of every restaurant she had been to in the last six months, along with vivid descriptions of the various meals she consumed in them. She succeeded in getting my mind off Kevin for the moment, and in stirring up a craving for linguini with white clam sauce even though I had eaten just a few hours earlier. The Captain's Palace was best for lobster fra diavolo, she said, while Luigi's was tops if you were in the mood for a grilled swordfish steak. She had some cold gnocchi left over in the refrigerator from two nights ago, as well as half a bottle of a white Bordeaux. Would I like to share a midnight snack with her? Well, sure. Why not? Seeing too much of Janet was likely to be fattening, but I was not planning on making a commitment any time too soon.

I watched her jiggle off the bed to fetch the cold gnocchi and she was definitely wider in the rump than I remembered her being an hour and a half ago. Funny how the inebriated mind can alter reality. Amazing how a case of advanced horniness can shave the poundage off a plump derriere. She was not merely a touch on the heavy side, I could see as I took a good second look;

she was downright *zaftig* with a roll of fat across the back beneath her armpits and a mound of belly that belonged in a Rubens painting. Had I really fucked her so passionately just a short time before? Did I actually browse face-down in the broccoli as she lay there with her heavy thighs splayed out and her enormous breasts hanging down each side almost reaching to the bed? Sure I did. I remembered it clearly. And lots of fun it was too. Fat girls were coming back into their own again, a rebellion against the jogging generation and all those bruised heels and damaged knee joints.

We ate the gnocchi and finished off the dry white wine and then we returned to Janet's favorite activity again, the one she liked even better than eating. She was an amazing cocksucker, starting in behind the balls practically in the anal region, then working her way up the stem until she had me swollen and inflamed like a purple mushroom cap. Sit on my face, Janet, and smother the life right out of me. What a way to go. I want to die with my face in your muff and my tongue six inches inside you. Janet was changing my entire perception of obesity. Fat girls were fun. They were heavenly. They had been getting a bad press for years. To hell with muscle and sinew. Janet smelled like a woman should—damp and sweaty and very crotchy. I stayed with her until four o'clock in the morning and when I finally stumbled down to the street to find my way home I thought I would need a wheelbarrow for my balls. They ached. They throbbed. I was numb and dead all over with fatigue except for the sensation below my belt. I needed about forty-eight hours sleep and I was lucky if I could squeeze in two, lucky if I could fall asleep at all before my alarm went off at seven to roust me in time for my eight-thirty meeting with Alex and the other partners. Damn! How was I going to get crosstown to my studio apartment in the West Seventies, the tiny L-shaped closet that was costing me nearly a grand a month? It was almost impossible to find a taxi at four in the morning when you were half-drunk and exhausted and badly in need of one.

Business was booming and the investors were ecstatic. Everything was rolling along smoothly. We were ahead of schedule, far ahead of our most optimistic projections of a few months back. The various segments of the operation were working as one, a well-oiled machine whose parts were in perfect synchronization. The seminars were booked to capacity everywhere we held them, a good percentage of the attendees signed up for the Acquisition Search Program, the inventory of potential buy-out candidates was the largest in existence, the coffers of the financial services division were bursting with cash, and our investment banking company was ready to go public with two or three deals by early autumn. Alex's report to the rest of the board could not have been more glowing. We all deserved a self-congratulatory pat on the back for launching such an elaborate and sophisticated money machine.

After the meeting Alex paid a visit to my office and closed the door behind him. "How're things going with you, old boy?" he asked. His face was developing the red flush and deep lines of the serious smoker and drinker. He lit up perhaps his tenth cigarette of the morning, crossed his legs, and settled in for a friendly chat.

"Right now I feel like I died a week ago and somebody forgot to bury me."

"Bachelor life not agreeing with you?"

"Agreeing with me all too well if dissipation is a sign of having fun. Another six months of it will finish me off altogether."

"I know it's none of my business, Paul, but . . . what the hell, we are friends after all. This thing with you and Elaine. My God! If I ever saw two people who were made for each other it's you two. Any chance . . . any chance of . . ."

"Of our getting back together? I'd go home in a minute if she'd have me. Right now she's so pissed off she practically sputters every time she sees me. Oh well. Some Texan told me a long time ago never to get caught with my banana in the wrong bowl of milk. That's exactly how he phrased it."

"And the kids? How're they taking it?"

"That's the hardest part. The kids and the jealousy. Whenever I think of Elaine in bed with somebody else I want to climb up the wall."

I observed Alex intently after delivering that line. I could not get rid of the nagging feeling that Elaine and he . . . that he at least was one of the men who called her up when I was not around. Had she succumbed? I could not imagine Elaine being attracted to him. Her tastes ran to youngish men in good physical condition, men with hard tight bodies. Alex hardly fit the description with his booze and tobacco and lack of exercise. Even his graying hair looked stained with nicotine around the edges. Still, Elaine might be inclined to make a business decision rather than a crotch decision her second time around, if there were to be a second time. I studied Alex's eyes but he gave nothing away. Cool. Friendly, Unflappable. The treacherous limey bastard!

"Moving was a lot of fun," I said to lighten my tone. "Forty-five liquor store boxes it took to move my meager possessions into a closet of an apartment. How the hell did people move during Prohibition anyway?"

Alex laughed and dinched out his filthy cigarette in the ashtray on my desk. It would take an hour and a half for the stench to leave the office.

"I must admit I never thought of that, fella. In a way I envy you. Every married man dreams of being a bachelor again for six months. Time off for good behavior. That sort of thing."

"That would be fine if wives didn't want reciprocal rights. Unfortunately, it doesn't work that way."

"Well, if you need anything let me know. Looking on the bright side of things, business couldn't be better. We're coining money like we invented it. In five years we'll be able to pack it in and clip coupons for the rest of our lives."

"This . . . this O'Malley thing doesn't bother you?"

"What do you mean?"

Had I gone too far? Voicing my gravest concerns to a man who . . . I didn't know what. How much more involved was he than I?

"He's going to be our next mayor most likely. And he's taking a tough stance against anyone in a suit and tie who turns a profit for a living."

"Yes, that attitude seems to be more and more fashionable in Washington, too. He's an old friend of yours, isn't he?"

"O'Malley? He and I grew up together."

"Why don't you give him a ring and see what's on his mind?"

"Good idea, Alex," I laughed. "I'm surprised I hadn't thought of that approach myself."

"Wake up and smell the coffee."

"Not now. Go away."

"How can you live like this? You have to take out the garbage once in a while."

Monica was definitely becoming a nuisance. What was the point of not having a wife anymore if you had a mistress who never let up for an instant? Life with Monica would be an endless round of shopping for furniture and hanging curtains in some dreary compound on Staten Island.

"I need some rest, Monica. I need a whole weekend just to catch up on lost sleep."

"You . . . you still love her, don't you?"

"Who?"

"You know who I'm talking about. Her."

Oh hell. Last night had been a mistake and I was going to pay for it most of the weekend, I could see. Monica and I went out for dinner and drinks after work on Friday. It was to be a farewell meal of sorts, a civilized end to an affair that began with an explosion of carnality and evolved into something worse than a loveless marriage. I worked it all out in my mind beforehand. "Monica," I was going to say over coffee and brandy, "this has to end for your sake more than mine." God, that was noble. Sacrificing my own interests for Monica's social development. "You've got to find someone who's in a position to share his future with you. I don't know where I'm going at this point. My life's too complicated, filled with too many obligations." She would accept the logic of that and the inevitability of a breakup. Then it would be over and we would remain friends.

None of it came off that way, naturally. "Monica," I began. "Don't say anything now," she interrupted. "Just take me back to your place and stick your cock inside me. I want to suck you off and I want you to eat me until I can't stand it anymore. I love you, Paul. I go crazy when we're not together."

So we left. And we did what she suggested for two solid hours until I passed out about one A.M. Now it was seven o'clock on a Saturday morning and she wanted to know if I still loved . . . HER. Monica never could mention Elaine by name. Elaine was always SHE or HER to Monica. Sleep from here on in was going to be impossible.

"I never pretended I didn't love Elaine. Yes, I still love her. I'm an old-fashioned family man beneath it all and I'm very dangerous to myself when I live alone. My life's a shambles right now."

Monica sat Indian-style on the bed with her lovely breasts sticking straight out from her chest. The damp sheets were entwined absurdly around my loins giving me the look of a grown man wearing diapers. I needed to fart badly, but that was another freedom I had to curtail in a mistress's presence.

"I thought things would be different when you finally got rid of . . . her."

"I didn't get rid of her, she got rid of me. And you don't jump from a solid marriage like we had with kids involved into another entanglement just like that. It takes time to make the adjustment."

"Entanglement! What a horrible word. It sounds like . . . it sounds like a prison sentence or something."

"I'm sorry, Monica. I really care for you but I'm just a bad deal for you right now. I can't give you what you want."

She jumped off the bed and walked over by the dining "L." She kept her back turned to me for several minutes without saying a word.

"Are you okay?"

"I . . . I think I want to kill myself."

"Don't say that, Monica. For God' sake. Life goes on. Nobody gets exactly what they want. Life's a bitch and then we die. That's the way it is."

"I thought we had something special going. We've been more than just lovers. We . . . we're like business partners almost. I cover for you in the office and . . . you know what I mean."

"What are you talking about?"

"I'm not stupid you know. I see what goes on there. All that money changing hands. Half those people you have accounts for don't even exist. And some of those characters parading in and out. They give me the creeps. But I keep my mouth shut and I never say anything about it to anyone because . . . well because I thought you and I were working together. Someday, I thought, when you got what you wanted out of it, we would go someplace and enjoy it together."

Was I hearing what I thought I was hearing? Was she actually threatening blackmail? Of course she knew better than anyone else what I had been doing for the better part of a year now. Monica wasn't brilliant but she possessed the powers of observation of a watchdog and the survival instincts of a cat. Street smarts. The hair bristled on the back of my neck and the perspiration on my face and chest became ice water. Monica was right at the very center of our operation and I put her there. Blindly. Stupidly. I thought I could press the flesh with her and then get rid of her with impunity when I wanted to. Now my vanity was pricked. Had she used me all along or did she really love me? Was she just turning vindictive to get even? I had to know.

"I can't believe what I'm hearing, Monica. I thought you really cared for me."

She whirled around and came back toward the bed. "I do love you, Paul. That's why I can't let you throw me out just like that. I need you more than anything. You're my whole life."

I'm your ticket out of Brooklyn was more like it. I knew I was crazy but Monica was beginning to convince me that I was stupid as well. She had me by the balls in more ways than one. My brain raced idiotically, searching for a way out of this maze I had put myself in. In the winking of an eye I understood that it was possible for a relatively stable middle-aged businessman to seriously entertain thoughts of homicide. The Vito solution. Fuck the Alex solution; that's what got me where I was. How much did Monica really know? Not the whole story certainly. I didn't have the whole picture myself. But she knew enough to be dangerous. She knew about the dummy accounts and the continuous avalanche of cash that had been cascading through our corridors. She knew enough to trigger an investigation that could blow the lid off the whole operation and put us all behind bars. I wanted to strangle her and I wanted to cry. I didn't know what to do. I reached out and pulled her toward the bed.

"For your own good, Monica, I wouldn't say a word about this to anyone. You said yourself there are some pretty unsavory people associated with our company. I'd hate to think what could happen if you decided to turn against them."

She stretched out on the bed beside me and hugged me tightly as I stroked her hair and shoulder. "I wouldn't do anything like that, Paul. I couldn't do anything to hurt you. I get crazy sometimes when I think maybe you're getting tired of me. I just want to be with you. If I couldn't see you anymore I . . . I think I'd want to die. I wouldn't care what happened to me then."

I stroked her hair slowly and stared up at the ceiling. Simplify! Simplify! Simplify! But how? Life was getting more complicated all the time. I wanted Monica to disappear and still she was there, more firmly entrenched than ever before, a walking time bomb threatening to explode any time I stepped out of line. I had to laugh at the irony of my situation. I had come down this road to liberate myself from financial anxiety and had enjoyed a wild sexual romp along the way. Now that I had more money than I thought possible seven months before, I had about as much freedom as a prisoner in a Soviet gulag. My wife could barely speak to me without sputtering, my kids were starting to hate me, and my body belonged to a compulsive neurotic who had the power to destroy me. I almost laughed out loud as I analyzed my predicament. For the moment it seemed hopeless. I couldn't see a way out. There was only one sensible thing to do. I rolled over and put my hand between her thighs.

"Oh, Paul. Kiss me down there. When you kiss me down there it feels like my pussy's on fire."

Chapter Twelve

"While a person who threatens violence to steal a wallet deserves strict punishment," said Kevin O'Malley at a midsummer press conference, "we should be equally tough on the thief in a three-piece suit who manipulates a ledger or a computer to steal millions. Crimes against business ultimately become crimes against the rest of society. I believe that stiff criminal penalties would serve as a strong deterrent against white collar crime. If I'm elected mayor in November I intend to lobby for legislation making white-collar crime punishable under the Racketeer Influenced and Corrupt Organization Act."

Elsewhere, a stockbroker in Richmond, Virginia, was indicted on four counts of embezzlement for diverting a hundred and sixty thousand dollars from his clients' accounts into his own. The Assistant Commonwealth Attorney said that he had decided to file criminal charges against the broker instead of merely making him pay back the money and fining him, the usual practice in these cases. Until now, most brokers would neither admit nor deny their guilt, accept a ten thousand dollar fine and a thirty-day suspension of their license, and return to work after an extended vacation. In this instance, the Virginia broker faced a maximum sentence of twenty years in prison and fines ranging into the millions.

In Boston the U.S. Attorney for Massachusetts was criticized by the First Bank of Greater New England for taking the toughest stand of any U.S. Attorney in the nation against cash-reporting violations. "We sure would like to know why it's so different here," said the chairman of the bank. "Are banks here worse than in other parts of the country?" He had expected the bank to be slapped with a civil fine for laundering five and a half million dollars in unreported cash. Instead, the U.S. Attorney was hitting the bank and its top executives with criminal charges that could put them behind bars and bankrupt them financially.

Halfway across the country, the Second U.S. Circuit Court of Appeals in Michigan ruled that a financial advisor could be held criminally liable for helping his clients launder cash. Previously, the courts had held that only the principals themselves could be charged with criminal violations while their brokers or bankers were guilty of a civil misdemeanor. The presiding judge in Michigan, however, set a precedent with his decision that ". . . one who willfully causes another to commit a crime is punishable as a principal."

In Philadelphia six brokers for a major financial firm were indicted on conspiracy charges for pocketing more than two million dollars from a gambling and money-laundering scheme. Their action violated the federal Bank Secrecy Act, authorities claimed. The firm they worked for faced nearly seventeen million dollars in fines while the individual brokers could serve a total of a hundred and ninety-eight years in jail and pay aggregate fines amounting to sixteen million dollars. Their operation was exposed by the jilted girlfriend of one of the brokers who also happened to be his former secretary.

In another case back in New York city, a small platoon of investment bankers and mergers and acquisitions lawyers was charged with criminal conspiracy for making millions of dollars in illegal trading profits. Apparently, those involved passed on inside information about companies that were about to receive tender offers from other corporations or greenmail specialists to clients who bought stock and options before the news was made public. Each individual faced a maximum of twenty years in jail plus millions of dollars in fines except for one investment banker who decided to cooperate and inform on his colleagues.

Throughout the nation the authorities were moving to close

the gap between crooks who used or threatened violence and were therefore subject to criminal charges, and their white-collar counterparts who did it all with smoke and mirrors and customarily were treated as though they had been caught jay-walking. Suddenly, the newspapers and weekly magazines were crammed with stories that turned my legs to Jell-O, particularly the one about the jilted girlfriend. Did things like that really happen? Adultery was getting awfully expensive.

Meanwhile, my partners at the Zurich Group seemed oblivious to it all. Nothing changed; no sense of apprehension was visible anywhere. Did they know something I didn't know or were they just so arrogant with success that they believed nothing could touch them? Or—and here again I had to ask myself if my instinctive paranoia was getting out of hand—could it be that they had less to worry about than I did? Was I the one in the hot seat? Did they set me up to be the fall guy? I was the financial man, the money maven, the expert with "yards and yards" of Wall Street experience. Were they protected better than I? Would they turn against me in a crisis and claim that I actually ran the show? Could their lawyers make a valid case out of the other partners' ignorance? "Nobody knew anything like this was going on. Paul was the money man, the one with all the financial expertise. We trusted him. We turned the financial end of the business over to him and this is what he did to us." They had all the connections and the wherewithal to buy themselves out of it. Somebody had to take the hit, if it came to that. Who else set up all the dummy accounts and turned on the Magic Money Machine?

Why not? It made sense. Or at least it did to me in my perplexed and agitated state. But whom could I talk to? Tommy, my confidant and spiritual advisor in affairs of the groin? Hardly. Not with all the money he had funneled through me. He was just as vulnerable as I was. Alex, the maestro, the man who set the whole thing up and quite possibly was fucking my wife? Not a likely choice. Kevin O'Malley, the candidate who would be king? He could probably be elected president on what I could tell him. Crimebuster from New York breaks up zillion-dollar money-laundering operation. A latter-day Tom Dewey with more political savvy. But what was in it for me except a kind of turncoat martyrdom? John Dean Goes to Wall Street. Not an appealing role, and one that would surely be dangerous to my health.

There really was no one I could turn to, nowhere I could go with my story without opening a giant can of killer worms. I needed time to let my slow moon take a couple of spins around the planet, time for the fog to lift so I could see the road ahead more clearly. I needed time to figure out if my imagination was racing away out of control, or if my most horrifying fears had any factual basis to them. Meanwhile, do your job and keep your eyes open and don't let anyone suspect for an instant that you entertained such notions. It was not the most enviable of positions.

Part-time fatherhood was also becoming a nightmare. My biggest problem was with Mark. Laurie seemed to be taking it better; she was more resilient. Half her friends' parents were divorced and she accepted it as a fact of life. Mark regarded my departure from the family nest as a personal rejection no matter how hard I reassured him that my feelings for him and his sister had not changed. He revealed a talent for manipulation that I never noticed before. Always a model student, he suddenly turned into a disciplinary problem in school. He cut classes, he was rude to his teachers, and Elaine and I were called in for several eight A.M. meetings with his counselor to see what could be done about him. I understood that this was Mark's way of bringing Elaine and me together.

The first time I tried to discuss his behavior alone with him in his room, he flew into a rage and socked me flush on the jaw. "I hate you! I hate you!" he screamed and then collapsed in grief on the floor with his back turned to me. It broke my heart. It shook me to the marrow. The real tragedy of shattered family life was evident before my eyes and I was helpless in the face of it. No words could help, no amount of reassurance had the slightest effect. Weekend visits to the family homestead to see the kids were painful and awkward. Mark punished me with his silence and I could almost feel him plotting his revenge, while Laurie was always busy with her friends. Most of the time I just hung around like an extra piece of furniture, trying unsuccessfully to get through to Mark and wondering what Elaine was doing on her day off by herself. I didn't really want to know.

My social life was a confused blur of alcohol and stray women. I was indiscriminate in my tastes and rarely remembered their names the morning after. I found myself in the ironic position of trying to hide my infidelities from a potentially vindictive mistress rather than from my wife. She would not be overly impressed by the knowledge that I was out to capture the North American Humping Championship. I did not want to do anything to make her too angry with me. What an absurd position to be in. I knew it could not last much longer. It was absolutely intolerable. It was just a question of time before I took action— some sort of dramatic and decisive action—to turn my whole life around. I did not know precisely what form it would take. But I did know it would not be too far off in the future.

Chapter Thirteen

"This is the opportunity of a lifetime, fella, the chance to rub shoulders with some of the biggest wheeler-dealers in Washington."

"I wouldn't miss it for anything, Alex."

"I only wish I could be there with you. Unfortunately, it's not on the agenda."

"Oh? I was under the impression we would all be going."

"Miles and Julian will be there to introduce you around. You and George. It doesn't look as though Ron or Mike will be able to make it either."

"What a shame. To have to stay home and miss a bash like this."

"I envy you, fella. Barbara would divorce me if I even suggested running off for a week on my own. You and George have the freedom and . . . well, after all, the two of you are the most important people in this operation."

"How's that?"

"You're our contact with the public. Hell, you two make the whole thing work. The rest of us are behind-the-scenes functionaries, administrators if you like. But without your talent, yours and George's, I don't have to tell you I don't think the concept would have gotten off the ground."

"That's very generous of you, Alex, but without your original

141

plan—yours and Ron's and Mike's—George and I wouldn't have had anything to work with."

"Well, we can sit here all day exchanging accolades, but the main thing is you're going. That's settled then. Splendid. The contacts you make on the cruise are going to be invaluable to the entire operation, *our* operation. I can't emphasize that enough."

"I'm looking forward to it, Alex. It should be quite an adventure."

George Burnham and I had just been selected to go off on a Caribbean cruise—a floating brothel, gambling casino, and non-stop open bar (it sounded like)—along with a sprinkling of U.S. senators, a squad of congressmen, and a battalion or two of businessmen, lobbyists, and assorted chain-pullers from Washington. It was the kind of working vacation most men would have given their right arm to be invited to. So why wasn't I overcome with joy and enthusiasm? Why did I suddenly feel like a hireling, not an equal partner, being handed a new assignment? I guess it was just a case of galloping paranoia getting the best of me again.

We flew down to Miami together on a Friday night. George was excellent company if you were in the mood for an endless stream of the latest jokes interspersed with descriptions of his latest sexual escapades. He was handsome, funny, and boyishly charming, and it was difficult to tell if he was completely devoid of depth or if he worked hard at glib superficiality. He possessed a unique talent for it despite his apparent intelligence. Even my attempts at serious conversation were adroitly deflected by his innocuous humor. After my fourth drink I brought the discussion around to religion.

"Do you believe in God?" I asked as ponderously as I could. "In life after death?"

"There has to be life after death."

"Why's that?"

"There's too much unfinished business hanging in the air," he laughed. "Heaven's a place where everybody meets again to get even."

I told him I had been depressed lately because I was separated from my wife and family.

"It's just as well."

"Just as well? Why?"

"Bringing a wife along on a trip like this is like bringing a ham sandwich to a banquet."

A minute later he was chatting up one of the stewardesses, a cute blonde in her late twenties, trying to get a fix on whether or not she was spending the night in Miami. She wasn't, but he managed to cajole a phone number from her for future reference. I had the feeling that not even World War III would be enough to wipe that dazzling smile from his face. He surrounded himself with an impenetrable veneer of humor and nothing could puncture it. Irrationally, I felt out of sync with my whole environment, with life itself. It seemed to belong to the Georges of the world. I had tried to turn myself into a George or an Alex but the fit was not right. My new role draped over me like a baggy suit. I decided to make one more attempt to disturb George's complacency.

"Have you been following all the financial news lately, George? All this business about cracking down on white-collar crime? It's all over the papers."

He turned to me with the smile fixed on his face. But his eyes were shrewd and alert and they held me directly. They were not the eyes of a frivolous man.

"What about it?"

"Does . . . doesn't any of it worry you?"

He studied me a moment longer, then seemed to relax as his smile grew wider. "I'm a salesman, Paul. Selling's what I do best. If I weren't with Zurich I'd be peddling stocks and bonds to the institutions for somebody else or refrigerators to Eskimos if I had to. It's all the same to me. I do my job and I expect to get paid for it. It's as simple as that."

George had clearly done some thinking of his own. "Hey, fellas. I'm just a hired hand doing my job, a dumb fun-loving salesman following directions. What the hell do I know about high finance and corporate shenanigans? I leave that sort of thing to people who are smarter than me." It was a totally believable part he had chosen for himself.

"Relax, Paul." George patted my arm and sat back in his seat. "You take life too seriously, that's your problem. It's not worth all the worry, believe me. Just relax and enjoy it and take it as it comes."

Take it as it comes. How reassuring. Relax, have fun, and stop worrying so much. How many times had I heard those sentiments expressed in similar language? How hard had I tried to adopt that philosophy as my own? I believed for a time that I had transformed myself successfully, but I knew now I was only deceiving myself. I felt like an imposter at a party with people I didn't really like or admire. They were all laughing and enjoying themselves and I was just pretending. I did not belong there with them even though I dressed as they did and spoke their jargon. How long would it be before they spotted the outsider in their group? How long would it be before I gave myself away?

The limousine met us at the airport and swept us eastward along I-95 toward Biscayne Bay and the Julia Tuttle Causeway which connected the mainland with Miami Beach. The driver had a head like a cobblestone beneath his peak-brimmed hat; he looked like he could demolish buildings with it. The car turned left onto Collins Avenue and traveled north along the water's edge. The changes that had taken place during the last few years were nothing less than startling. Mostly gone now were the seedy hotels and boardinghouses and the hordes of senior citizens rocking themselves to death on the porches. The town had made a serious effort to lure young professionals in order to rebuild the economy, and the campaign was apparently successful. Sparkling new condominiums lined the avenue overlooking the Atlantic and glitzy shops and restaurants dressed up the sidestreets that were badly run down the last time I saw them. It was quite a transformation in so short a time.

George and I were staying at the Coral Star Hotel, a new pleasure palace not too far from the Eden Roc and the Fontainebleau. The air outside the limo was sweltering, almost unbearably hot and humid. Without air-conditioning your brain would turn to oatmeal in this climate. Even my tropical suit weighed down on me like a suit of armor. George, of course, looked as cool and dapper as he did before our flight.

The temperature inside the hotel was thirty degrees colder

than the evening air. We had an hour and a half to kill before our meeting with Miles and Julian, time I wanted to spend alone. I needed a shower to clear my brain from the effects of the alcohol I consumed on the plane so that I could analyze my situation clearly. Just how vulnerable was I at this moment? My independent activities alone—the laundering of money for various clients plus the diversion of cash for my own use—were enough to put me in jail for several years on embezzlement and conspiracy charges. In addition to a sojourn in some federal penitentiary, I would almost certainly be saddled with fines that I would be paying off for the rest of my life. There would also be the IRS to contend with, taxes on unreported income as well as penalties and fines amounting to several times my tax liabilities. And that was only the beginning.

These crimes would be dwarfed in comparison to the Zurich operation. I was Chief Financial Officer and Treasurer of an organization whose coffers were bursting, virtually overnight, with millions of dollars that seemingly appeared from nowhere. Where did the money that was financing the investment banking and the factoring and lending divisions come from? "I have no idea, your Honor." You mean you're the chief financial executive of a corporation that created seed money out of thin air, and you never questioned where it came from? "That's about the size of it, sir." Didn't it occur to you that there might be a conflict of interest in enticing others to acquire businesses, charging them for your services, then maintaining a controlling financial interest in these newly acquired companies by collateralizing their assets? "Well, not exactly. It struck me as a clever way to do business." And did you not know that news of pending takeovers and tender offers was being passed along to certain individuals who profited from this privileged information? "No, sir, not me. I didn't do anything like that." What were you doing then on a cruise ship in the Caribbean wining and dining people in positions of power? "I just went along to boogie, your Honor. To have some fun and see if I could fall in love for a few days."

Under close scrutiny my predicament was not only as bad as I imagined, it was worse. I had compromised myself to a point of no return. My options from this point on were fairly obvious. It was too late to simply cut bait and paddle away, assuming that I wanted to. I had Monica to worry about, and even if she kept her mouth shut there was still a chance that the Zurich Group and my role in it might be investigated sometime down the road. I would never have peace of mind with that fear lurking in the background. A second option was to continue as I was doing, hoping that I would never be exposed and we would all get away with it indefinitely.

I didn't have any statistics readily at hand, but chances are that more crimes go undetected than not. My gut feeling, however, was that the longer you persisted in a larcenous enterprise, the greater the chances of getting caught. A third course of action would be to approach the authorities, arrange some sort of a deal for myself and work to convict the others. Surely they were out to fry bigger fish than me, real criminals who ran entire networks of underworld activities and used people like me to front for them. But then what? I would be looking over my shoulder for the rest of my life, afraid to cross the street or talk to strangers. My family might be in danger unless we all entered a government witness program, changed our identity and disappeared from view. It hardly seemed workable.

And there was yet another alternative, one equally as dangerous as cooperating with the authorities but at least with the advantage of keeping my family out of it. It was daring and ambitious. It would be effective and would serve the interests of justice without endangering those closest to me. Pulling it off successfully would require a tremendous amount of creativity and ingenuity, as well as a king-sized helping of luck. Perhaps I could turn the tables on them, beat them at their own game. I could be working against them while appearing to be working with them. I thought I could manage it if I set my mind to it and worked it all out carefully beforehand. It would certainly be a challenge, the most challenging job I would have taken on since the beginning of my career, probably the greatest of my life. Just thinking about it got the adrenaline flowing and the heart pumping at full speed. For the first time in ages I felt the old spark rekindling. I was going to start having some fun again.

George was at the bar in the cocktail lounge when I went

down. The atmosphere was a veritable explosion of ultramodern glitz and sparkle. Your senses were bombarded from every direction by glittering lights, thumping music, and a general cacophany of voices and laughter. Even the air smelled artificial, cold and devoid of any natural odors. Approximately every fourth barstool was adorned with the unblemished beauty of a high-priced hooker—smiling, alluring, and expensive-looking. I thought back to the first time I visited Dallas, the same occasion I learned about "slick meat" so poignantly. I went down to the hotel bar for a nightcap, only to find myself being stared at by three aggressive call girls at the end of the bar. One of them winked and beckoned me to take the stool beside her. I smiled and looked away, and two minutes later she was at my side with her right hand firmly gripped around my testicles.

"You ain't some kind of faggot, are you, honey?" she asked.

"No, I just don't feel like paying for my pleasure, that's all."

"No need to be so unneighborly. Least you can do is come over and buy a working girl a drink."

I learned my second lesson about Texas that night. In oil-rich Dallas at the time it was common for oil men to mingle with the hookers after work and buy them a round or two of champagne whether they intended to go upstairs with them or not. Not to do so was considered an unfriendly act—just as unfriendly as ordering slick meat in a steak house apparently. I filed this information away for future reference.

George was sipping a Perrier on the rocks with a twist. He hardly touched alcohol at all and this was another thing that annoyed me; I didn't trust people who were so carefully guarded all the time. I ordered an extra-dry martini, something I did not ordinarily do since gin made me a little too crazy for my own good. But that's the kind of mood I was in.

"Feeling better?" he asked.

"Wonderful, George, wonderful." What the hell did he mean by that anyway? "I just needed a little rest to clear my mind a bit."

"I know what you mean. We can all use a long vacation. We've been putting out a thousand percent since we started this operation."

The incongruous duo, Miles and Julian, entered the lounge,

craning their necks in the darkness to see if we were there. I waved and caught their attention and they came over. Julian was all smiles and hearty handshakes, bursting with camaraderie as though he had just been reunited with his dearest friends. Miles's attempt at a smile revealed a row of white splinters for teeth. He looked like a piranha stuffed into a pin-striped suit.

"Welcome, my good friends, the snowbirds from New York," said Julian, hugging the two of us.

Miles offered his limp right hand and said nothing.

"How do you like the Coral Star, the jewel of Miami Beach?" asked Julian.

"It's about what I expected," I answered too quickly. They both stared at me quizzically, not knowing how to take it.

"It's fabulous," said George, the salesman and diplomat. "I've never seen anything like it."

"I'm so happy you like our little establishment since we are delighted to be your hosts during your stay with us."

"I . . . I didn't realize you were the proprietors here."

"I own nothing, my friend, except the suit on my back and a small boat in the bay. But our investors . . . many of the same ones who contribute so handsomely to Zurich . . . are the true proprietors as you put it. Come now. Let's find a table and make ourselves comfortable so we can discuss business privately, shall we?"

Julian led us to a large table in the far corner, a table big enough for six. Within moments a bottle of chilled Dom Perignon was presented to us by an attractive waitress in a sequined minidress. Julian nodded his approval and the cork was popped and our glasses filled with great fanfare. Julian swept his arms wide, taking in the whole room.

"You are our guests while you are here. Anything you like . . . and I mean anything," he winked, nodding toward the barstools, "do not hesitate to ask for."

We lifted our glasses in a toast and sipped the sparkling white wine that felt like liquid diamonds on my tongue. Miles stared at me intently from behind his rimless glasses. His eyes darted back and forth from George to me, then settled on me.

"So things are going well in New York," he said. It was not quite a question.

"So it seems. We keep turning them away at the seminars and signing them up into our program. Everybody wants to be a deal-maker these days. It's practically a religion."

Miles stared and did not reply.

"We've got the biggest inventory of businesses for sale in existence and as of last week, yesterday actually, we've officially closed on an even two dozen. No cash down from any of the buyers. Which means we've got a lockhold on all of them through ZFS."

Miles and Julian looked at each other and smiled.

"In addition," I continued, "we're ready to go public with three of our own deals by October at the latest. A computer firm in Denver, a genetic engineering outfit in Salt Lake City, and a racetrack in New Jersey. If the market continues the way it's been going, we can probably sell the shares at the top end of our price range."

"And the institutions, George?" Miles asked. "They are receptive to these companies?"

"I've already talked the deals up to eight major portfolio managers and half a dozen hedge funds. There'll be no trouble moving the stock."

"Excellent," Miles replied, showing us his pointed teeth again. "Any problems you foresee that we should know about?"

George and I exchanged glances for an instant, then I replied. "I mentioned this to George on the way down and it's something that's been bothering me. This new crackdown on white-collar crime. Atlantic Investments in New Jersey's been indicted on seven counts of stock manipulation, illegal campaign contributions, perjury, insider trading, money laundering, and half a dozen other charges. Mike Dolan's been forced to resign as CEO and he's looking at maybe ten years in jail plus God knows how many millions in fines. This is going on all over the country and it seems to be getting worse."

Now it was Miles' and Julian's turn to exchange looks. Julian leaned forward and spoke in a low, measured voice. "There is absolutely nothing to fear, my friend. I guarantee you this is nothing more than pretense or sabre rattling, as you call it. Mike Dolan is very well protected and I assure you he will not spend ten seconds inside a jail cell. Any fine will be a token, a fraction of what you mention, which will be taken care of for him. The whole thing will be swept aside in a matter of months, as soon as the November elections are over."

"The whole point of this pleasure cruise," added Miles, "is for you to meet some important people who are very good friends of ours. Senator Philips, Congressmen Moczinski and Jameson, the very people who are yelling the loudest are actually working for us. The layers of protection that surround this organization are absolutely impenetrable. Rest assured, this nonsense you read about in the newspapers is nothing more than a charade designed to keep the voters happy. Nothing will come of it."

"It is good you are concerned," Julian said. "It shows you are thinking. That is good for all of us. But your fears are groundless."

"I was certain they were. But it's good to have your reassurance. I feel much better now that we've discussed it."

"Excellent!" Julian clapped his hands. "Come, George. Let's you and I retire to the bar. I think Miles has some personal business he wants to discuss with Paul."

What was this all about? The two of them rose, George's smile as dazzling as ever as though he hadn't a worry in the world. I was left alone with the dwarfish Miles Ross. Though I stood nearly a foot taller than he did, I felt as if I were in the presence of a great white shark who could eat me up alive if he chose. The prospect of going one-on-one with him was somewhat disconcerting. He went through an elaborate ritual of extracting a filtered cigarette from a silver case, inserting it carefully into a long bejeweled holder, and lighting it with a heavy gold lighter.

"You and I are very much alike, Paul," he began. "You're a cautious man and so am I. You've got a good head for business and numbers as I do. George is pleasant and he does his job well, but he doesn't have your head. You and I communicate well. I think we understand each other perfectly."

I had no idea what he was getting at. "I agree," I said. "I've always admired the way you think."

"For this reason it upsets me when I see a man like you losing control over his personal life. When a man's personal life is in order, his business life is in order too. When his personal life falls apart it affects other areas as well."

"You're referring to my separation from my wife no doubt."
The arrogant bastard. Prying into affairs that didn't concern him.

"Your separation is only symptomatic of a more alarming
problem. Believe me, I wouldn't bring this up if it didn't concern all of us. What a man does for pleasure is his own business
as long as he keeps it under control. I don't have to tell you how
many corporate presidents and members of Congress have their
dalliances on the side and keep their family intact at the same
time. It's best for everyone that way. No mess, no fuss, no scandal."

"I agree. Unfortunately in my case I . . . "

"Their indiscretions also provide us with a wonderful opportunity as well, if you follow me," Miles went on. "It's commonly
known that the incredible power Roy Cohn enjoyed was due to
his leverage over half the politicians in the country. He had the
goods on everyone. Who was fucking whom, who liked boys,
who liked girls, who liked dope. The man was perhaps the most
successful procurer of modern times."

I nodded. I had a good idea now what he was leading up to.

"In your case you've put yourself in the position of a man who
can be compromised rather than one who does the compromis-
ing. When we first met your life was a model of discretion.
Solid, clean, unblemished. In a surprisingly short period you've
made yourself vulnerable."

I was beginning to understand how David Stockman felt when
he was "taken to the woodshed" for indiscretions of his own by
President Reagan. Miles was showing me his whiphand and I
suddenly felt as though I were ten years old again.

"This girl Monica who's become such an important part of
your life . . . she's been with you quite some time now."

"She was my secretary before we started Zurich, yes."

"She has a good working knowledge of our operation. She
functions pretty much like your right hand when you're out of
the office."

Miles wasn't asking questions; he was stating what he knew
were facts. I felt as sober as a Baptist minister despite the alcohol. The noise and glitter of the lounge receded into the background. Nothing existed except the sound of Miles Ross's voice
and the look in his unblinking eyes. I nodded yes.

"Has she become a problem to you in any way?"

He knew everything. He understood me better than I did my-self. I lived my life inside a fishbowl. For all I knew my phones were tapped, my apartment was bugged. My paranoia hadn't gone far enough. My first reaction was to protect Monica. I could not be responsible for her having an "accident" on her way home to Brooklyn some evening—a slip off the subway platform, a hit-and-run driver, a fatal mugging outside her apartment. I could not live with that.

"She's not a problem, Miles. She's discreet and totally loyal to me."

Miles smiled and my blood froze. All I could see was a row of sharp nicotine-stained teeth inside a mouth that filled my universe.

"She has to be removed, Paul, but not in the way you think. Violence is so unnecessary. All it does is anger the authorities and upset the public. We will have a talk with her, offer to make her life a lot more comfortable than it is right now, explain some facts of life to her. She'll be agreeable, I'm sure of it. You have no objection to this?"

"Not if it's handled like that, no."

"You're not so infatuated that you can't live without her?"

"It's all over with now. I was planning to break it off as soon as I got back anyway. I want my family back and that can't happen until she's out of the picture."

"This is the best solution for everyone then. The girl benefits, we have one less problem to worry about, and you are relieved of an unpleasant emotional confrontation."

"I agree."

Miles rested a tiny claw of a hand on my right arm and flashed his teeth once more. "It will be taken care of then. She'll be gone by the time you get back. Consider it done."

Chapter Fourteen

The three-day cruise to nowhere should have been a bacchanalian revel for me as well as a working holiday. But I was so completely sobered by my conversation with Miles that I could not unwind for a moment. I drank vats of rum punch and larger still quantities of beer and wine with no evident effect on my brain. All my sensory organs were on full operational alert; my entire neurological apparatus was on a war footing. I felt I could hear a pin drop on the other side of the Atlantic. My wits were as finely tuned as they had been in ages.

Miles and Julian were both very much in control, and George and I were gradually introduced to everyone who mattered on board. Quite an assemblage it was too. Alex had not exaggerated the importance of those who would be along for the ride. I counted eight congressmen, two United States senators, and the governor of a large northeastern state. I also got to meet more bank presidents than I've ever seen assembled in one place, a squadron of Wall Street stock traders, the chairmen of four major brokerage firms, eight portfolio managers, enough lawyers to staff the faculties of half a dozen law schools, CEOs of twenty different corporations, a dozen or so silent types who looked as though they ate razor blades for breakfast, and incongruously enough, three dentists from upstate New York. There were more voluptuous women aboard ship than you can find during

153

lunch hour in midtown Manhattan, the oldest of them no more than a couple of years over thirty. The highlight of the cruise for me was meeting a popular country-and-western singer who spent the entire three days with a bottle of bourbon cradled in one arm and a full-breasted blonde in the other.

"What do you think of these singers and their anti-nuke benefits?" he was asked by some banker in plaid Bermuda shorts and steel-rimmed glasses.

"Buncha fuckin' idiots! Fuck 'em all! Blow 'em all clear to hell. Shit, git it over quick. Jes don't kill no alligators in Loosiana 'cause I married a couple of 'em."

"How many wives you had now anyway?"

"That's my fuckin' business. Pussy is pussy. I'm a sinner, I know it. Soon I'm gonna hafta reckon with the chillin' hands of death."

By the end of the first day out to sea I had been handed more than enough business cards than I needed to paper a wall, and both George and I distributed a gross or two of our own. Indeed, other than eating and drinking and playing musical beds, swapping business cards was the principal activity of the cruise. Along with setting up lunch dates. My lunch card was booked for three straight weeks after my return to New York. I was thinking of hiring Janet, the buxom divorcee from P.J. Clarke's, as my restaurant consultant, then thought better of it when I contemplated the outcome of my affair with Monica. No more close encounters of that kind. Perhaps I should think seriously of abstaining from sex altogether. Become a Trappist monk and give up all the sensual pleasures. Rigid self-discipline was my only salvation.

Miles was as good as his word. When I returned to the hot and clammy city Monica was nowhere in sight. In one way it was a relief since he did me a favor by removing a proverbial thorn from my side. But the more I thought about it, the more my pride was pierced. Just how difficult was it for Monica to extract herself from me? What was the price of her forced separation from the man who was her "whole life" to her? Was it a painful decision or did they make it easy for her with a better opportunity than I represented? How could a woman who threatened to throw herself in front of a moving train if I tried to leave her give me up without a fight? I had to find out how she was taking it.

I called her at home for three nights running before I found her in. The idea crossed my mind that both our phones might be tapped but I didn't give a damn; I had to talk to her.

"Hello."

"Monica?"

There was dead silence on the other end, then:

"Oh, it's you."

"Are you all right? How are you doing?"

"Just fine, if you really want to know."

"Of course I want to know. Are you okay?"

"I . . . I can't talk to you."

"What do you mean?"

"I'm not supposed to."

"Is that part of the deal?"

"I'm not going to make any trouble if that's what you're worried about."

"That's not what I'm worried about. I'm concerned about you."

"I'll be just fine, so you can put your mind at ease about it."

"Did they offer you money? Is that it?"

"Some, yes. Plus . . . I'm not supposed to tell you."

"Tell me! I want to know."

"I'll be moving soon. They offered me a job in Florida."

"Florida?"

"Miami Beach. At some new hotel."

"Doing what?"

"Oh, I don't know yet. Public relations, something like that. The money's good. Twice as much as I was making with you."

"Public relations! Shit, Monica. Do you know what you're getting into?"

"I . . . I've gotta go now, Paul. Somebody's coming over. The man who offered me the job. I can't talk to you anymore."

"Are you sure, Monica? Are you sure this is what you want?"

"I can't have what I really want, Paul. Nobody gets what they really want, you said to me once. But it's better than taking the subway back to Brooklyn for the rest of my life."

"My God, Monica. I . . . I don't know what to say."

"I loved you, Paul. I know you don't want to hear that, but it's true."

"I loved you, too, in my own crazy way."

It was the first time I told her that and it did not come out easily.

"I've got to go now, Paul."

"Goodbye, Monica. Please take care of yourself."

I hung up the phone and wailed like a baby for nearly an hour. It was the most heart-wrenching cry I had since my break-up with Elaine. Once again the reality of what I had been doing overwhelmed me in a flash. We all pay the piper for our actions sooner or later. There's no escape from that. I did not love Monica but I was truly fond of her and cared about what happened to her. And now it had come to this. The final goodbye. Not the clean goodbye I wanted before I left for Miami. A shitty and painful goodbye tinged with evil. A fitting goodbye considering the sordid condition of my life. How could I have been foolish enough to expect anything else? Everything was of a piece.

If there was ever any doubt in my mind, Miles's solution to the "Monica problem" convinced me that I was dealing with professionals. Removing Monica from my life was accomplished in a manner that demonstrated just who was in control. It was a masterful exercise of power and discipline. Ruthless and efficient. And more than a little bit humiliating.

Elaine and I had dinner together for the first time in months. She met me in the city at a small French restaurant in the West Forties, adjacent to the theater district. Her hair hung loose in soft waves that fell to her shoulders, and she wore a light green summer dress that tightly hugged her body's twists and turns. She was more beautiful than ever and she looked eight to ten years younger than her real age.

We had a drink at the bar while our table was being prepared and talked mostly about the kids and how they were doing. It was a typical Gallic restaurant. The waiters were just arrogant enough short of being completely obnoxious. Manhattan waiters regarded smiling as a sign of weakness. The more they bullied the customers, the more the public was willing to pay for the food. It was a curious social phenomenon.

I ordered wine immediately as we studied the menus. Veal, chicken, fish, and the usual French-style steak coated lavishly with crushed peppercorns. I refused to order lamb in a French restaurant. I like my lamb pink inside, not purple. The French prefer it almost raw and scowl at anyone who likes it cooked. I didn't need that kind of a confrontation tonight, so I ordered sweetbreads with chanterelles in a wine sauce and Elaine ordered poached salmon. A fat woman to my left lit up one cigarette after another and she bristled when I asked her to blow her smoke in the other direction. Her husband pretended not to hear and he looked away.

"I forgot how much I always liked this place," I said.

Elaine stared into her drink glass and said, "We used to come here whenever we didn't feel like eating in Joe Allen's. Whenever we felt like splurging."

"Which we did whether we could afford to or not. We were never ones for keeping our eyes on a budget."

"I always left that up to you. I never knew how tight we were financially until . . . well until that crazy night last winter when you finally decided to unburden yourself. I still can't figure out why it took you so long."

"I . . . oh what's the difference? It's all water under the bridge now. It's over with."

"Is that why you asked me to meet you here tonight, Paul? To talk about money again?"

"No. Well, yes and no, but not the way you think. It's more complicated than that."

"Everything's complicated lately, isn't it?"

"Yes, unfortunately. It seems to get worse all the time."

The waiter brought our salads and sprinkled ground pepper on them from a pepper mill that looked like a baseball bat. He could have set a homerun record with it. The fat lady had been glaring at me since I spoke to her about her cigarettes and I made an effort not to respond in kind. I wondered what it was like being married to someone like her for the past twenty-five or thirty years; what it was like knowing there were another twenty years left to go. Did they each feel trapped in their own private boredom or had they made some sort of psychological accommodation to their fate? They had not spoken more than three words to each other since we arrived.

"There are so many things to talk about, Elaine. I don't know where to start. I love you so much. I miss you terribly. I hate being away from you and the kids."

She fiddled with her salad, her eyes growing moist as she stared down at the artichoke hearts and dark green spinach that glistened with an oily sheen. "I don't like being separated from you either. I love you too. That's why I was so devastated when I found out what you were doing. I still don't understand what possessed you. Should I just chalk it up to midlife crisis or what?"

"It's nothing as cut and dried as that. I mean, I didn't go looking for someone else because I felt a mid-forties panic coming over me, nothing like that. You have to understand the mental condition I was in at the time. I used to have seizures of silent hysteria on the train worrying about money. I literally wanted to die."

"So you went and fucked your secretary. It was a perfectly rational solution to our financial problems. How could I be so stupid not to have seen it clearly before?"

The woman's glare took on a new dimension. She lit a fresh cigarette defiantly, convinced that I was the arch villain in a real-life soap opera. Her husband furrowed his brow as he shifted his eyes back and forth from Elaine to me as though he were watching a tennis match. This was clearly better than staying home and watching television. They were getting their money's worth whether they liked the food or not.

"No, Elaine, it wasn't a solution to our financial crisis," I said calmly. "What I've been doing with Alex and the others is the solution, and that's something else we have to talk about. Monica just fit in with it at the time. She came on to me and I decided to let it happen. I'm sure you've been tempted with other men. You'd be dead if you weren't. I'm sorry it happened but it did and it's all over now."

"So where do we go from here, Paul? Do we put it all behind us and pick up where we left off? Is that what you want?"

"Well, I do know that the longer people live apart, the harder it is to get together again. If we're going to salvage our marriage we have to do it soon before it's too late, before too many other things come into our lives and we reach the point of no return."

The waiter brought the wine, a 1982 Margaux. I went through the ritual of inspecting the label, sniffing the cork and tasting the wine which the French take more seriously than religion. I nodded that it was fine and the waiter filled our glasses less than halfway up and left us alone again. Elaine's eyes brimmed over with tears and they ran in rivulets down her cheeks.

"I want our marriage to work again, Paul. I don't like not being a family anymore. It's terrible. I didn't realize how close we were until . . . until this happened."

The woman to my left disapproved of Elaine's feelings. She nearly snorted out loud before giving in to a hacking cough that convulsed her throat. Elaine and I held hands across the table and we both broke out in broad grins for the first time in months.

"You miserable bastard. I do love you. I just need a little more time to . . . to adjust my thinking. I'm not as decisive as you are." Elaine wiped the tears away with her napkin. The waiter arrived with our entrees in the midst of all this emotionalism and nearly beamed with joy. We were doing honor to his restaurant. The only thing missing was Charles Aznavour or Yves Montand wailing about unrequited love in the background. He rewarded us by immediately pouring a generous splash of wine in our glasses and twisting the neck of the bottle with a flourish. When he disappeared we attacked our food with a sexual hunger. The sweetbreads were excellent; I had never tasted better. Midway through the meal Elaine and I exchanged plates as we had often done in the past and finished each other's food. I thought the waiter would have an orgasm as he came by to ask if everything was all right. We rewarded him by linking our arms around each other's and sipping wine with our arms locked. I had seen Jean Paul Belmondo do that with Jean Seberg in some old movie, and never forgot it. Such elegant foreplay. It was even sexier than watching Albert Finney devouring oysters with Diane Cilento in *Tom Jones*. Better than fingerfucking beneath the tablecloth in a restaurant.

"I don't suppose either one of us knows what we're doing," Elaine said lightly. We both felt as though a great dark cloud was beginning to break up, letting down a ray or two of sunshine.

"At least you can't say it's been boring."

"You son of a bitch. If you ever think of cheating on me again I hope your balls fall off."

Elaine was never one for mincing words and I was superstitious enough to believe in the power of curses. We finished the food and lingered over the final glass of wine from the bottle. I probably shouldn't have brought it up but I wanted to know. I waited until the mood was relaxed and we were settling back into our old selves before I asked.

"I'm sure you've been going out with other men during the past few months, but . . . nothing happened between you and Alex, did it?"

"Alex? Don't be ridiculous. I've always admired his business sense but . . . physically? You've got to be kidding?"

"I didn't think so but I wanted to be sure."

"It wasn't for lack of opportunity though. I shouldn't tell you this since you're still involved with him, but the man's a letch. Not a brazen, out-in-the-open letch, but a sneaky devious letch. Clumsier than I thought he'd be. I feel sorry for Barbara."

"Who else called you up when I moved out? Anyone I know?"

She hesitated for a moment, then said, "I don't think we should get into this, Paul. The last thing I need now is to torment myself with questions about how many people you've been to bed with, and I don't think you should think about that either. It's unhealthy for both of us.

She was right of course. My sado-masochistic curiosity would not do either of us any good. It was enough to know that our marriage might be saved, that our feelings for each other had intensified during our separation. Everything else was trivial by comparison.

"Do you want coffee?" I asked. "A cordial? Frangelica or Amaretto?"

"Not here," she smiled seductively. There was a look in her eye that told me things were returning to normal again.

Making love to my wife in the same bed I had lured so many

strange and varied women to had an illicit quality about it. If the idea bothered Elaine in the least, she gave no indication of it. We reached for each other hungrily, undressing each other with expert hands, making up for the months we had been apart with an exquisite urgency that bordered on violence. We did not linger. We did not work up to a level of orchestrated passion slowly as we had in the past. This time for us was a spontaneous explosion of pent-up desire. We purged ourselves instantaneously of all the months of frustration and denial. I don't think it lasted more than ten minutes, but it was infinitely satisfying. In less than a moment it dawned on me that our marriage had lasted as long as it did for a very good reason. Our union was so exciting because it was rooted in extremes. We loved each other wonderfully and we also fought like hell. Our time together was either exhilarating or maddeningly frustrating. There were no in betweens, there was no dullness in our lives. It was a manic-depressive existence but it worked for us.

Afterward we kept our arms around each other and lay side-by-side without talking. Maybe it was a time for silently considering the road ahead without pushing things too quickly. For better or worse we fit together comfortably and we both understood that. Finally, it was I who broke the silence.

"Feels good, doesn't it?"

"God, I missed you so much," she whispered.

"It's been a season in hell for both of us. Is it possible for temporary insanity to last almost a year or do you think I'm really crazy?"

She thought about that for a moment, then said, "I think we both got a little too greedy for our own good, Paul."

"Oh?"

"I've done a lot of thinking during the last few months. I've tried to analyze exactly what happened, exactly what went wrong with our lives."

"And?"

"Part of the blame was mine, I know that now. I still don't understand the Monica business completely. It's going to take me a long time to get over that. But the financial pressure was partly my fault. I didn't want to hear about the problem. I still don't. The idea of giving up what we've worked for and taking a step backward terrifies me. I enjoy living nicely and I want to be able to do everything we can for the kids. I've gotten spoiled, Paul, and so have you. I know I pushed you in my own not-too-subtle way. I've got to be honest about that."

On one hand it was good to hear her say all this, but on the other hand it annoyed me. It sounded as though I didn't have a mind of my own. "I didn't need much of a push," I said. "I had one foot dangling over the line all along."

"Still, I've got to be honest. I wanted you to do something, whatever you had to do to keep us from going under. I thought Alex was the answer and I'm sorry now I encouraged you to fall in with him."

"What do you mean 'fall in with him'? When I was a kid my mother used to warn me away from boys who might have a 'bad influence' on me, and now my wife is taking the blame for my falling in with bad company. I do have a mind of my own you know."

"You don't have to snap at me. I was only trying to shoulder my own share of the responsibility. I know you have a mind of your own. It's just that . . . sometimes you can't figure out what it's trying to tell you," she said, and then erupted in a fit of giggles. Her laughter took most of the punch out of her remark and, despite my initial reaction, I found myself laughing along with her.

"Let's face it, Paul. You're a typical Gemini. You're always scattering yourself in six directions at the same time. Every alternative looks good to you so you either try them all out simultaneously or else you don't do anything."

"Yes, well there is some truth to that," I laughed. "But you're not much help either when you start pushing my buttons without weighing all the consequences. I can get into enough trouble by myself without a push from you."

Neither of us said anything for a while, both of us preoccupied for the moment with our individual thoughts. There was a lot left to talk about; we both knew that. The tough part was yet to come. A way had to be found out of the financial quagmire I was stuck in before we could even begin to plan on putting our marriage back together. It was far more complicated than merely deciding whether or not to kiss and make up.

"Just how much trouble are you in, Paul? Is it as serious as you thought it was at the beginning of the summer?"

"Worse I'd say. Every time I think I've learned everything there is to know, I uncover a new layer of activity I never saw before. It's like a series of boxes within boxes. You never get to the end."

"But what can you do about it? Can't you just quit and walk away from it?"

"It's not that simple. I . . . I'm too deeply involved, too close to the center of things."

"You're making it sound impossible. There's got to be a solution. There always is to every problem." She was sitting up on the bed now, staring down at me with great concern. The worry lines crinkled her face, adding years. For an unguarded moment she looked her age. It would feel good to tell her everything I knew and everything that had to be done. But that was not possible. The less she knew, the better off she would be. Ignorance was her best protection.

"Well there is a solution all right and I've just about decided to put it to work. But it's not going to be pleasant. If I'm telling you less than you want to know it's for a good reason. Please believe me."

"But what about us? What's going to happen to us?"

"What do you mean?"

"Us. Me and the kids. The house. Everything. What's going to happen?"

"You'll be completely removed from it. It won't touch you. We'll keep on the same as we are now for a while. I'll stay in the city and I'll pay all our bills. Nothing's going to change. Later on, when the dust settles, then we can talk about . . . you know . . . where you and I go from there."

"But suppose . . . suppose . . ."

"Suppose something happens to me?"

The stricken look on her face said everything.

"I've got some money put aside. Quite a lump as a matter of fact. I'm going to give it to you. Just put it away in a metal box somewhere and don't ask questions. Down in the cellar in that alcove behind the boiler with those old skis and tennis racquets. Forget about the banks. They're fishbowls. It'll keep you going for quite a while if . . . if there's some reason why I can't send you monthly checks any more."

I had never seen Elaine look so terrified before. If she thought I was exaggerating my predicament before this evening, there was no longer any doubt in her mind about how serious it was. The fact that I was willing to entrust her with my pirated booty was proof of that. It was my insurance fund for her and the kids. To her it showed my family came first. She cuddled beside me and rubbed my graying chest hairs with her free hand. As terrible as the situation was for all of us, Elaine still had her sense of humor. She reached below the sheets and wrapped her hand around my dick.

"This is the most unusual separation I ever heard of," she said.

Chapter Fifteen

I taxied down to the Dublin House to visit Tommy Gilmartin at ten-thirty the next morning. I wanted to see him early before the lunch trade came in and occupied his attention for the next three hours or so. It was a crisp September morning with the smell of wet leaves and freshly mown grass from the park heavy in the air. By noon these pastoral aromas would be suffocated beneath a blanket of exhaust fumes and curbside garbage. My mood was light and cheerful, senselessly optimistic considering the kind of corporate combat I was about to engage in.

"A bit early for you, isn't it?" Tommy smiled when I walked in.

"I think I'm getting senile, Tommy. The world's caving in on me and I'm walking around with a smile on my face."

"Oh? What's up?"

"Do you have a minute? Let's sit at that corner table over there so we can discuss business in private."

Tommy had put on some weight over the summer and he was more disheveled than ever. He was raking in money ten times faster than he could spend it and he looked like someone you would throw a quarter to if you passed him on the street. The air in the bar was a bit sour, a rancid blend of stale beer and liquor and yesterday's cigarette smoke. The floor smelled as though it had been wiped with a dirty mop. The casual observer would never recognize the place for the gold mine it was.

"How're things at home, Tommy?"

"Pretty much the same as ever. My kids're driving me crazy and my wife averages about three doctors' appointments a week. Nobody can find anything wrong with her, but if you tell her it's all in her head she starts bouncing dishes off the wall. How about you? You . . . you and Elaine still . . ."

"Still separated. We're trying to patch things up. I'm getting too old for bachelorhood. It's enough to kill anybody over forty."

"What about the other one . . . what's her name?"

"Monica. That's over with. It was fun while it lasted but adultery is far more complicated than most people realize."

"The way you do it, it is. You've got a knack for turning everything into a circus. . . . So tell me what's up. I know you didn't come down here this early in the morning just to shoot the breeze."

"The party's over, Tommy. Or at least it will be soon and I want to protect you and the others before things start heating up."

"What happened?"

"Nothing yet. But I'm anticipating trouble. I'm looking down the road ahead and it doesn't look too smooth to me. I think it's time to get out. Maybe I'm being too cautious but I don't think so."

Tommy looked over at the three solitary drinkers with their shots and beer chasers at the bar. He studied the movements of his bartender, a new man named Seamus he recently imported from Ireland. When he turned back to me he had a half-smile on his face, a knowing smile, a look that said he expected something like this would happen sooner or later.

"I didn't expect it to last forever," he said. "To be honest with you, I never felt all that comfortable with it. I always had mixed feelings. What do I have to do now?"

"Nothing. We quit cold turkey, just like that. I'll close out your account and see if I can purge it from the record as though it never existed."

"But what do I do with . . . you know . . . all the cash from here on in?"

I was almost shocked by his question. On one hand he seemed relieved that he would not have to continue doing something that troubled his conscience, on the other hand he was annoyed that he no longer had an immediate outlet for his cash.

"Well, it's obvious, Tommy. Your options are limited. You either play it straight from here on or . . ."

"And pay taxes on it to the fuckin' IRS you mean?"

I couldn't believe this guy. "Or else you find somebody else to take it in," I said. "It's up to you. All I'm telling you is that I can't do it anymore. It's getting too risky. Christ, Tommy. I'm trying to save your ass as well as my own."

"Yeah, well I guess you're right," he grumbled. "I been reading the papers, too, about all these assholes who've had their hands in everyone else's pockets all their lives suddenly finding religion. Fucking hypocrites. They've got their own bundle stashed away somewhere and now they're trying to cool the action for everybody else."

I was stunned. Maybe I was naïve, but I had not expected this kind of a reaction from him. He was actually angry with me for shutting the window on him, as though I were part of the establishment conspiring to make him pay his taxes. The crazy bastard regarded everyone with a white collar and tie as a natural enemy, friendship notwithstanding. And he was one of the few I had been honest with, never extracting a cut for my services, relying on commissions alone.

"So what happens now?" he insisted somewhat belligerently.

"What do you mean?" I suddenly felt dizzy. A sense of déjà vu struck me with the certainty that I had carried on this conversation verbatim in an earlier lifetime. He stared at me intently without a trace of a smile on his face.

"I've got a box full of bearer bonds and whatnot plus a stack of cash I need to get rid of. Where do I go from here?"

"Well, I . . . I suggest you put it into some real estate. Use the bonds as a downpayment for a piece of property or as collateral for a loan. Maybe you can work a deal with somebody to take cash under the table and deduct it from the selling price. This way he gets to pay less taxes on his gain. It goes on all the time."

"I know about that angle. Maybe I shoulda done it all along," he sneered.

"Now wait a fucking minute, Tommy!" I was rippling, ready to take him outside on the sidewalk if I had to. "You're acting like this is all my fault or something. You knew from the beginning we were both taking our chances with this. You're blaming me because the authorities've decided to crack down? I can't believe you. I've got more to lose than you do, damnit!"

Tommy stared at me for a long moment without saying a word. Then his face split in half with a wide grin that had more mischief than humor in it. It was the same smile of resignation he used to wear in the backfield before hurling himself against a solid wall of muscle and beef.

"Still got that old temper," he said through the grin. "You never could.take the needle without blowing up."

"Fuck you," I answered with a grin of my own. "You crazy bastard, you haven't changed a bit."

The tension was at least partially dissolved, the critical moment had passed for both of us. Being friends with Tommy always did have a volatile side to it. His solution to a crisis was to lash out at the nearest body.

"I know it's not your fault, Paul," he said more calmly now, settling back against the bench and sagging into himself a bit. "It's just that . . . well it was a nice deal while it lasted and I hate to see it end. It gives me one more thing to worry about. You think . . . you really think the feds're getting serious this time? They've rattled the cages before, usually just before election time, and then they drop it like a hot potato after the votes are tallied up."

"People are going to jail, Tommy. Maybe I'm making too big a deal out of it, but I don't think so. A lot of people are getting nailed now who were never touched before. And they're throwing the book at them, not just a fine and a slap on the wrist like in the past. It's for real this time. At least it looks that way to me."

"You're probably right. It's better to play it safe I guess. I'll be all right. I'll find a way. How about you? Where do you go from here?"

"That's a good question and I wish I had an answer for you. It sure as hell puts a damper on my style of doing business. Maybe I'll have to go out and sell vacuum cleaners for a living. Maybe I'll come to work for you. Can you use an honest bartender?"

"Hah!" His laugh was spontaneous and genuine. "I'd have to watch you closer than these Micks I bring into the country."

He said it with a smile but I think he half meant it. I had a fleeting insight into how I must have looked to others. Hell, the people I did business with knew me primarily as their laundry-man, a guy who was at least as crooked as they were despite all the financial mumbo jumbo. Birds of a feather doing business together. What else could I expect?

"What the hell. You're probably well fixed by now anyway," Tommy said with that mischievous grin on his face again.

"The hell I am. I wish that were the case."

"You must have a million or two stashed away by now."

"Whatever I've got is only chicken feed next to your pile. I'm a piker compared to you."

I felt a bit soiled when I left Tommy shortly after eleven, just as his establishment was beginning to attract a steady stream of pre-luncheon drinkers. Tommy had been dealing for so long with crooked cops and politicians and inspectors on the take that he couldn't believe anyone with half a brain would seriously think of going straight. I was convinced before I left that he would quickly find a new outlet for his cash. There was no way he was going to let a bunch of gutless bureaucrats turn him into an honest man—a sucker to his way of thinking—in an inherently dishonest world. People like Tommy regarded solid citizens as patsies who went up to bat every day with two strikes against them. There was always a way to beat the system, he believed; always a new loophole to replace one that was being closed. Perhaps he was right. Perhaps I was getting myself all worked up over something that would pass in time. It was true that I was reacting more out of fear than a sense of morality or idealism. Elaine saw me clearly; I did analyze six different sides to every problem, and they all seemed equally valid to me. But this time I was not going to scatter my energies or allow myself to be paralyzed with indecision. I had decided on a plan and I intended to stick by it, for better or worse. The knowledge that the friendship Tommy and I had enjoyed over the years would never be the same again troubled me more than anything else.

"I understand you're having lunch with Steve Roberts today,"

Alex said as he poked his head into my office just before noon. I had a hundred thoughts buzzing through my brain after my meeting with Tommy, and I had not begun to focus yet on my lunch date with Roberts, a lawyer from Miami. I met him on the cruise to nowhere and he seemed especially anxious to get together with me after I returned to New York.

"Hi, Alex. Yes, I'm meeting him in half an hour at '21.' "

"Splendid." He stepped over the threshold to my office and immediately lit up a cigarette, a gesture that never failed to drive me nuts. He sat in the chair beside my desk and I had to fish an ashtray from the bottom drawer to accommodate his ashes. His eyes looked red around the edges as though he had been drinking for a day and a half without any sleep. Just inhaling the exudations from his pores was enough to give you a hangover.

"I hear you and Steve hit it off pretty well down in Miami."

"We had a few drinks together and got along just fine. He was anxious to have lunch with me when I got back to the city so we set this thing up."

"Steve and I go back a long way together. I knew him up in Toronto after I left the U K and we kept in touch when the both of us came down to the States. He set up shop in Miami . . . oh, I guess it was ten years ago by now. We've been partners in a number of deals over the years."

"Well, thanks for filling me in on the background. I had no idea you and he knew each other at all."

Alex was silent for a moment as he inhaled deeply from his cigarette, and let the smoke seep out slowly through every aperture in his head. For a full minute after he dinched his butt out in my ashtray, little puffs of smoke wafted from his mouth and nostrils. It even seemed to be coming out of his eyes and ears. I couldn't believe that anyone could travel around in such an atmosphere throughout his entire adult life and still be alive.

"Steve Roberts can be a very big asset to this operation," Alex said slowly and quietly. "I can't emphasize that enough. He's extremely well connected. Of all the people you met aboard that cruise ship, Steve is perhaps the most important . . . senators and congressmen notwithstanding."

There was such an emphatic tone to Alex's voice that I did not know exactly how to respond. He sounded as though he had just come down from the mountain with tablets containing the ten commandments in his possession. I merely nodded and invited him to continue.

"Steve will tell you exactly what he has in mind in a lot more detail, but I wanted you to be prepared before you sit down with him."

"I'm glad you popped in, Alex. I wasn't sure exactly what to expect before now. I didn't realize what a heavyweight the man was."

What galled me more than anything else was being kept half in the dark most of the time. I got my information in bits and pieces from Alex whenever he felt like doling it out. A morsel here, a tidbit there, just enough to keep me effective but never more than I had to know at any time. Knowledge was power and there was no point in dispensing more of it than was absolutely necessary.

"Well, I won't detain you too long, fella. You've got a twelve-thirty date and crosstown traffic is always brutal any time of day."

Sure, Alex. It was time for me to trot off and do my errand like a good little messenger boy.

I arrived at twelve thirty-five and I was ushered to a table across from the bar on the main level. I ordered a campari and soda with a slice of lemon and hoped I would not have to wait too long for Steve; I wanted to be completely sober when I dealt with him. Protocol at the "21" Club was always amusing to observe. Certain regulars like Robert Mitchum had reserved tables out in the open in full view of the gawkers at the bar. He liked to be seen but not approached, and celebrity-watching was the main attraction of the high-priced bar and restaurant. Others, like former mayor John Lindsay and real estate moguls Donald Trump and Harry Helmsley, preferred to be tucked away partially out of view with maybe just an earlobe or the nape of the neck visible to the public. Possibly, they did not want too many people to know exactly whom they were dealing with.

There was a table for every whim and taste of the high and mighty, for those who wanted to bask in the limelight and those who demanded either partial or total privacy. It was a standing joke that actor Carroll O'Connor loved to sit at the most visible table in the restaurant while complaining loudly to whomever he was with about his loss of privacy since he became a star.

Steve Roberts finally showed up at ten to one as I was halfway through my second drink. We shook hands and when he asked me what I was drinking he told the waiter to bring the same thing for him. There were two things that struck you immediately about Steve Roberts. The first was that his real name most likely was anything but Roberts. It might have been Schiavone, it might have been Greenblatt, it might have been Moscinski, but it sure as hell wasn't Roberts. The second was the stark incongruity between his hair and his face; he had twenty-year-old hair and a face that looked fifty. I was not a great fan of toupees, but tasteful hairpieces carefully designed to suit the physiognomy of the wearer were at least understandable on movie stars and other performers. Steve Roberts, however, was sporting an outlandish helmet of thick brown curls that nearly obscured his forehead. The face beneath it was a deeply chiseled range of crevices, gullies, and ravines baked indelibly in place by half a century's exposure to the sun. The youthful exuberance of his artificial hair only called attention to the devastation below it. Had he chosen to go *au naturel* instead of camouflaging his baldness he would have been a virile man who looked his age instead of an old fart trying to pass for thirty-five.

He smiled and his teeth jumped right out at me. They were a startling white in contrast to his dark leathery skin, and they were perfectly shaped as though pressed from a machine. I noticed that his shaggy curls obscured a tiny hearing aid in his left earlobe. The pinkish skin-colored device did not blend well with his own coloring. I was having lunch with a cyborg, a man who was half flesh and blood and half modern technology.

"So what's shakin'?" he asked in a breezy manner that suggested middle-aged cool.

"Quite a bit as a matter of fact. I don't know how much Alex filled you in on, but we're juggling a dozen different deals at the same time now. We can't keep up with all the action that's coming our way."

"That's what I hear, that's what I hear. Alex hasn't backed a loser yet and I don't expect he ever will."

He was dressed in his own approximation of Wall Street conservative, but there was a touch of the hoodlum in the way he brought it off. The stripes in his dark suit were a little too wide, more like chalk stripes than pinstripes. His white shirt was shiny and patterned, and his red tie was far too light, closer to a pastel pink. The sparkling diamond on his right pinky did not help too much either, nor did the billowing hanky in his breast pocket which precisely matched his tie. I could not imagine what law school he had graduated from.

"How're things in Florida?" I asked.

"Great. I hate this fuckin' city. Every time I leave Florida and head north I get nosebleeds and freeze my ass off. I don't know how you people can stand it." His voice was gravelly as though he had a couple of pebbles lodged down there among his vocal cords.

"We're all masochists I guess. We thrive on smelly crowds and lots of pressure that turns your stomach into an earthquake at three o'clock in the morning."

"Tell me about it. I grew up in Jersey City just across the river. As soon as I was old enough to beat my meat I headed for the sunshine and I haven't been sorry since."

That did not jibe too well with Alex's brief biography of him before I left the office, but I let it pass. The less I knew about some of these characters, the better off I would be. Nobody I knew told the truth anymore.

We ordered lunch—a "21 Burger" costing twenty-one dollars for me and calf's liver for him—and another round of drinks, my third as if anyone was counting.

"I hear good things about you from Alex. From Miles and Julian too. They tell me you really know your way around the financial world."

"I've spent half my life advising other people what to do with their money, so I guess I've learned a few things along the way."

"You head up the financial side of things, right?"

"George and I both take care of the money part of the operation, investor contacts, sales and marketing, deciding how big the deals should be and which ones to bring out first, that sort of thing."

"Yeah, but from what I hear you're the one with all the juice."

I'm the one with all the juice? What the hell was he getting at? Why was he pumping me up bigger than George? I wished I knew what was really going on. I got nervous when people made it sound as though I were the linchpin of the company.

"I'm the one who's structuring the deals that we're going public with. The first one's due out in less than three weeks now. George is the salesman who's peddling them to the institutions, making sure we have strong institutional demand out there so there's good support for the shares in the aftermarket."

"That's one of the things I wanted to talk about. This IPO I think you people call it . . . it looks like a sure thing or what?"

"The stock's called Zenedex and we're bringing it out at eight dollars a share. One of our clients bought the company last May from the founder, some inventor out in Salt Lake City who ran out of operating funds. We set up the financing for the buyer like we do in eighty percent of our deals, which gives us effective control over the company's assets."

"What kind of business they in?"

The waiter arrived with one of the plumpest hamburgers I've ever seen and Steve Robert's liver which was about the same color as his suntan. I waited until he left and then answered.

"The original owner had been doing genetic research for fifteen years or so when he finally came up with a chemical compound that's supposed to aid sexual performance. It has to do with something called polypeptides, a natural chemical in the body."

"Does it work?" Steve asked with half a grin as he slowly ground his liver between his perfect teeth.

"Who knows? About as well as any other miracle drug, I guess. If there's anything to it you can be damned sure one of the big pharmaceutical firms will be announcing their own version before you know it. The only thing that matters is that the public *believes* it's going to work. Perceived reality is more important than the truth where the stock market's concerned."

"So what's the bottom line? The stock comes out at eight you said, right? Then what happens?"

"It should be a hot issue, meaning that there's more demand for the stock than there are shares available. After the offering the price should jump to . . . I don't know. I remember when Genentech first went public. The price doubled overnight and stayed there for a while before collapsing like a lead balloon."

"So you figure the stock will pop right away to maybe fifteen, sixteen a share?"

"Say twelve to fourteen just to be on the safe side. You know the old saying? Bulls make money, bears make money, and pigs get burned. It doesn't pay to get too greedy."

"So a quick four or five points is what you're saying. What the hell, fifty percent's not a bad return for a hit-and-run investment. How about the downside? What can go wrong?"

"There's no such thing as a deal that's a hundred percent fool-proof, but this is as close to it as you're likely to find. There's always maybe a three or four percent chance that something might go wrong, the whole market taking a nosedive if the president has a heart attack, that sort of thing. But I really don't see that as a problem. The funds kill each other for as many shares of a deal like this as they can get their hands on."

Steve finished his liver and sat back in his seat. I could see him twisting his mouth to pry the meat out of his teeth with his tongue. He reached for the matchbook on the table and used the cover to complete the job, then fished a long green cigar from his breast pocket. The size of the cigar was awesome; it looked as big as the dick on a horse. I accepted his offer of one in self-defense, even though I had a theory that cigar smoking had homosexual connotations. I was not going to sit there choking on his fumes without a weapon of my own.

"So here's the deal," said Steve. He reached inside his jacket and extracted a thick brown envelope with his right hand, then plopped it on the table between us. "There's two hundred grand in there for starters. I'll get more to you over the next week or so, probably as much as another half mill. Put it all in this Zebodex or whatever the fuck it is you said. But not in my name for Christ's sake. I want it put in three different accounts. Here, I'll write the names down for you. Just open up the accounts and put an equal amount in each one."

I stared at the money, then at him writing down the names, then back at the money, afraid to touch it for some reason. I had handled scores of packets just like it, but for some reason I did not want to touch this one. He handed the list to me and I gazed at the names, addresses, and social security numbers without any of them registering.

"When I get the rest to you I'll give you the names for each account and how much to put in each one. I'll leave it up to you when to sell the stock. What the hell, you're the financial expert, right?"

Steve looked at me with a whimsical cast to his eyes, then he lowered his gaze down to the envelope. Finally I picked it up and stuck it into my briefcase.

"You . . . you want it all in . . . in Zenedex, right?" I had to stop a minute to think of the stock's name.

"Why not? It's practically a sure thing, right? Any problems with that?"

"No problem. I'll see you get as much stock as you want. Alex said to give you priority, so if I have to cut back somebody else's allotment I will."

He smiled broadly, flashing his white teeth at me again.

"I like doing business with you. Alex said you knew what you were doing and he's right."

He took a long suck from the end of his cigar and blew out a stream of heavy smoke. He curled his lips and tongue around it as though he were giving head. If I could have crushed my own torpedo out without offending him, I would have.

"Something else you might be interested in," said Steve.

"What's that?"

"You know a lot of guys on the floor of the exchanges? Traders? Brokers? Guys like that?"

"Quite a few. Why?"

"I hear a lot of them like to sniff nose candy. Helps them cope with all the pressure. Makes them feel they're smarter than the next guy."

"I've heard that too. But I've never been involved in anything like that."

"Well it could be worth your while to find out about it. Who likes what. Who's looking for a good supplier. You know what I mean."

"How so?"

"We handle some of the best shit coming into the country. Absolutely prime cut. Any outlets you find for us, you get to keep twenty percent of the action."

"Sounds good. I'll ask around and let you know."

I paid the bill and made my move to leave, feigning a two o'clock appointment. I left him sitting at the table having oral sex with his Macanudo and staring at the famous faces. When I stepped outside into the daylight, the bright afternoon sun struck me full blast. I squinted like a kid leaving a movie house after a Saturday afternoon double feature. My head was spinning and my stomach churned like a tropical storm working its way up to hurricane force. I felt like throwing up.

Chapter Sixteen

I knew what I had to do. My plan of action was as clear to me as though it were emblazoned in the sky. When I got back to my office I was completely sober. Sober and sweating. I could feel my shirt sticking to my skin even though the temperature was comfortably cool, somewhere in the mid-sixties. I nodded to Sylvia, the dour blue-haired grandmother they hired to replace Monica when I was down in Florida, then retreated into my office. The fact that I apparently could not even be trusted to hire my own secretary was one more thing that irked me. In one way I could not blame them, but it was still humiliating and unnerving. For all I knew, Sylvia might have been Miles's maiden aunt who was there to keep an eye on me. We regarded each other with mutual suspicion.

Alex was out for the afternoon, so at least I did not have to answer his questions about my lunch date with Roberts while he blew smoke in my face. I had a lot to do during the next few hours and did not want to be interrupted. Seated behind my desk, I directed my attention to the files in the bottom drawer. I had always been a meticulous record-keeper. When you did business with the kind of people I had been dealing with for so long, it was smart to keep your facts straight. From the beginning I had kept a notebook detailing every cash transaction that came my way—who made it, on what date, and the exact amount. I was not concerned about my personal clients, people like Tommy Gilmartin and the others I serviced in my pre-Zurich days, only the heavy hitters referred to me by Miles and Julian and my partners. Technically, it was not illegal for anyone to roll a wheelbarrow filled with cash into a bank and deposit it. The onus fell upon the financial institution to report it, in this case on me because I was the chief financial officer, the one with "all the juice" as Roberts put it. Since I had come to the end of the line as far as I was concerned, I thought it best to do the prudent thing and cover my own ass, something I had been taught to do in the Marine Corps a quarter of a century ago. I walked over to the file cabinet across from my desk and located the proper forms, then spent the next hour and a half filling them out in detail—depositor's name, social security number, date, and the amount of cash involved. By the time I completed the accounting with the name of Steve Roberts and his aliases with the two-hundred-thousand-dollar offering, my hand was shaking visibly and I was soaked with ice-cold perspiration.

Next I turned my attention to the more delicate matter of protecting my own people and making them invisible, "disappearing" them from the records so to speak. This involved an even more time-consuming procedure of "flattening" each account, mailing out all remaining cash and bringing the balances down to zero. I did the paperwork myself, not trusting Sylvia to do it for me. The next step would be to access our computer after hours when no one was around and erase all their names from the account files. At five-thirty I had a sandwich sent up from the deli down below and waited for the rest of the staff to go home. Naturally, Sylvia was the last to leave. She eyed me suspiciously as she finally donned her coat at five to six, or so it seemed to me; she was unaccustomed to seeing me stay this late in the office. By six-thirty the corridors and empty offices were filled with an eerie silence, and the fading sun on the far side of the river cast lonely shadows along the walls. I felt all alone and extremely vulnerable, like a child in the woods without his parents for the first time when the evening darkness begins to infiltrate his campsite. But was I really alone? As soon as I started to work the empty silence of moments before was filled with strange stirrings in the corridor outside. I thought some workmen had arrived to perform a job I wasn't aware of—or worse, that one of my partners had returned to catch up on some work. At least half a dozen times I left my seat to make sure no one else was present in the office.

Silence.

Were the noises in my mind or were they real? Visions of some goon slipping up behind me and slitting my throat addled my brain. My fingers fumbled with the keyboard and it took me an eternity (it seemed) to tap out the right code so that I could access the computer. Each time I thought I had located the right one, the damned machine told me I was not authorized to proceed any further. I had visions of alarms going off in some central monitoring station, alerting security that a snooper was poking his nose where it didn't belong. Any moment I expected a computer SWAT team to descend on the premises and apprehend me. The job that lay ahead was spooky enough without me looking over my shoulder every thirty seconds to make sure no one was creeping up behind me.

By eight-thirty I had checked, rechecked, and triple-checked every action I had taken since lunch. I had been operating on automatic pilot for the past six hours or so, doing things that had to be done without dwelling consciously on them. I was existential man gone berserk, driving ahead relentlessly in a deterministic frenzy. I dared not pause long enough to weigh the consequences of my actions for fear that cold logic would paralyze me with indecision. I did not want to be distracted by reason. Finally, there was nothing left to do. My immediate task was done. Phase One of my plan was completed. As maddening as it had been, it was only a warm-up for the exercise ahead. Phase Two would soon begin and it would be far more difficult than anything I attempted in the past. I was about to graduate from Triple A baseball to the major leagues. Almost literally overnight.

The leaves were beginning to turn along the Hutchinson River Parkway as I drove up to Connecticut. The New England Thruway was faster and more direct, but the Hutch was a prettier ride particularly this time of year. There was a special aroma in the air of the seasons changing over, a hint of wood-smoke and apples and crispness that is partly in the imagination and partly real. I lived in California once for an entire year and I missed the changing of the seasons the most, along with the feeling that everything was possible as one cycle ended and another one began. Endings and beginnings. Death and renewal. Reincarnation within one's own lifetime. In California life seemed an endless repetition with each day the same as the one that preceded it. But here the change in the weather and in the natural environment spurred me on with a senseless optimism. It gave me something to look forward to.

The gravel in the driveway was banked along the edges and there were bare spots in the middle. The trim around the windows and beneath the gutters needed a coat of paint. My eyes picked out the little details now that I was hoping to rejoin my family sometime soon. When I was breaking away I managed to block them out. Oddly enough, the myriad domestic chores that drove me nuts a few short months ago seemed to hold a warm allure for me. I realized now that I preferred them to the chaotic self-indulgence of bachelorhood. Why does it take so long to learn the things we should have known instinctively?

My unexpected arrival came as a great surprise to Laurie and Mark. They greeted me more exuberantly than they usually did on my planned visits, perhaps sensing a subtle change in the domestic atmosphere. Elaine was even more surprised than the kids since I had not called ahead. Why didn't I? Perhaps on some sinister subconscious level I was testing her feelings, hoping to catch her on her way out to meet someone else. I understood immediately that my sado-masochistic impulses pushed me very close to self-destruction at times.

She hugged me tightly and kissed me, then questioned me with the concerned look in her eyes. She was obviously happy to see me, an instinctive response that dispelled any lingering hint of jealousy I harbored. Is anything wrong? Are you all right? These were the questions I read in her face as I walked past her into the living room. I felt at home as though I had never left it, unlike on my previous visits when I shuffled through the place like a man who had lost his way.

"How's everybody doing?" I asked.

"Fine. Everybody's thrilled as you can see. We just didn't expect you tonight, that's all."

"I like being unpredictable. It keeps everyone on their toes."

"You should have called ahead. We would have held dinner for you."

"I ate a heavy lunch today so it's just as well. What's everybody doing?"

"We were watching a movie in the den. Some silly science-fiction thing about people from another planet who look like lizards."

"They *are* lizards," Mark corrected her. "They only dress up like humans so they can take over the earth without using violence."

"They're ugly, Daddy," Laurie said. "When they take off their skin they're really scary."

"Sounds great."

"Are you sure you're not hungry? I can heat up some pot roast for you. It's no problem."

"No thanks. I'll let you buy me a drink though. Do we still have any bourbon around here or did you finish it all without me?"

"Why don't you kids go watch the end of the movie? Dad and I have things to talk about."

Mark and Laurie were happy to be sent off on their own. They were eager to get back to the movie they had seen at least three times before, and they regarded any time their mother and father spent together as a positive development in their lives. Elaine and I went into the kitchen where the air was still heavy with the lingering aroma of potted meat and gravy and assorted spices. The smell of Elaine's cooking never failed to give me an appetite and tonight was no exception, but I was determined not to give in to it. I had lost ten pounds during our separation and wanted to keep them off. I packed two glasses with ice cubes and filled them halfway up with Jim Beam, then topped each drink off with a frothy head of seltzer water. Elaine handed me a lemon and I cut off two long peels of skin that were moist with lemon oil, rubbed them around the rims and dropped them into the glasses.

"So."

I held up my glass and Elaine clinked hers against mine and took a sip.

"So what's going on with you?" she asked.

"Everything's moving quickly. Life's a big blur right now. If I can keep things under control it shouldn't take much longer. Another month or so and it'll all be over."

She stared at me with the same puzzled look in her eyes that had been there since I walked in.

"I wish I understood what was going on."

"No you don't. I wish I *didn't* understand what was going on. But I do and I'm taking steps to change things around."

"You . . . you're not in any danger, are you?"

"Of course not. There's nothing to worry about."

"Don't talk to me like that. Be honest, will you, for God's sake!"

"What do you want me to say to you? I'm embarking on a treacherous course that could end up destroying me? No, I don't think it's as serious as that. But I am doing things that are designed to blow the whole operation apart, and I don't think my colleagues are going to appreciate it. What are they going to do about it? Your guess is as good as mine."

"But . . . what happens afterward? What are we going to do?"

"What do you mean?"

"Your livelihood! Your way of making a living! What are you going to do when it's all over?"

I put my glass down and rested my hands on her shoulders, smiling at her.

"My greedy little beauty. That's what got us into this mess in the first place. Don't worry. I'm not coming away from this empty-handed."

"You bastard! Again you're blaming me?"

"Shhh. I didn't come here to fight with you."

"You son of a bitch," she hissed so the kids couldn't hear. "You're still trying to lay the blame on me."

"No I'm not. It wasn't your fault. I'm a big boy and I knew what I was doing. I was joking. If we lose our sense of humor, Elaine, we'll wind up in the loony bin."

She softened and leaned her head against my chest and I wrapped my arms around her. We were together again. For better or worse. Christ, it wasn't easy.

"Let's lighten up the mood a little," I said. "Here, I've got a present for you."

I walked over to the counter and snapped my attaché case open. Inside, stacked neatly in orderly piles, were half a dozen rows of twenties, fifties, and hundreds. Some of them stunk of stale booze and cigar smoke, and some of them of transmission oil. The combined effluvia was redolent with middle-American ingenuity and entrepreneurial talent. God bless America. I had served its middle class well and here was my reward.

"Ninety-four big ones, honey. Our nest egg in case that rainy day arrives."

Elaine looked at me, her eyes wide open and staring.

"Ninety-four thousand dollars?" she whispered with reverence.

"Never saw that much in one place before, did you? Neither did I. It's amazing how small a place it fills up. You'd think it would take a suitcase to carry it all, but there it is."

"But how . . . how did you . . ."

"Don't ask. What you don't know can't hurt you." Or me, I thought to myself. It was clear that, if the key to a man's heart was good home cooking, the combination that unlocked Elaine's emotions was a stack of legal tender. Oh, I knew she loved me well, but a box full of greenbacks was icing on the cake.

"What are we going to do with it?" She was still dumbstruck with awe, not quite compos mentis.

"Let's close it up before one of the kids walks in. Later, after they've gone to bed, maybe we can take our clothes off and roll around in it."

"It wouldn't make a very nice mattress I don't think," she laughed.

At eleven o'clock, after nearly half an hour of threats, cajolery,

and bribery, we managed to get Mark and Laurie into their bed-
rooms and the lights turned off. Bribery worked best. It's amazing what you can get people to do if you only meet their price.
And it saves a lot of fuss.

Elaine and I went down to the cellar with the money and I
hauled out the heavy metal box from the space behind the
boiler. This was where we kept the sundry and varied docu-
ments one accumulates during a decade and a half of marriage—
both our wills, titles to the cars, insurance policies, a stack of
one-ounce gold coins in case the doomsday criers turn out to be
right, some of Elaine's more expensive jewelry, and mementos
from the past worthless to anyone except ourselves. I trans-
ferred the bills from my attaché case into the fireproof box and
barely managed to get the lid closed over them.

"Are you sure this is the safest place?" Elaine asked.

"It's the safest place I can think of. It's fireproof, this is the
only part of the house that would remain intact after a tornado,
and any rat that can eat his way through this steel deserves to get
the money."

"Why do you have to make a joke out of everything? Can't you
be serious for a minute?"

"I am serious. The box is well hidden back there and it's safer
than the bank. Shit. If the feds wanted to nail me, the first thing
they'd do is put a lock on any bank box we had."

"I guess you're right. It just makes me nervous, all that money
sitting there like that."

"You'd be more nervous if it *wasn't* sitting there. Then what
would you do when the cash flow dries up?"

That last remark was all the convincing she needed. What
precisely does one do when the great money machine stops
cranking out legal tender? Sit home and cry? Go out and rob a
bank? Or go down to the cellar and grab a fistful of twenties?
Case closed. It was nice to have an option like that. It helps to
take the edge off your hysteria. Puts an end to those three A.M.
anxiety attacks. I had suffered through too many sleepless nights
worrying about money and it was good to know I had put them
all behind me. For the moment at least.

We went back up to the kitchen and I made another round of drinks, then I put my arm around her and pulled her close to me.

"I'm horny," she said.

"Is that what money does to you?"

"That's what you do to me. I think that whatever happens to us, whether we ever get back together again or not, we'd probably continue to sleep together for the rest of our lives."

"I do believe you're right."

I slid my hands inside the waistband of her sweatpants and pushed them down around her ankles. She stepped out of them and stood there in her panties, those gorgeous long legs as lean and firm as ever. She was damp when I touched her down there.

"That's the prettiest picture I've ever seen," I said.

"Prettier than ninety-four thousand dollars?"

"Those legs of yours are worth at least a hundred grand to me."

Chapter Seventeen

Zenedex was scheduled to go public in a week and a half, which meant I had a lot of work to do in a relatively short time. Time was the enemy unless you knew how to use it properly. Then it could be your friend. Time had to be my ally during the next ten days or else my scheme to destroy Zurich would blow up in my face.

We were bringing out five million shares of stock at eight dollars a share which would raise forty million dollars for a company that had no earnings history at all, just a chemical concocted in a laboratory that was supposed to help impotent men sustain an erection. This itself was not unusual. Genentech had raised much more from its IPO with nothing more than a promise to be in the vanguard of a new technology called genetic engineering which the public knew nothing about. Investment advisor Marty Zweig raised three hundred million dollars in 1986 on the premise that he could continue to pick stocks that would outperform the market. Mario Gabelli pulled in four hundred million dollars with more or less the same idea. In bull markets the public literally gorged itself on the low-priced shares of companies that consisted of three guys with an office, a telephone, and a copy machine out in Denver. Senseless? Of course. But it happened all the time.

The strength of any new offering depended on the support the shares received in the so-called aftermarket. The investment banking firm that did the underwriting tried to hype the stock beforehand in an effort to create a demand for the shares by the institutions, the hedge funds, and ultimately the investing public. The underwriter hoped the Street and the market would "take the shares away." If this were the case word got around that it was going to be a "hot issue," meaning that there was more demand than there were shares available, and the price would spurt immediately after the offering.

What investment bankers feared the most was a lukewarm reception for their deals. If there was no demand out there, the hedge funds and institutions got out early, dumping shares back in the market and pushing the price down. The only way an underwriter could support the price under these circumstances was by buying back the shares itself. Many small investment banking firms had gone bankrupt buying back their own paper. They used up capital supporting the prices of their own deals and eventually got buried under an avalanche of stock that nobody wanted. John Muir & Co. collapsed in 1982 doing exactly that. Yves Hentic & Co., a small broker-dealer based in Jersey City, went belly-up in 1986 when its deals went sour. If an underwriter *failed* to support its IPO's the net result was essentially the same. No one would ever take it seriously again and its effectiveness as an investment banker was lost forever. It was a high-risk game that got nasty at times, but the stakes were high. Successful underwritings made millions for everyone connected with them, so it was worth the gamble. But the sharks and barracudas were always out there watching, waiting for someone to fumble the ball so they could capitalize on their mistake and earn millions for themselves.

Zenedex was Zurich's first attempt to take a company public, and it was critical that the offering succeed. It was possible to blow a deal after two or three successful ones and still survive, but almost impossible to recover if your first venture failed. It was like a fighter turning pro after three years in the amateurs and getting knocked out in the first round by some bum nobody ever heard of before. Alex and the partners had done their due diligence well, and every indication we had said that Zenedex was going to be an enormously attractive deal. The stock was tight and there were very few shares available for the small investor, those with less than fifty thousand dollars to put into it. All the partners had set aside shares for themselves, but it was 144 stock—insider stock that had to be held for two years before it could be sold. Alex's friend Steve Roberts had come up with eight hundred thousand dollars, cash money of course, and took down a hundred thousand shares in the various accounts he set up for himself. Miles and Julian, most of the people I had met on the cruise to nowhere, and all our heavy investors were loaded to the teeth with stock—all except me and, curiously, George Burnham, who had done such an excellent job of selling Zenedex to the institutions. When I asked him why he hadn't taken down any shares for himself, he shrugged his shoulders and said he had invested every last cent he had in a condo down in Florida. I, too, pleaded poverty, although I had an option to buy stock at ten dollars a share within the next two years if I chose to exercise it. I had originally feared that my lack of personal commitment to Zenedex would attract unwanted attention to myself, but thanks to George I was not alone. Alex merely smirked as though he thought the two of us were crazy. "You two are missing out on a sure thing," he said. "It's money lying in the street waiting to be picked up."

Maybe. Maybe not. Not if I could accomplish what I hoped to during the next ten days or so. My timing had to be impeccable, precisely right. If I moved too quickly I would tip my hand and give the others a chance to launch a counterattack. If I acted too slowly my assault would lose its impact. I needed to register a clean knockout in the first round. A lethal blow delivered with force and surprise. If it didn't work and we had to fight to a decision, I might as well pack my bags and head for cover now. I was sure to come out a loser in any battle that lasted past the first round.

The euphoria that filled our corridors during the week before the offering was palpable. You could open your mouth and taste it, slice it with a knife. Mike Rosenbaum walked with a sprightly air despite his three hundred and fifty pounds. Ron Bishop looked like the goose that laid the golden egg and I could see he was the type to get a trifle obnoxious once he had some real money in the bank. Miles and Julian called from Miami to make sure all systems were GO and we had everything under control. Toward the end of the week everyone was walking on Cloud Nine, rubbing their hands and smiling in anticipation of the killing to come. There was tension in the air that was almost sexual, the kind you feel when you finally get to screw that someone special you've been dreaming about for the past two months.

When I thought the right moment had arrived, I went down to the lobby of our building and made my phone call. I wasn't positive that the telephone in my office was bugged, but neither could I be sure that it was not. He answered after the second ring. It was time to tell my story.

Chapter Eighteen

I got to the restaurant early and fiddled nervously with my swizzle stick as I waited for him to arrive. He was precisely on time, almost to the minute, and the maître d' ushered him to my table. I had deliberately asked for one in the back that was hidden from view and afforded us as much privacy as possible. The last person I wanted to be seen talking to was a writer and reporter, particularly one with a reputation for tackling controversial subjects.

Harry Winkler had written biographies of several well-known financiers, as well as articles for various newspapers and magazines, concentrating mostly on financial and political subjects. I had known him for years and usually avoided him like the plague since he was constantly snooping around for information I did not want to see in print.

This time was different. This time I needed a literary Aunt Blabby who could be counted on to spread bad news with all the venom he could muster. Harry was about the same age as I, perhaps a year or two older, and his usually shaggy beard was trimmed closer to his jawline than it was the last time I saw him. His hair was thinning, thinner at the top than mine and it also looked darker than I remembered. I'd swear the son of a bitch was using Grecian Formula or Morgan's hair color restorer on it. He appeared trim and physically fit, as though he had been working out lately. He told me once that he had boxed for a while as an amateur and was undefeated after fifteen fights, but I never knew whether to believe him or not.

"Glad you could make it, " I said, standing up to shake his hand.

"You're a pisser, you are. I called you up four times and you finally called me back . . . six months later. I can get the mayor on the phone faster than I can get some of you Wall Street guys."

"Yes, well, maybe the mayor with all his problems has less to hide than Wall Street does these days."

The waiter stopped by to see if we wanted a drink and I ordered another bourbon and soda for myself.

"Give me a beer, whatever you've got on tap," said Harry. "No, fuck it. I'll have a Jack Daniels on the rocks with a twist. This is some kind of an occasion I guess."

We made small talk for a while, mostly about the soaring real estate values in Connecticut since we moved there. He lived in Cos Cob, a few towns down the shoreline from Soundview. "Best investment I ever made," he said. "The stock market's for suckers. The only people who make any money there have inside information."

"And they end up going to jail eventually, like Ivan Boesky and Dennis Levine."

"Serves them right. Boesky passed himself off as a brilliant stock trader for years. He even wrote a bestseller telling people what a genius he was and how the average schmuck could make a pile of money following his advice. What a pair of balls. I could make money, too, if I had a plant like Dennis Levine feeding me privileged information."

"There are very few geniuses," I agreed, "only people with better connections than the next guy."

We both ordered veal marsala with risotto and sauteed zucchini, and I selected a 1982 Bordeaux from St. Estephe. What the hell, I had the feeling this was going to be a last supper of sorts.

"So what's the story?" he asked, slugging back his sour mash whiskey while we waited for the food to arrive. "You avoid my phone calls for months, then all of a sudden I hear from you out of the blue. What's going on?"

Slowly, with great precision and deliberation, I told him everything going back to my conversation with Alex last winter. The only part I left out was my activity involving Tommy Gilmartin and my other personal clients. And Monica of course. The story evolved easily and naturally, and I told it calmly as we sliced our way through the tender strips of veal and drank the dry musty wine from St. Estephe. I did all the talking while he listened in silence, listened and drank and ate. I observed the professional side of the man for the first time. The bluster and bravado were nowhere to be seen. He was all business as he listened and recorded, filtering impressions through an invisible but palpable screening mechanism, a sixth sense that writers develop to separate the real from the fanciful—a good bullshit detector as Hemingway once called it. I finished just as he was spearing the last piece of veal with his fork. He swallowed the food, washed it down with a sip of the red wine, then looked directly into my eyes.

"That's quite a story," he said without a trace of a smile on his lips. "Just what is it you expect me to do with it?"

"Well, I . . . as you said, it's quite a story. It's an exclusive. I want you to blow the lid off the whole operation."

"Two questions. First, why me? You've been avoiding my calls for six months or longer, and now all of a sudden you open up to me like this?"

"I've been avoiding your calls because I had something to hide before and I expected you to try to find out what it was. But now I've decided to go public with it and I called you because . . . well, we've had our differences in the past, but I think you're honest and thorough and I do admire you as a writer."

"My second question if fairly obvious. How do I know you're not hustling me to make a killing for yourself? Maybe you've got a vested interest in seeing this deal go belly-up. How do I know?"

"I don't own a single share of stock, nor am I short a single share. I won't make a red cent if the stock runs up to fifty or if it crashes down to zero. I'm only telling you this because I know

now that I'm in over my head. The situation's a lot more crooked and a lot more dangerous than I ever dreamed it would be, and I'm the one who's been set up to take the fall if the authorities crack down on Zurich."

"What kind of proof do you have? Did you bring any documentation?"

This much I expected. I opened my attaché case and removed copies of the sheaf of forms I had filled out, detailing the cash deposits made to Zurich since we opened up for business last spring.

"These are yours," I said. "The originals were mailed down to Washington a week ago."

He pulled a pair of half-moon glasses from the breast pocket of his jacket and rested them on the tip of his nose a bit self-consciously. "I hate these damned things," he explained. "I can pass for thirty-eight most of the time, but as soon as I put these on everybody knows I'm full of shit."

He studied the list carefully, his eyes resting longer on familiar names with large cash deposits next to them.

"Jesus! You guys've been operating a regular laundromat over there for the rich and famous, the high and mighty. You mailed these down to Washington you said?"

"A week or so ago. Those copies are for you to hang onto."

"What . . . what made you decide to do that? You're not dealing with Boy Scouts you know."

"Like I said, I figured things had gone too far and I was the one sitting in the hot seat. I did it to cover my own ass."

"Cover your own ass! You're crazy, you know that? If I were you I'd buy a fake beard and a wig and head for cover. Christ! I could get shot just sitting here with you."

"That's why we have to act fast. The sooner we go public with this and blow the whole scheme apart, the safer it is for me and everybody else who knows. They'll all be scrambling for cover themselves. I'll have them on the defensive."

"The defensive! Hah!" He emitted a loud raucous laugh that shot across the restaurant. "On the defensive for how long? You'll be looking over your shoulder for the rest of your life. Are you sure you want to go through with this? Have you thought it all out carefully?"

"It's too late to turn back. The information's already been mailed to the feds and this is the next logical step. It's my only way out of a bad situation."

"I don't get it, I really don't. You get mixed up with guys like this in the first place, then you decide to rock the boat when you find out they're nastier than you thought they were."

"It's a long story, believe me. If you've got three or four hours some day we can get into the motivation. But for the time being, why don't we just stick to the facts? Are you going to use all this or not?"

He looked down at the sheaf of forms on the table, then looked at me and smiled. He yanked the reading glasses off his nose and stuck them back in his pocket. He picked up the papers and slipped them into his own briefcase, along with the microrecorder he had used to tape our conversation.

"How can I not?" he asked. "You've given me a story that would be a crime to keep to myself. A crime in more ways than one, I might add."

"Just one thing," I said. "A favor if you will. Can you keep my name out of it? Can you refer to me as a reliable source or something like that?"

He looked me squarely in the eye without a hint of a smile on his face. He was strictly business, as ruthless in his own way as any stock manipulator I had ever known.

"I'll see what I can do. But I can't make any promises," he said.

Chapter Nineteen

I could not sleep, I could not sit still for more than two minutes at a time during the next few days. Life became a twilight zone for me. Minutes seemed like days, days were stretched out longer than weeks. All my senses were racing on overdrive, as though they had been finetuned by a master mechanic. I saw all things clearly, tasted and smelled everything more keenly than before, heard every sound and utterance as though they were blasted through loudspeakers, and felt the slightest imperfections in every object I touched. My entire sensory apparatus was honed to a fine point. If only we could be aware of what was happening today instead of daydreaming about a future that never arrived, or dwelling regretfully on the past. In truth, this part of my life was the most dangerous time I had ever known. And it was also the most thrilling and exhilarating.

Notwithstanding all the personal peril I was in—perhaps even because of it—I would not have traded it for anything.

The final weekend before the offering was spent in a state of acute anticipation. I couldn't even get properly drunk, and it was not due to a lack of trying. My body seemed to be absorbing the alcohol and transforming it into a new source of energy. I could not speed up time, I could not deaden the anxiety. I had no idea what Harry was going to do with my story; I had not heard from him since our lunch date and I had the feeling he would not appreciate a phone call from me. Everything was out of my hands now. I had set my plan into motion. Now it existed apart from me, an external thing with a life and momentum of its own.

On Sunday evening I did something I had never done before. I put on my sweat suit and a pair of running shoes and jogged down Central Park West. I entered the park at 72nd Street just as the sun was sinking behind the high-rise buildings down by the river. Already the evening shadows were beginning to lengthen along the streets, and the shapes of the trees and foliage in the park grew indistinct with the fading light. I jogged deeper into the darkness, daring whatever was in there to come and get me. Nothing could be heard except the chittering of squirrels, the croaking of frogs by the pond, and a growing cacophony of animal nightlife coming awake. The darkness enveloped me and I jogged further into it. I felt that nothing could touch me, nothing in the darkness inside the park was more ineluctable than I.

Chapter Twenty

Everyone came to work early the day Zenedex went public. The deal was tight; there was not a single share of stock to be had by anyone other than the institutions and the high rollers with a pipeline into Zurich. I entered the trading symbol into the monitor on my desk and waited for the stock to break syndicate. The moment it was cleared for public trading, a bid and ask price would appear on the screen followed by the price of each transaction as it traded in the aftermarket. All morning long we made phone call after phone call, trying to get an indication of the demand for the stock at each member firm. The consensus was positive; demand for stock by the general public appeared to be strong. With heavy retail buying taking place in the aftermarket, the price would shoot up and the Street would be taking the stock away from us.

Finally, at a quarter to twelve, a price quote flickered on the screens at brokerage offices throughout the country. Zenedex 9½ 9¾. A loud spontaneous cheer rang up and down the corridors outside my office. Alex came dashing in a minute later, a green torpedo clenched between his teeth in place of the usual cigarette.

"Congratulations, fella! You did it! We're off to the races!"

"*We* did it, Alex. It was a team effort all the way."

198

"Whatever. It's a smash. We're going to make a bloody killing."

Then he was out the door, shaking hands and slapping backs along the way. Mike and Ron danced out of their offices, each puffing away on his own cigar and looking for all the world like fat cats who had just feasted on a meal of roast canary. The phones were jangling off the hooks. Miles and Julian called from Miami after seeing the price quote in a local brokerage firm. Steve Roberts called me up—collect if you can believe it—to tell me what a genius I was.

"I told you you got the fuckin' juice," he said.

"Well thanks, Steve. But I really . . . "

"I leave it up to you to get me out when the time is right. You're the boss. Don't bother to call me up. Just do it!"

I almost cried when I hung up the phone. Was I out of my mind? Steve was going to murder me. When the initial euphoria had tempered a bit, George Burnham entered my office and extended his hand.

"Congratulations, Paul. You did a splendid job."

"Congratulations yourself," I said somewhat embarrassed. "You're the one who moved most of the stock with the big boys. You're the one who really did the job . . . even if some of the people around here seem to think I deserve most of the credit."

"Well . . . okay," he smiled a bit shyly. I had never seen him so reserved or subdued before. "I am a good salesman I guess. But you packaged it just right. So congratulations to both of us."

There was something about his manner that caught me by surprise. In his modesty and self-effacement, he revealed a depth to himself that I never noticed before. It was a side of his nature that he kept well hidden on our joint adventure in Florida. Why? I suddenly realized that I did not know him at all.

Throughout the day the stock traded between 9 ½ and 10 ¼, and it closed out the trading session at 10 ⅛, a first-day move of more than twenty-five percent from the offering price of eight dollars a share. By any standard of measurement it was a booming success. Everything had gone so smoothly and seemed so well under control that I began to wonder if I had acted prematurely. Maybe I should have kept my mouth shut and gone along for the ride. Made my killing with the rest of them and worried about the next step later on. Chances are they would never have gotten caught, they were all so well connected.

Yes, but . . .

Ivan Boesky was well connected too.

Still . . .

Idiot! It was too late to have second thoughts now.

In doing the right thing, I may have made the biggest mistake of my life so far.

Chapter Twenty-one

The next day was relatively calm compared to the first. Zenedex opened at 10 ¼, traded as high as 11 at one point, and closed at 10 ⅝, a half point higher than its close the day before. Everything was so serene, as a matter of fact, that I questioned whether my actions were going to have any impact at all. Perhaps my well-laid plans were all for naught and nothing I had done or could ever do would deter them from achieving their ends. I was only one man, insignificant in the face of all this power and wealth. How does an individual stop a juggernaut from laying waste to everything in its path?

The following morning I found out. The story exploded on page one of *The New York Times* and continued for two full columns in the business section, right next to the stock tables. I usually bought the newspapers on my way in to work and read them at my desk with a cup of coffee for company. Thank God I decided on a more leisurely pace today. I carried the papers back up to my apartment and planned to read them over a plate of ham and eggs before sauntering down to the office. Harry Winkler's byline in the upper lefthand column on page one of the *Times* caught my eye immediately. Mesmerized, I read his copyrighted article in slow motion like a second grader reading about Dick and Jane. It was all there, everything. He had barely left out the pauses as I chewed my zucchini. It was only after I finished the story and read it a second time that I noticed he had not mentioned me by name. I was an "unnamed source," a "key figure in the operation" who had provided the press with "bona fide documentation." Thank God for small favors. And thank God I was not in my office when I unfolded the newspaper and saw the headline for the first time. There was no doubt in my mind, none whatsoever, that my partners would be able to put their heads together and figure out who spilled the beans.

I did not know where I was going, but I did know that I could not go to work or stay in my apartment much longer. Any moment now the phone would start ringing. "Paul! This is Alex. Have you seen the *Times* today?" "Paul! This is Miles. We're coming up from Florida to cut your balls off." "Paul! This is Steve Roberts. I thought you had the juice, you rat bastard!" No, I would not be taking any phone calls today. No, I would not be receiving any visitors. I had visions of burly men in dark raincoats hanging around in the lobby of my building, waiting for me to make my exit. I had to leave immediately. I had to make myself invisible.

I packed a bag, took the staircase down to the cellar, and left the building through the rear door past the garbage cans and a large gray rat with a long tail scrounging for food. I hailed a cab over on Broadway that was letting out a thin black man with a maroon suit and a wide green hat; he looked like a neighborhood pimp coming home from work, and for a bizarre instant I wished I could trade places with him. He had the demeanor of a working man coming off the night shift, and his lifestyle at the moment seemed more stable than my own. Instinctively, without thinking consciously about it, I instructed the cabbie to take me out to the airport. If you asked me then where I was going, I don't think I could have told you. But some part of me knew; some primordial corner of my brain that deals with survival had taken over after the rest of my gray matter became paralyzed with terror.

As I was sitting in the airport lounge waiting for the plane to board, it suddenly occurred to me that I was out of work. For the first time in twenty-five years I had no job. I giggled idiotically and suppressed a hiccup. It felt nice, sitting there in my corduroy jeans and sneakers, knowing that I could do anything I wanted to do the rest of the day. The rest of my life for that matter.

Chapter Twenty-two

The mountain peaks in the background were covered with snow, although it was too early in the season to do any skiing, even in Utah. I wanted desperately to call Elaine, to let her know that I was all right, but I knew it was best not to make contact with her. If she did not know where I was, if she had not heard from me, she could say so honestly to whomever questioned her. My colleagues would be calling her by mid-morning at the latest when I failed to show up for work. The authorities would be swooping in at any time now that the details of the scam were public information. Most likely the partners, and our network of investors, would be making themselves scarce in the aftermath of the story. It was either that or stay put and tough it out, but that seemed unlikely since their position was virtually indefensible. The reporters would be hovering outside the doors of Zurich like so many vultures lusting after a decaying carcass. The networks would also be camped outside with microphones and cameras. It was sure to be a media circus and I did not think my colleagues would want to hang around and face it without consulting our lawyers first.

I taxied up to Park City and checked into a quiet motel near the slopes under the name of James Dixon. I had ten thousand dollars cash in my bag that I had kept for precisely this emergency, and I paid the desk clerk two hundred and forty-five dollars for a week in advance. I was afraid to go near our condo, figuring it was only a question of time before it was put under surveillance.

The slopes which I could see through my window were white on top near the peaks with patches of brown down below where the snow was thinner. In two or three weeks they would all be blazing white under the sun, inviting the first impatient skiers of the season. Already the sky was cloudy with a promise of snow. The air was cool and fresh and cleansed me as I inhaled deeply. If only I could find a way to purge myself and start all over, find a way to filter out all the garbage in the future. If only it were that easy.

I spent my first evening in Park City prowling through my favorite haunts up and down Main Street, consuming an inordinate amount of Killian's Irish red. At three A.M. I found myself in Andre's hunkered over my twentieth, or perhaps my thirtieth, beer of the evening. I seemed to be attached to a large attractive redhead wearing a down ski vest, but when or where I met her or what her name was I didn't have the foggiest idea. She was at least as drunk as I and she hung heavily on my left shoulder for support. At one point she began to sing rather loudly and off-key, and a moment later—so it seemed in my inebriated state—she was gone, departed from my life as curiously and mysteriously as she entered it. As bleary-eyed and brain-scrambled as I was, I was aware that I would be paying a severe price in the morning for the evening's dissipation.

I awoke, if you can call it that, hours later in a lumpy bed with sunlight slanting through the window. I could tell I was still alive by the dull throbbing sensation directly behind my left eyeball. The hangover was localized, centered around the forefront of my brain, but when I tried to sit up the wreckage shifted lower into my stomach, and finally permeated my whole body with awful pulsating pain. My tongue was dry and cottony and filled my entire mouth. I had a lump somewhere in my throat, as though one of my tonsils had blown up to the size of a grapefruit. It hurt when I tried to swallow it. The absurdity of my pursuers finding me in this desperate condition was too ridiculous to contemplate. I had to put myself back together in a hurry.

Shortly before eleven, one o'clock New York time, I managed to saunter down to the Yarrow, the huge luxury Holiday Inn that was only a ten-minute walk from my motel. I bought a *Wall Street Journal* in the lobby and headed for the restaurant to read it over a cup of black coffee. I turned immediately to the inside back page and there it was; Zenedex was written up in the Abreast of the Market column directly above Heard on the Street. Zenedex had earned the dubious distinction of heading the list of over-the-counter stocks that were the biggest percentage decliners in the previous day's trading. Heavy sell orders had been placed starting with the opening bell and continued throughout the day. Speculators pounced on the stock as well, shorting it in anticipation of a steep market drop so they could buy back shares at a lower price later on and close out their short position at a profit. A total of two million shares were traded, 40 percent of the entire float. No stock can take that kind of hammering without suffering a near-fatal injury, and Zenedex was no exception. It closed at 7 ¼, down 3 ⅜ from yesterday's close for a loss of 32 percent. The carnage was expected to continue today.

Without waiting to finish my first cup of coffee of the morning, I threw a dollar on the counter, scooped up my jacket and gloves, and raced toward the door. There was a Merrill Lynch office down the street, midway between the hotel and Prospector's Square. The time in New York was a little past one which left slightly less than three hours' trading before the four o'clock bell. I was oblivious to the cold and to my self-inflicted pain as I tore down Kearns Boulevard with the newspaper bunched into a ball in one hand and my coat tucked under my other arm like a football. People stared after me as though I were a madman but I paid them no notice. I was a monomaniac with one destination in mind; I had to get to a quote machine as soon as possible, and God help anyone who was using it when I got there.

The visitors' lounge was empty except for a solitary rustic who looked as though he had slept in his clothes last night. He reeked of dirty socks and body odor. After my initial revulsion it occurred to me that a casual observer might have taken us for birds of a feather. I looked like hell myself and the emanations from my mouth and pores were enough to make a bear beg for mercy. He scarcely acknowledged my presence which was just fine with me. I rushed over to the quote machine and punched in the symbol for Zenedex. It was trading at 6 ¼, down a point for the day so far. It had actually opened higher at 7 ⅜ and gotten as high as 7 ½ before the selling commenced with a vengeance. Everybody who owned the stock was feeding it out a little at a time trying to get the best price they could for it, and the shorts were having a field day for themselves. Every time there was an uptick, they slammed it down with a new wave of selling.

At two o'clock New York time my body developed an insatiable craving for hangover food. I had not eaten a solid meal since my plane ride from JFK, and all I could think about was pizza with pepperoni, hot dogs with mustard and spicy onions, and a deep dish of chocolate chip ice cream. But this was Utah, not New York City, so I went to a Tex-Mex place around the corner and settled for a bowl of chili with little cubes of raw onion sprinkled on top, and a Mexican pizza. The pizza was especially fiery, loaded as it was with jalapeno peppers, slices of black and green olives with pimientos, and Monterey Jack on a bed of crisp tortillas. It was a wonderful substitute for New York City hangover fare and I could see that I could easily become addicted to it. I managed to stuff myself to bursting and my stomach started to bubble with a volcanic fury.

When I got back to the brokerage office, the derelict was still immobile in his chair, lost in his own private pain. He had barely moved since I left. Someone else was checking stock prices on the machine, and I had to rein in my impatience as I waited for him to finish. He was a stock market junkie, eager to engage me—or anyone for that matter—in conversation. People like him filled brokerage offices all over the country, picking the brains of losers like themselves in an effort to find the One System that would allow them to beat the market. Invariably they got burned following one piece of bad advice after another. They spent their lives talking about the one or two stocks they owned that were up and ignoring the dozen or more that had taken a dive into the sewer. I did not want to talk to him today. I was depressed enough as it was so I ignored him when he asked me what I thought of National Semiconductor.

Zenedex was 5 ⅝, a victim of continuing selling pressure. I hung around until four o'clock New York time, two o'clock local, and watched the stock close at 5 ¼, the low for the day. The volcanic fury in the pit of my stomach, a product of last night's beer and this afternoon's hot spices, was aggravated by a case of jitters that gripped me after the close. I had visions of my partners and our army of investors confronting me outside on the sidewalk with their pockets turned inside out, demanding that I make up their losses. I would be haunted by their faces, apoplectic with rage, for the rest of my life. I did what I did because I felt I had to do it. But I did not feel proud of my accomplishment. Quite the opposite in fact.

Chapter Twenty-Three

Broker-Dealer, Investment Banker Zurich Goes Under

Victim of "Bear Raid"

BY RONALD HARRINGTON
Staff Reporter of THE WALL STREET JOURNAL

NEW YORK—Zurich Financial Services, a broker-dealer, investment banker, and merger-and-acquisition firm, was put out of business yesterday, apparently the victim of a stunning "bear raid" on the first new issue it brought to market.

The end came when the firm's clearing agent, Pendleton Securities, liquidated all Zurich's stock holdings to meet capital requirements. According to a Pendleton official, the liquidation followed the Securities and Exchange Commission's declaration that the financial services firm was in violation of the agency's net capital rules. The price of Zenedex, Zurich's first public offering, fell from its offering price of $8 a share last Tuesday to $1.88 by the close of business yesterday. The shares had traded as high as $11 the day after the offering. For purposes of net capital rules, any issue with a market value below $5 a share cannot be counted.

Zenedex first attracted the attention of institutional investors and large retail accounts because of its work with certain naturally occurring body chemicals called polypeptides, which the company claims aid sexual performance. It was considered to be a "hot issue," meaning that demand for the stock is so strong there are not many shares available for the average investor to buy until the stock is traded publicly. In cases of this nature, small investors usually have to pay a higher price for the shares than those who got stock before the offering paid for them. Last Thursday, however, two days following the offering, the *New York Times* carried a story maintaining that gross financial improprieties had been taking place at Zurich since it opened for business last spring. According to the *Times* article, Zurich had been functioning as a cash laundering operation for its clients, including many well-known politicians and businessmen. Other irregularities mentioned by the news-

paper include: merger-and-acquisition
activity performed without full disclo-
sure to Zurich clients, insider trading
violations, and similar practices.

Following the *Times* story, the institutions and large individual investors, who had loaded up on Zenedex
shares before the offering, began selling the stock heavily. They were
joined by hedge funds and speculators
who sold the shares short. In a typical
bear raid, investors sell shares they
don't own in an effort to break down
the price of a stock. Their goal is to
buy back the shares at a lower price
and make a profit. Short selling is not
illegal unless it is done in a concerted
effort by a group of investors acting
together in a conspiracy to defraud
shareholders. In this instance, it
would appear to have been under-
taken as a reaction to the negative
news story.

Efforts to reach Zurich officials
were not successful. The Securities
and Exchange Commission has already begun its own investigation
into the incident, and the Federal Bureau of Investigation is said to be interested in the matter as well.

Chapter Twenty-four

The sky opened up over the Wasatch mountains and huge powdery flakes floated down like feathers from the clouds. By early afternoon the streets of Park City and the mountains that encircled it were covered with a billowing white blanket. Winter had arrived in all its pristine glory, and the local beer drinkers on Main Street shrugged off their lethargy in anticipation of the first run of the season. There was a universal stirring, a collective awakening with the advent of the first snowstorm of the year.

I watched the swirling whiteness outside my window as I packed my bag and prepared to check out. Two weeks in hiding was long enough for me, more than long enough for anyone. It was time to put my life in motion again, to go out and face the world and find out what it had in store for me. I was also anxious to see Elaine and the kids again. God how I missed them! My fugitive days were over. It was time to join the living.

My rental car was waiting outside the motel. It was a gray Honda Civic, tight and compact and efficient as it sat there in the snow. I threw my bag in the back seat, turned on the wipers and the rear window defroster, and put the car in gear. It held the road nicely as it bumped over the snow. The snowflakes were large and dry with no hint of wetness or sloppiness in them. They fell off the windshield and the hood of the car imme-

211

diately without clinging or turning to slush. I turned right on
Park Avenue, then swung left onto Deer Valley Drive. I was going to our condo to re-establish contact with the real world. First
I would call Elaine and tell her where I was. Then I would step
into my skis and take a run down the mountain. No, perhaps I
would ski first and then call Elaine. I needed to flush out my
system before I spoke to anyone.

There was no sign of a stake-out as I pulled in front of the
door. No sign of any visitors at all, official or otherwise. This surprised me somewhat since I half expected the place to be cor-
doned off by armed troopers with helicopters circling overhead.
In a way I was disappointed. I wanted my re-entry to be dramatic, not a non-event like this. A little fanfare would have made
it all seem worthwhile. Instead it appeared on the surface as
though the world had forgotten me and no one cared where I
was or what I was doing. I felt a surrealistic sense of isolation and
aloneness. I wanted to shout, "Hey, look at me! I'm the guy who
bankrupted Zurich!" I turned off the ignition, pulled my bag out
of the back seat, and went inside the condo.

It smelled a bit musty after nearly nine months of neglect.
Particles of dust floated in the shafts of sunlight that slanted
across the living room in front of the fireplace. It needed a good
airing out so I opened the louvered windows a few inches to help
circulate the airflow. The skis were locked inside the shed outside the back door where we left them. We had them waxed and
sharpened at the end of our vacation in February so they would
be ready to ski on when we returned the following season. I
struggled into my boots and buckled them tight near the instep
and looser around the shinbones. I flexed my knees and bent
forward to stretch them to my shape.

The sky was blue in patches here and there and the dry flakes
continued to come down as though the snow would never let up.
I skied down the smooth wide cruising trail toward the chair lift
below, enjoying the cold sharp air as I sucked it into my lungs. I
made one run after another, pushing myself harder than I
should have this first time out after the long layoff. I wanted to
make this part of my journey last as long as I could, forever if
possible, but that could not be. It had to end sooner or later like
all things both good and bad in life, and it was late afternoon

when I returned to the condo. The sun was fading off to the west and the air was noticeably colder than when I started out.

I did not see anyone immediately, but I could feel his presence as I stepped inside. It was palpable, a thing a blind man would have felt. If you asked me how or why I knew I could not have answered, but I was certain who was waiting for me inside before I set eyes on him.

"Hello, Paul," he said. "I was freezing my ass off so I closed the windows. I hope you don't mind."

"Make yourself at home. Can I get you a drink?"

"I've already helped myself to some of your vodka, thanks. You . . . you don't seem very surprised to see me."

"I guess I'm not. I don't know why but I half expected you to be here. In a way it's a relief. It . . . it could have been someone else a lot worse than you."

"I'm glad you don't think of me as an ogre or anything like that. When did you begin to suspect anyway?"

"Not until the very end, just before the offering. I saw you with different eyes for the first time. Before that you struck me as a bit of an airhead, George, a fun-loving salesman with his brain in his dick. You pulled it off very well I must say."

"My mother always told me I should have been an actor."

"What's your real name anyway?"

"Brian Halloway. Special Agent, Federal Bureau of Investigation, if you want the whole title."

"You'll always be George to me. I'm sorry," I laughed.

"I've been called a lot worse than that," he said joining in.

I poured myself two fingers of Jack Daniels over ice and sat down on the sofa across from him. I observed him carefully, seeing him in different ways than I had before. It was like looking at a diamond that you think you know until the changing light illuminates the many facets in it.

"So, George. Why don't you bring me up to date? I've been out of touch the last couple of weeks."

"Yes, we've noticed. It hasn't been boring getting to know you, I'll say that much for this case. You're a one-man demolition crew, do you know that? Nobody could figure out what the hell you might do next."

"Neither could I. I amaze myself sometimes."

"Answer one thing for me. Turning in Steve Roberts and his friends and giving the story to the press. Did you do all that because you were on to me?"

"No, I honestly didn't. I decided to do it weeks ago when we were down in Florida. I knew I was in over my head and I didn't want to go along with it anymore. You . . . you had me completely fooled until the end, after I already set everything in motion."

George/Brian stood up and held his glass out toward me. "May I?" he asked.

"Help yourself. I think I'll join you."

We replenished our drinks and I went over and fired up a chemical log, then placed two real logs on top of it.

"I used to build a fire from scratch," I said. "Paper, kindling, the whole bit. Now I cheat with this chemical shit first. It saves a lot of time."

George smiled and said nothing.

"What I don't understand," I continued, "is why you infiltrated the group in the first place. I didn't know myself how shady the whole operation was until afterward, until we set everything up and I got to meet some of our . . . investors."

"We've been following Alex Jordan around for three years now. We knew about his relationship with Miles and Julian and that whole crew down in Florida, and this was our opportunity to nail him. Fixing me up with a set of credentials and getting an entree through one of his buddies . . . who is one of our operatives actually . . . was the next step. We had the goods on him and were ready to close in and shut down the whole organization before the Zenedex thing . . . when all of a sudden we get word that . . . you, you crazy bastard . . . had started to launch a one-man counterinsurgency action of your own. So we decided to hold off and find out exactly what you had in mind."

I sat there stunned, truly numb and speechless for the first time in my life. They were on to everything from the start. I had been living my life in a fishbowl all year long, with the authorities peering in and observing my every action. They knew everything. Where did that leave me now? I had to know.

"Where . . . where do I stand now?" I asked. I could hear the shakiness in my voice.

"Are we going to try to throw you in jail along with the others? Is that what you want to know?" George laughed and put his arms down on the coffee table. Then suddenly he grew serious.

"If we were going to charge you with anything I would have had to read you your rights before I said hello. There'll be a trial of course. You'll be asked to testify and tell everything you know. Hell, that shouldn't be difficult for you. You've already put it all on tape for *The New York Times*. We are aware, Paul, that you've committed some improprieties of your own, and you've certainly contemplated the possibility of turning yourself into a major league thief. But we're willing to overlook all that in return for your testimony. We want to put these guys away, Paul, and you're the one who can help us do that. Shit! You've already ruined them financially."

Again I sat there stunned and speechless, trying to sort out exactly what had happened to me during the past nine months.

"You should be aware, Paul, that there's an element of personal danger in what you've done." George's tone was somber. "You've pulled the rug out from under some very heavy hitters. There's always the chance that . . . that they might try . . . "

"I've thought about that. Christ have I thought about it."

"You can go into a federal witness program after it's all over. You and your family. Change of identity, a new set of credentials, altered appearance and relocation to a different part of the country. I want you to know that."

I thought it over for a second and a half and said, "Thanks, but no thanks. I can't live my life like that. No way."

"I didn't think so but I wanted you to know your options."

"I'll be all right. I think. They've got enough to worry about without adding murder to the list."

George did not reply.

"What's the next step now?" I asked.

"Well, for starters I think you should pick up that telephone over there and call your wife. She's worried sick about you."

"Poor Elaine, I haven't been the easiest guy in the world to live with."

"After that we'll drive down to the airport and catch a plane back to JFK."

"I don't even have to pack," I said, nodding to the nylon valise that was still sitting in the middle of the floor where I put it when I came in.

"The media's going to be all over you when we get back east. The less you say to them the better off we'll all be. Save your talking for the jury until this whole thing is done with."

I smiled at George in anticipation of all the attention that would follow. In a way I was looking forward to it.

"This is the biggest scandal to hit Wall Street since the Ivan Boesky-Dennis Levine thing. The public thinks you're a fucking hero," he said with some irritation. "I guess you might as well start getting used to it."

Chapter Twenty-five

My old buddy, Kevin O'Malley, was elected Mayor of New York City on November 4th. In February, less than a month after his swearing-in ceremony, he presented me with a Good Citizenship Award for my "outstanding service to small investors all over America." The *New York Post*—or perhaps it was the *Daily News*—had dubbed me the "Robin Hood of Wall Street" in the aftermath of the scandal. But the media was by no means unanimous in its appraisal of my role in the Zurich affair. The *Wall Street Journal* argued in a scathing editorial that Alex Jordan and the others had committed no real crimes, that both the Ivan Boesky and Zurich scandals were precipitated by ineffective attempts by the federal government to regulate the securities markets, that people like Boesky and the Zurich investors actually contributed to stock market efficiency, and the newspaper called for the abolition of the SEC, insider trading, and cash reporting regulations. The *Journal* went on to say that I was no better than the rest of my compadres at Zurich, and I had only turned against them to save my hide.

But public opinion was decidedly on the side of the Robin Hood school of thought. Middle America had been convinced for years, if not decades, that well-connected insiders were earning hundreds of millions of dollars for themselves at the expense of small investors with no access to privileged information. They

217

were happy to see fat cats like Alex, Miles, Julian, Steve Roberts, and the other investors brought to heel. The fact that an outfit like Zurich had been shot down in flames by one crusading individual touched a romantic vein. I played the role shamelessly and found my niche championing the rights of small shareholders throughout the country. A public opinion poll revealed that there was no sense of moral indignation over the affair. Seventy-two percent of the people polled said that they would hide cash from the federal government, and 76 percent maintained they would buy stock on inside information if they felt they could get away with it. Their resentment against the high rollers, it turned out, was in being excluded from their club. It was resentment against wealth and privilege and a desire to see powerful people brought to their knees.

The trial was scheduled for the spring, and appeals would probably keep the case alive in the courts for the next two years at least. I doubted that anyone would end up spending a day in jail, although I'm sure that tens of millions of dollars in fines, and possibly more, would be disgorged by the time all the pieces fell in place. A handful of senators and congressmen would be forced to resign their seats, and at least a dozen high-level executives would be taking early retirement.

In March I heard from Monica for the first time in months.

"Where are you?" I asked.

"I'm still down in Florida. I just wanted you to know. I'm getting married next month."

"Oh! Who is he?"

"His name is . . . don't laugh, okay? His name is Paul, the same as yours. He's one of the managers at the same hotel where I work."

"I . . . I don't know what to say, Monica. Congratulations, I guess. I'm a little bit jealous."

"I still think about you a lot."

"I think about you, too, Monica. I really do."

"I think about when we went out to that motel by the airport the first time. Remember?"

"How could I forget? How could I forget any of it? I get horny as hell every time I picture you in my mind."

"I shouldn't say this but I'd like to be with you once more before I get married. Is it terrible for me to feel this way?"

"No it's not terrible. It's perfectly natural but it wouldn't be a good thing, not for either one of us."

"Are you . . . did you and HER get back together again?"

"Yes, Elaine and I patched things up. The kids are happy as hell and we both feel good about it."

There was a pause on the other end, then she said:

"I've been reading about you in all the papers, Paul. Are you going to come out of it okay?"

"Better than I deserve, I'm happy to say. Life is full of funny twists and turns. If you told me six months ago that things would turn out like this, I would have said you were crazy."

"I guess you must feel pretty good about it then."

"Did you see the movie *Taxi Driver*? Remember the main character who started off by trying to assassinate a politician and winds up killing some pimp instead. He was a psychopathic killer who was acclaimed as a hero. Whenever I start to take this all too seriously, I think of Robert DeNiro in that role. It puts life back in perspective for me again."

"Well, I'm happy for you, Paul. I guess I better hang up now. I . . . I just wanted to say goodbye to you before . . . before I . . . "

"I'm glad you called Monica. I'll always remember you. I'll always be your friend if you need one. Best of luck to you."

"Goodbye, Paul. I'll never forget you either."

Chapter Twenty-six

I opened my own firm in April, just as the first warm breath of spring air could be felt beneath the biting winter winds. I called my company Peoples Investment Center. It had just the right populist touch I wanted to capitalize on my newly acquired media image. Robin Hood Financial Services, a name suggested to me by my public relations agent, was too damned obvious. It was blatantly exploitive and I thought I'd be the laughingstock of Wall Street if I attempted to go with it. I started small with just a secretary and two young sales trainees for staff. My thought was to concentrate on the lower end of the market, the small investor who was all but ignored by most of the established firms, the kind of people Merrill Lynch used to go after before it became a multinational money center. I would give them good advice for modest fees, put them into mutual funds and low-priced stocks with good earnings potential. I had had enough of the heavy hitters to last me the rest of my life.

Broken branches and small patches of unmelted snow were scattered across the lawn when I pulled into the driveway. Pretty soon it would be time to get out the rakes and the other garden tools and begin the annual spring cleanup. For the first time in my life I actually looked forward to it.

The house smelled like a food lover's paradise when I let my-

self in. I could hear the television in the family room where
Mark and Laurie barricaded themselves after school each day.
Elaine came out to greet me looking powerfully seductive in a
pair of tight slacks and a green sweater that accentuated the
blue-green sparkle in her eyes. She kissed me on the lips.

"How'd it go today?" she asked.

"Great. We're off to a good start. Most of the publicity's been
good so far and we're opening up more accounts than we can
handle. If it keeps up I'll have to hire three new brokers by
June."

"I'm glad to hear it because the money's going to come in
handy. I discovered a leak in Mark's room inside his closet near
the back. That roof's not getting any younger you know. We're
probably going to need a new one pretty soon."

"Shit!"

"And this stove is driving me crazy. The oven keeps shutting
off and I can't regulate the temperature any more. I'd like you to
come with me Saturday to look for a replacement."

"How much is that going to cost?"

"Close to a thousand dollars I would guess."

"A thousand dollars!"

"We've got to spend the money, Paul, unless you feel like eating out every night. We've got all that cash down in the cellar.
Why don't we use some of it?"

"I . . . I'd hate to start dipping into that now."

"But why? What else is it good for if we can't spend some of
it?"

"I like having it as . . . as an insurance policy so to speak."

"An insurance policy for what?"

"For whatever."

"We'll have to spend it all eventually anyway. Mark's getting
closer to college and then we'll have Laurie to think about. The
last time I looked tuitions were up over fifteen thousand dollars
a year."

I could feel that old familiar tightness gripping my chest
again. The same viselike sensation that used to seize me on the
train a little more than a year ago. Please, God, don't let that
start all over. I can't go through that again. Just when you
thought you were one step ahead of life, it had a way of closing in

and trapping you. Snared. Backed up against the wall. There was never any end to it.

Well, if that's the way it was going to be, then I was up to the test. There was no question in my mind that if I was ever threatened with financial ruin again, I was capable of doing whatever I thought was necessary to keep myself from going under.

THE END